CW01431048

CL(

'Do you think you could get me into films?'

'Maybe – it you look as good out of your clothes as you do in them.'

Jake couldn't believe his luck when the pretty traffic warden began to peel off her uniform. The jacket slid to the floor, followed seconds later by the starched white shirt.

He whistled silently when he saw the white lace half-cup bra which supported her staggering breasts, pushing them upwards and together in an intoxicating display of satiny female flesh.

The skirt was next . . .

Also available from Headline Delta

Exposed
Indecent
Undercover
Amateur Nights
Amateur Days
Bianca
Compulsion
Two Weeks in May
The Downfall of Danielle
Fondle in Flagrante
Fondle on Top
Fondle All Over
Hot Pursuit
Kiss of Death
The Phallus of Osiris
Lust on the Loose
Passion in Paradise
Reluctant Lust
The Wife-Watcher Letters
Amorous Appetites
Hotel D'Amour
Intimate Positions
Ménage à Trois
My Duty, My Desire
Sinderella
The Story of Honey O
Three Women
Total Abandon
Wild Abandon

Close Up

Felice Ash

HEADLINE
DELTA

Copyright © 1995 Felice Ash

The right of Felice Ash to be identified as the Author of
the Work has been asserted by her in accordance with the
Copyright, Designs and Patents Act 1988.

First published in 1995
by HEADLINE BOOK PUBLISHING

A HEADLINE DELTA paperback

10 9 8 7 6 5 4 3 2 1

All rights reserved. No part of this publication may be
reproduced, stored in a retrieval system, or transmitted,
in any form or by any means, without the prior written
permission of the publisher, nor be otherwise circulated
in any form of binding or cover other than that in which
it is published and without a similar condition being
imposed on the subsequent purchaser.

All characters in this publication are fictitious
and any resemblance to real persons, living or dead,
is purely coincidental.

ISBN 0 7472 4779 X

Typeset by Keyboard Services, Luton, Beds

Printed and bound in Great Britain by
Cox & Wyman Ltd, Reading, Berks

HEADLINE BOOK PUBLISHING
A division of Hodder Headline PLC
338 Euston Road
London NW1 3BH

Close Up

Chapter One

'I know the company's in trouble, but it can't be that bad, surely?' groaned Emma.

Tom ran his hand through his dark hair and looked at her enquiringly. 'Do you know something I don't?' he asked, pushing the books across the desk towards her. 'The money coming in is less than the money going out – doesn't that suggest something to you?'

Emma picked up the nearest book and studied the figures, although she already knew them by heart.

'The way I see it, we have three options,' stated Tom. 'We can move – Soho's just too expensive now . . .'

'Not a viable option,' Emma pointed out. 'The lease still has a year to run.'

'Or we can lay everybody off and just use them as we need them on a freelance basis . . .'

'Which means we risk them not being available when we do want them,' she interjected. 'Besides, we've already let several people go this year and everyone left is running around doing the work of three people.'

'Or we can stop trying to hold on by the skin of our teeth and get into something more lucrative until business picks up again.'

'*If* it ever picks up again,' commented Emma gloomily. 'I

1

suppose if we get the chocolate commercials it will keep us going a while longer.'

Tom and Emma were partners in a film and video production company, which until a couple of years ago had been extremely successful making commercials, corporate videos and promotional films.

But the boom period was over and businesses that until recently had happily spent vast amounts of money on promoting themselves, their products or their services, had now tightened their belts and cut budgets.

Which meant that production companies like theirs were in trouble, with too many people competing for what little work there was around.

Emma stood up and began to pace the office while Tom put his feet up on the desk and watched her, idly admiring the curves of her body, which were accentuated rather than concealed by the severe grey business suit she wore.

Emma was always worth looking at, he reflected, with her smooth fall of shoulder-length blonde hair framing a sensual kittenish face. Even at moments like this, when her brow was furrowed in concentration, she exuded the sort of ice-queen sexiness that most men found irresistible.

He certainly did.

Tom's pleasant looks and affable manner concealed a voracious sexual appetite, which he indulged at every possible opportunity. As Emma paced, his gaze dropped to the contours of her backside swaying erotically beneath her tight-fitting skirt.

His eyes narrowed as he imagined himself slowly raising her skirt to reveal the tops of her sheer black stockings, then her suspenders, then a pair of filmy little panties. Was she wearing black underwear? Or possibly grey?

Whatever colour it was, he knew it would be sexy – Emma always wore sexy underwear and it never failed to turn him on.

He remembered one occasion when they'd been working late and Emma had perched on the edge of the desk to take a phone call.

Her skirt had ridden up to offer a tantalising glimpse of lace-edged, peach silk lingerie. While she'd continued to talk, he'd unbuttoned her front-fastening skirt and let it fall open to reveal the intoxicating sight of her camiknickers, suspenders and shapely, stocking-clad legs.

Ignoring the hand she'd raised to wave him away, he'd caressed his way up her thighs, then stroked the bare flesh above her stocking tops. She pressed her thighs together and mouthed at him to stop, but as she was holding the phone in one hand and writing notes with the other, she was unable to prevent him from following his natural inclinations.

He stroked her belly over the sheer peach silk, then circled over her bush with the tips of his fingers. Of their own volition her thighs drifted apart and he continued his slow circling down over her pubic mound and between her legs.

The strip of satin encasing her honeypot was already damp and he massaged it until more of her creamy juices soaked through.

Emma finished her call and put the phone down. Before she could protest, he pulled aside the crotch of her loose-fitting camiknickers, bent his head and buried his face in the soft, moist folds of her pussy. She gasped when he teased her clit with his tongue, then drew it gently between his lips and sucked.

He felt her hands in his hair then she drew up her legs so

her feet in their high-heeled shoes were on the edge of the desk, her knees bent and widely parted.

He licked and kissed his way into her honeypot, thrusting his tongue in as far as it would go, then flickering over her clit until she moaned softly and sank back onto the desk, her blonde hair fanning out around her.

Tom straightened up, unzipped his trousers and entered her, plunging in as far as he could go. She wound her long legs around his waist and they fucked long and hard, work forgotten, at least for the moment.

Tom had long ago lost count of the number of times such scenarios had been enacted in either his office or hers.

Unfortunately it hadn't happened for over a year.

Not since Emma had discovered him screwing the temporary receptionist in the editing room and had announced coldly that their marriage was over. It had been the second time in six months that she'd found him being unfaithful to her, and after the previous time she'd made it quite clear that one more transgression would be the last.

And it had been.

She'd moved out of their house in Highgate and nothing he could say would induce her to move back in.

Unfortunately Tom was a creature of habit – most of them bad – and throughout his adult life he'd made a pass at any woman he'd found attractive, a habit he'd subsequently found impossible to break.

At least Emma had seen the sense of them continuing to work together, which was a mixed blessing because Tom could rarely spend any time in her company without wanting to fuck her.

The fact that he was now free to pursue openly any woman who took his eye was some consolation, but it was still a matter of daily regret for him that he could no longer pull Emma down onto the desk whenever the urge took him.

Pull her down onto the desk and slowly unbutton her blouse to reveal her firm, pert breasts with their candy-pink nipples. Then tease them to hard points with the tip of his tongue, circling them tantalisingly while she arched beneath him, her hips already moving in an erotic rhythm . . .

Tom came back to reality as Emma suddenly stopped pacing and glanced at her watch.

'We'll discuss this tomorrow. It's time for our meeting with Sophia Brentwood and we can't afford to be late.'

'Can't you go on your own?' asked Tom hopefully. 'I thought I might edit some stuff for a new promo video.'

On her way out of the door Emma turned to smile at him gleefully.

'Not a chance. She's obviously taken a shine to you and, with five companies pitching for this work, we need to exploit any advantage we have to the full – and in this case that means you.'

Sophia Brentwood owned Brentwood's Chocolates and she was taking a long time to decide which of the different production companies currently pitching would get to make a series of commercials.

To Tom's discomfort she patently found him attractive and made no attempt to hide it. The one thing he found a complete turn-off was a woman making the running. He was a man who loved the chase and actively disliked the roles being reversed.

Not that Sophia was unattractive. Although nearer to fifty than forty, she was nevertheless a good-looking woman with a lush, ripe figure.

But Tom liked to be the one making the moves and the way she looked at him, like a cat considering a particularly succulent morsel, made him very uncomfortable. A fact which afforded Emma a considerable amount of amusement.

Rising reluctantly to his feet, Tom reached for his jacket and briefcase. 'Don't you dare leave me alone with her,' he warned.

'You're a big boy – you can look after yourself,' she told him airily, as they made their way outside into the bright sunshine to flag down a cab.

'How many more meetings are we going to have to attend before she finally makes up her mind?' he demanded. 'She's really making a meal out of it.'

'Aren't they all?' muttered Emma.

It was true that in recent months they'd spent much more time chasing work than actually making films. Prospective clients expected wining, dining and wooing, often only to decide not to commission anything after all.

It wasn't a happy state of affairs.

Brentwood's was currently their best shot at a large chunk of work in the near future, a fact that they were both only too aware of.

'So it isn't just a case of the best track record,' said Sophia Brentwood, admiring her own immaculately painted bright-pink nails, 'the chemistry must be right too.'

Tom and Emma both nodded politely, while Tom resisted the temptation to glance at his watch again.

'After all,' Sophia went on, 'to be able to work together successfully we need to be on the same wavelength. You'll need my input to be able to reflect accurately the ethos of Brentwood's Chocolates.'

She smoothed a strand of glossy red hair back from her brow and looked at Tom meaningfully.

He wished gloomily that he got a tenner for every minute

he had to sit and listen to a client, or in this case a potential client, talk complete bollocks.

In an ideal world, they won the commission, were given a brief and then produced the first in a damn good series of commercials. After the initial briefing, the less the client had to do with the actual production, the better.

But life never worked out like that and clients had an annoying habit of expecting to be consulted every step of the way, just because it was their money.

They were always changing their minds about what they wanted, watched budgets with an eagle eye and, worst of all, often insisted on attending the shoot.

How he was expected to direct a commercial with the client looking over his shoulder, making fatuous and unworkable suggestions, was a mystery to him.

He could tell Sophia Brentwood would want a well-manicured finger in every pie that was going – including his own, if the way she was looking at his crotch was anything to go by.

'. . . so I thought we could discuss it further over dinner tonight,' she concluded.

Tom was jerked out of his reverie by a sharp jab in the ribs from Emma. He pasted an enthusiastic smile on his face and said, 'Great idea. Is there anywhere particular you'd like to go?'

'I thought I'd cook something myself,' she told him gaily. 'I've just moved into a new flat and I'd like to show it off – if you've no objection that is.'

Tom didn't care where they ate – he just wished the bloody woman would make up her mind and stop wasting their time. But at least the company wouldn't have to foot the bill for another lavish meal for three.

He was horrified to hear Emma say, 'Unfortunately, I'm

7

already committed to something this evening – but I know Tom isn't doing anything, so I'm sure he'll be delighted to accept.'

It was obvious that this was what Sophia had been angling for all along. There was a lascivious gleam in her eyes which Tom found very off-putting.

'Then I'll see you at eight o'clock,' she said to him, scribbling her address onto a slip of paper. 'Come hungry.'

'How could you?' demanded Tom as soon as they were out of the building.

Emma laughed out loud at the outraged expression on his face.

'No difficulty guessing what's on Sophia's menu for this evening,' she mocked.

Tom took her elbow and steered her into a nearby bar. 'I need a drink,' he said grimly.

'Only one,' she warned him. 'You can't afford to be found wanting in the performance stakes. You're probably up against some *stiff* competition.' She collapsed with laughter again.

'A pint of bitter and a vodka and tonic,' Tom told the barman.

'Make that two vodka and tonics,' Emma amended his order. 'You can't go round there reeking of beer.'

'I'm not going round there at all,' Tom said determinedly. 'I'm going to phone and cancel.'

'You can't do that!' exclaimed his ex-wife, aghast. 'We can say goodbye to the work if you do – she'll be *furious*.'

They sat in a booth at the back of the bar and Tom stared moodily into his glass. 'She should want to use us because we're good, not because she's got hot pants for me.'

It was a sultry May afternoon with thunder threatening

and it was warm in the bar. Emma removed her jacket and leant back in her seat. Through the thin material of her black silk shirt Tom could see the pert thrust of her nipples.

Was she naked under the shirt or was she wearing a silk camisole or possibly a little lacy bra? he wondered.

At thirty-one, her breasts were still deliciously firm and taut and she certainly didn't need the support of a bra. The shirt was unbuttoned far enough to reveal a hint of creamy cleavage and it was having its usual effect on him.

'Considering that you'll screw anything with a pulse and a pussy, I don't know why you're making such a big deal about it,' she said tartly. 'You spend most of your waking hours trying to get your evil way with any female who happens to be in the same room, but when you actually meet a woman who makes it clear she's attracted to you, suddenly you don't want to know. I can't think what gets into you sometimes.'

Tom wondered what her reaction would be if he slipped his hand up her skirt under the cover of the table.

Probably the same as the last time he'd done it – he'd experience a sudden lightning pain in the kidneys.

'*I* like to be the one to make the running,' he muttered. 'I'm telling you, Em, I'm not doing it. If the situation was reversed, do you think for one moment I'd be sitting here demanding that you sacrifice your fair white body for the chance to make a few piddling commercials?'

'No, but that's only because you can't stand the idea of any other man touching me – even now when we've been separated for a year.'

Without replying, he strode over to the bar and ordered another couple of drinks. It was true – he'd always been terminally jealous where Emma was concerned. He'd have personally punched the lights out of any male client who tried to put the make on her, even if it meant losing a vast amount lucrative work.

And the idea that she might be sleeping with some new man in her life sent him into a frenzy of jealousy. But Emma had kept her private life strictly private since they'd split up and he had no idea if she was seeing anyone.

He hoped not.

'Come on, Tom,' said Emma coaxingly when he'd returned with another round, 'all you have to do is what comes as naturally to you as breathing. What's so difficult about that?'

She put her elbows on the table and leant towards him. He caught a faint whiff of the perfume she used and saw that the valley between her luscious breasts had deepened.

Damn it, why wouldn't she let him screw her any more?

It wasn't as if she didn't enjoy it for fuck's sake. She used to moan and writhe beneath him and wind her long, silken legs around his waist, begging him to bring her to yet another climax.

Why deny them both the pleasure?

It was sheer bloody-mindedness on her part.

When she'd left him he'd assumed it was to make a point and that she would come back eventually. He'd apologised. coaxed and even begged, but to no avail.

He was baffled, but still told himself it was only a temporary separation. For now, he'd settle for them becoming lovers again.

'We're all depending on you,' she continued persuasively. 'If we don't get this one, we won't be able to pay any of the incoming bills, let alone the ones already overdue. I'm running out of excuses and our creditors are running out of patience.'

She smiled at him beguilingly and pushed the fall of

blonde hair back from her face. Her slanting blue eyes were fringed by thick dark lashes and she fluttered them at him appealingly.

Tom took a thoughtful gulp of his drink. It had been a long time since Emma had last looked at him like that. It felt good.

'I'll tell you what I'll do,' he said at last.

'What?' Her tone was hopeful.

'I'll fuck Sophia Brentwood if you'll let me fuck you.'

'You *can't* be serious!'

Tom grinned at her. 'You bet I am. Why should I be the only one to make the ultimate sacrifice? It isn't as if we haven't done it before. You give me your word that we can get it together again and I'll go round there tonight and give it my all. The money would keep us going for a while at least – and give us the chance to look for more work.'

'That's practically blackmail,' she protested.

'Call it what you like, but either you agree right now or I'm going to call her and cancel.' He felt around in his pockets for some loose change.

Emma folded her arms and met his gaze steadily. 'Okay then, go ahead and call her. You've got as much to lose as I have.'

Tom rose to his feet and crossed the bar to the payphone. He was put through right away.

'Hello, Sophia, I'm just calling to . . .' He broke off as Emma reached across and cut him off.

'All right – I'll do it,' she agreed reluctantly.

'When?' he demanded, his dark eyes gleaming with triumph.

'Does it matter?'

'It does if you're going to make it a date for 3 July 2007. It has to be within a week.'

11

'All right, within a week – and only if we get the work.'
Her tone was grudging in the extreme. 'But don't expect
me to enjoy it. Now for goodness' sake phone her back and
pretend you were going to ask what wine she'd like you to
take.'

The painting over the fireplace alone would have paid for a
dozen commercials, thought Tom, as he sipped a glass of
champagne in Sophia's flat that evening.

He hated champagne – all bubbles and no substance, but
he had yet to meet a woman who didn't want to drink it by
the bucketful.

Sophia had greeted him wearing a black evening gown,
which plunged virtually to the waist. The expanse of
smooth-skinned cleavage that was revealed had temporarily deprived him of speech and he'd wordlessly
handed her the bottle of Chablis he'd brought, while
striving to regain control of his vocal chords.

He had to admit she had a stunning figure. Full, high
breasts tapered to a small waist cinched in by a narrow gold
belt. Her hips and backside were far too voluptuous for
current fashion, but the way she moved them was an
education in itself. Watching her walk across the room,
Tom knew that he'd undoubtedly have made a play for her
at some stage – if she hadn't got it in first.

But part of him felt degraded by the idea of having to
perform sexually to get work – it wasn't a situation he'd
ever experienced before.

But his more pragmatic self took the attitude that sex was
sex, and that he'd be a fool to look a gift horse in the mouth.

After all, it wouldn't exactly be a hardship to give her
what she wanted. The fact that she was at least ten years
older than him didn't do her a disservice in his eyes – an

attractive woman was an attractive woman as far as he was concerned.

Looking around the opulently furnished flat, which bore all the hallmarks of an expensive interior designer – right down to the paintings and antiques, which had obviously been chosen to blend in with the rest of the decor – Tom mentally upped the commercials' budget.

If Sophia could afford this little lot, she could afford to pay a reasonable rate for their services. The budget they'd originally submitted had been slashed to the bone to be as competitive as possible, but it could always be revised.

First he'd better make sure they got the work.

Over dinner, which Sophia claimed to have cooked herself but which Tom suspected had been sent in by the Italian restaurant around the corner, he set out to be as charming as possible.

He barely tasted the food, good though it was, because he was mesmerised by the sight of Sophia's unfettered breasts rolling around under the low-cut bodice of her dress. Every time she moved, or reached for something, one or both of them threatened to escape, until Tom felt a light film of sweat form on his brow.

He didn't know whether it was deliberate or not, but over coffee in the sitting room, as she held out a dish of mints, one large, caramel-coloured nipple popped out of her dress.

'Would you like a mint?' she purred.

'I'd rather have you,' he told her, reaching out and pulling her shoulder strap down to reveal a firm, heavy breast. His hand closed over it and he savoured the weight in his palm, rubbing his thumb delicately over the hard, erect nipple.

Sophia moaned and her head dropped back against the

sofa. Tom took the opportunity to slip her other shoulder-strap down, then feasted his eyes on her fantastic breasts for a few moments as she sat naked to the waist.

Her skin was tanned to a light honey colour and in the lamplight had the sheen of shot silk. Tom caressed one golden orb while sucking gently on the prominent nipple of the other.

He planned to take his time, but Sophia had other ideas.

Leaning across she unzipped his trousers, then knelt in front of him between his parted legs. His cock was already rearing skywards as she took it between her full, pouting lips. Tom groaned, his hands fully occupied with her breasts, as she sucked hard on his appreciative member.

Her mouth felt like hot, wet velvet as she took him further and further in, her tongue swirling around his ramrod-hard shaft as she explored every contour. The sensation was like being drawn into a whirlpool of heated volcanic mud.

She sucked and licked for a long time, so long in fact, that with great reluctance he eventually had to withdraw, afraid that he'd come before he'd satisfied her.

He pulled her back onto the sofa and swiftly stripped off his clothes before removing her dress to reveal a pair of high-waisted scarlet panties over a matching suspender belt.

He caressed her hips and belly, before stroking the tight-fitting silk panties where they clung to the voluptuous curves of her ample backside.

He slid his fingers along the indentation between her buttocks and followed it down between her legs. He was gratified to discover that the crotch of her panties was already damp and rubbed it delicately until the damp fabric became sodden.

She raised her bottom so he could ease her panties down her thighs, revealing a luxuriant dark-red bush, through which her deep-pink clit protruded expectantly. He rubbed the shaft with his forefinger and she let out a low moan as he intensified the pressure. He could feel the slick little sliver of flesh quivering under his finger as he manipulated it expertly.

She came quickly, letting out a loud cry, then, before the shudders which accompanied her climax had died down, she climbed astride him on the sofa and reached for his cock. She paused above him, the bulbous head of his large member poised at the entrance to her honeypot, then bore down hard so he was sheathed right up to the hilt inside her.

Tom didn't know when she'd last had a man, but from the ferocious way in which she rode him it had obviously been a while. She used him for her own pleasure, sometimes rising and falling above him, sometimes rocking backwards and forwards.

She rode him for a long time, until at last he lifted her off and pulled out. She reached out for him and he laid her onto her back before thrusting smoothly into her again. He'd let her control their movements earlier – now it was his turn.

He plunged slowly in and out of her slippery, warm interior, revelling in every thrust.

Beneath him, her curvaceous backside rotated erotically against the slub silk-covered sofa. He slid his hands under her and jammed her hips further against him, feeling her generous buttocks overflowing into the palms of his hands.

He quickened the tempo until they were moving together on the sofa at a frenzied pace. At last, in a long drawn out series of spasmodic shudders, he pumped his hot juices into her then sank down panting onto the welcoming cushions of her voluptuous breasts.

Several hours later, Tom left the flat and staggered out into the deserted streets of pre-dawn Kensington to look for a cab. He hadn't dared to phone for one from the flat – Sophia was asleep and the last thing he wanted to do was wake her.

After their session on the sofa they'd sat drinking brandy for a while until she'd taken him into her bedroom. Tom was no stranger to sexual excess but, even so, he ached all over after the bout that followed, which had lasted several hours.

It had culminated with him screwing her face-down over the end of a Victorian chaise longue, while she ground her buttocks into his groin and urged him on to greater efforts. They'd eventually collapsed on the bed and fallen asleep, his hand cupping one of her breasts, his detumescent cock nestling between her damp thighs.

When he woke up he decided that the wise course of action was to beat a discreet retreat, in case she wanted a repeat performance.

He thought he'd acquitted himself fairly well, but there was no point in pushing his luck – there was no way he could get it up again that night.

He'd left an affectionate note saying he'd had to go because he had an early shoot, but that he'd call her later.

A cab cruised into view and he waved it down, collapsing thankfully onto the grimy plastic seat and giving his address to the cab driver.

All in all, it hadn't been a bad day.

And the best part was that he'd get to screw Emma again. He could hardly wait.

Chapter Two

Propped against the pillows in her double bed, her tousled blonde hair tumbling around her shoulders, Emma sipped a cup of steaming coffee. She didn't usually have time for the luxury of breakfast in bed, but this morning she'd woken up at the crack of dawn and had been unable to go back to sleep.

She glanced at the clock, wondering if it was too early to ring Tom and find out how he'd got on last night.

Seven-thirty.

Much too early.

It would be better to wait until he arrived at work.

Emma would have put money on it that Tom's evening with Sophia would result in them getting the commercials – he'd always had the knack of rubbing women up the right way.

She'd spent the previous evening mentally kicking herself for agreeing to his outrageous proposal. She should have let him cancel his evening with Sophia rather than give in to him.

Now, when the memory of just how good sex between them used to be was blurring around the edges, she was about to get an unwelcome reminder.

Their life together had been great – except for Tom's seeming inability to keep his dick in his trousers. She'd never been able to fathom why he kept screwing other women, yet professed to love her and often told her she was the most sexually exciting woman he'd ever known.

To add insult to injury he was pathologically jealous when other men paid her any attention.

Which they frequently did.

It wasn't as if he was advocating an open relationship – at least that would have been fair – no, he seemed to want to screw around whenever he felt like it, while she remained completely faithful.

Since they'd split up, she'd deliberately kept her social life in a separate compartment. She knew it was killing him not to know whether she was in another relationship.

As it happened, she wasn't. She'd been so furious when she'd walked out on him that she'd decided to steer clear of any involvement in the future.

Instead she had a string of casual lovers, which at the moment suited her just fine. She always had someone to go for a meal with, or to the cinema, or the theatre.

And more to the point, she always had someone to go to bed with.

Otherwise being with Tom all day would have been unbearable. She still fancied the bastard more than any man she'd ever met, but she was damned if she was going to be available now they'd separated.

Placing her cup and saucer on the bedside table, Emma turned restlessly onto her side. The trouble was he only had to look at her in a certain way for her to become wet between the legs, and since she'd weakly let him blackmail her yesterday she'd been in a permanent state of arousal.

Damn Tom for being such an attractive, libidinous rat. He probably thought that once he'd screwed her again she would welcome him back into her bed.

With open arms.

And legs.

Well that wasn't going to be the case. She'd get it over with as quickly as possible, then make it clear it wasn't going to happen again.

However good he was.

And as Emma remembered just how good Tom was, her hand drifted languorously between her legs . . .

Jake was one of the best lighting cameramen in the business and had been with the production company for five years. A tall, broad-shouldered, tough-looking individual, Jake invariably wore faded jeans and a battered leather jacket. He had tousled light-brown hair, blue eyes and the sort of rough-edged sex appeal that had made Emma wonder more than once what he would be like in bed.

When she arrived at work that morning, she found him pleading with Rosa, the office administrator.

Jake was a man who loved sex, but shied away from involvement. As soon as one of his girlfriends showed signs of wanting to become a permanent fixture, he was off. More than once some unfortunate girl had turned up at the offices looking for him, whereupon Jake usually bolted, leaving Rosa to deal with the situation.

'Look, all you've got to say is that no one called Jake works here – or has ever worked here. Is that too bloody much to ask?'

'I'm employed to keep the place running smoothly, not to field calls from your discarded girlfriends,' pointed out Rosa caustically, her dark eyes flashing. She tossed back her glossy black hair, which made her silver hoop earrings swing mesmerisingly backwards and forwards. 'Morning, Emma,' she added, as her boss came into the room.

'Morning,' returned Emma. 'Is Tom in yet?'

'Nope.'

'Ask him to come and see me when he arrives, will you please?'

She poured herself a cup of coffee from the pot and went off to her office, smiling to herself as Jake and Rosa resumed their altercation.

Emma had dressed for work this morning with even more care than usual in a cream linen dress over a cream lacy bra, panties and suspender belt. She knew Tom liked her without a bra, preferring her in a skimpy camisole or bare breasted beneath her clothes, and she didn't want him to think she'd dressed to please him.

She planned to get the sex which she'd so ill-advisedly promised him, out of the way, just as soon as she could.

She didn't want the thought of it hanging over her, like some erotic sword of Damocles, making her unable to concentrate on anything other than the demanding throbbing between her legs.

Just as soon as they got the go-ahead from Sophia Brentwood she'd insist they did it as quickly as possible, which would hopefully be today.

If they got the go-ahead, that was.

It would be almost worth losing the work to witness Tom's chagrin if his sexual prowess didn't have the desired result.

It was eleven o'clock before he put in an appearance, looking distinctly bleary-eyed. He certainly gave the impression of having been up all night.

'Well?' Emma greeted him coolly, feeling the old familiar excitement he could always arouse in her churning around in her stomach.

Tom threw himself down onto the small sofa in her office and stretched out his long legs, his face expressionless.

'Well?' repeated Emma impatiently.

He grinned at her wolfishly and rubbed his eyes.

'We got it.'

'My, my, you must have been good,' she commented, uncomfortably aware that the crotch of her panties was already sodden with anticipatory moisture.

'I certainly was. I admired her new flat, cooking and person, in that order. It seemed to go down quite well – as indeed I did later.'

Emma thought that might easily have clinched the deal – Tom could have won prizes for his proficiency at cunnilingus. Just the thought of it made her want to lie back on the desk with her knickers off and legs spread, impatiently awaiting the erotic ministrations of his mouth and tongue.

She walked over to the door and turned the key in the lock before turning to face him.

'Okay, where do you want it?' she asked, her tone brisk, in an effort to disguise her excitement. 'The desk? Or maybe the sofa? Let's get it over with quickly so I can get some work done.'

'If I had a hard-on, that would be enough to make me lose it,' he remarked casually, yawning and folding his arms behind his head. 'I'm sorry to disappoint you, but you're going to have to wait. The gorgeous Sophia has had my all for at least the next twenty-four hours and after being denied access to your delectable knickers for over a year, I certainly don't intend to settle for a quickie.'

Emma bit her lip in frustration. 'When then?' she demanded.

Tom rose to his feet and stretched. 'I'll let you know,' he told her amiably, and left the room.

He ambled past the open door of Rosa's office, where he could see her talking quietly but persuasively into the telephone. He presumed she was chasing up some of their outstanding money. Getting the work was difficult enough, but getting the money in once the work had been done was getting harder and harder in the current depressed economic climate.

'. . . then I'm going to take it in my hot, wet, welcoming mouth and work it in and out . . . in and out . . . faster and faster until you . . .' murmured Rosa into the phone, her ripe cherry-red lips very close to the mouthpiece.

She was talking to her new lover, a rather puritanical merchant banker. She knew he was in the middle of a meeting but she'd told his secretary that she had some urgent information for him, about the deal he was negotiating.

As soon as he'd come on the line she'd launched into a description of what she planned to do to him that evening and he'd listened without making any attempt to hang up, just saying, 'Is that the case?' and, 'Really?' from time to time – presumably for the benefit of his business associates.

Rosa knew he was annoyed with her for ringing him at work, but excited by her call nevertheless.

'. . . sucking . . . and licking . . . and kissing, then I . . .' she continued, wondering if he was flushing and mopping his brow. She doubted it – if there was ever a man who liked to stay in control it was Peregrine.

But she could make him lose it sometimes.

Like tonight.

Rosa claimed to have a Romany grandmother and she

22

certainly looked the part. She had a mass of dark curls framing her wanton, high-cheekboned face and tumbling down around her shoulders. Her thickly fringed dark eyes had a come-hither gleam which men seldom failed to respond to – that and the animal heat which she exuded like a particularly provocative perfume.

Her curvaceous, high-breasted body was tanned to a silken biscuit-brown and tapered down to a pair of long, shapely legs. Today she was wearing a short, khaki silk skirt which left most of them on display. Her breasts were veiled by a thin shantung tee-shirt, but the material was so fine that her bra was clearly visible beneath it and anyone looking closely enough could make out the dark circles of her nipples.

'. . . until tonight.' Rosa finished her call and put the phone down.

That should have Peregrine panting for her by the time he picked her up after work this evening. He'd no doubt want to drive straight to his flat and hump her immediately, but she had other ideas.

Smiling to herself she switched on the computer and got down to some work.

Emma had reached such a fever pitch of frustration that by mid-afternoon she called one of her current lovers.

Marco owned a trattoria in Islington and when she arrived he was sitting in the deserted restaurant doing some paperwork.

'Where is everyone?' she asked, gratefully accepting a glass of chilled Orvieto and sinking into a chair. Usually at this time the staff were bustling about between the kitchen and the restaurant, resetting the tables for the evening.

'I sent them home,' he murmured, coming to stand

behind her and slipping a hand down the front of her dress.
'I haven't seen you for a couple of weeks.'

Emma closed her eyes and leant her head back against
the hard bulge of his groin as his exploring hand slipped
under her bra and found the hot, throbbing point of her
nipple. She pressed it into the palm of his hand and rubbed
her head against his hard-on like a cat.

With his other hand Marco undid the buttons down the
front of her dress, then her front-fastening bra. Her swollen
breasts sprang free and he caressed them avidly, bending
down to nuzzle her neck.

London was still in the grip of an early summer heatwave
and her temperature, combined with her current state of
sexual arousal, made Emma feel as if she was burning up.
Her skin felt like it was on fire as she murmured, 'It's so
hot.'

Without a word Marco withdrew from her, then returned
a few moments later with a chunk of ice which he ran over
her breasts, making her gasp in shock. Cool drops of water
trickled down her body as the ice melted against her heated
flesh. Her nipples were already rock hard and standing to
attention, but at the touch of the ice they became like small
bullets.

'Mmm,' purred Emma appreciatively as he pulled her
dress down to the waist and ran the ice down her back. She
stood up and turned to face him, then sat on the edge of the
table and reached for his zip. His cock sprang out eagerly,
the glans glistening and swollen like a ripe, purple plum.
She grasped it firmly in her hand and lay back on the table,
her legs apart.

'Fuck me,' she invited him.

He didn't need any urging. Reaching beneath her, he
slipped her cream lace briefs down her slender legs,

revealing the golden down of her pubic hair. She kept it clipped short and it curled softly around her swollen labia.

Marco bent his dark head and dipped his tongue into the bubbling moisture that spilled from her over-heated honeypot. She wriggled her bottom on the snowy surface of the fresh tablecloth and he grasped her hips to keep her still. He knew she wanted him inside her immediately but, although he had been born in Basingstoke, Marco had enough Latin blood in his veins not to rush things.

With the tip of his tongue he licked and flickered his way along the folds of her labia, pushing softly into each hidden crevice. Her pulsating clit received particular attention, as did the slick entrance to her pleasure-tunnel.

Emma groaned and her head thrashed from side to side as he nibbled and sucked at her clit. She was in such a state of arousal that she came immediately in a sudden shuddering explosion of heat which left her flushed and trembling.

She felt the bulbous end of Marco's shaft butting up against her pussy and raised her hips to meet his smooth, determined thrust. He smelt of oregano and wine as he moved against her in the still, sultry afternoon.

The vibrations caused by the traffic rumbling along outside, were echoed by the ones they were making themselves as the table rocked its way erratically along the tiled floor.

Emma lay on her back with her head hanging off the edge of the table, her legs drawn up almost to her shoulders, as Marco screwed her energetically.

Her dress was bunched up around her waist and dimly she heard the sound of the pepper grinder and salt cellar tumbling off the table and crashing onto the floor below.

He thrust away for a long time until he let out a hoarse cry and she felt the delicious hot spurting inside which signalled his release.

She'd just been on the brink of her second climax and, unwilling to let it go, wriggled her hand between them and continued the stimulation until she gasped and came again.

A while later, they sat at the table drinking more chilled white wine, Emma naked, except for her high-heeled shoes, stockings and suspender belt, and Marco fully dressed again. Emma had shaken out her dress and hung it from the back of a chair in the hope that the worst of the creases would fall out, but she had to admit that it looked like a rag.

'Why haven't I seen you for so long?' he demanded. 'I call you, but you're always busy.'

'It's work,' sighed Emma, 'or rather the lack of it – it seems to take up so much of my time.'

She didn't add that by never seeing any of her lovers too frequently, it was easier not to get involved or have them getting too possessive.

'Come in for a meal one evening this week,' he urged her. 'I'll cook it myself and we'll eat together.'

'Maybe,' she prevaricated, then reluctantly decided it was time to go. She pulled on her bra, pants and the crumpled dress before kissing Marco goodbye and going back out into the afternoon sunshine.

'Who needs you, Tom?' she muttered to herself.

'My, my – what happened to you?' asked Rosa, taking in Emma's dishevelled appearance. 'Better not let Tom see you like that – he might think the worst, and then there'll be trouble.'

'Nothing I do is any business of Tom's any more,' Emma reminded her sweetly.

'Everybody knows that except Tom,' observed Rosa, fanning herself with a sheaf of papers.

'Where is he anyway?'

'Brentwood's. La belle Sophia phoned and off he went. Great news about getting the work, isn't it.'

Emma collapsed in a chair and, with a frown, studied a run in her stocking.

'It certainly is,' she agreed. 'Did you strike lucky prising money out of any of our wretched clients?'

Rosa ran her fingers through her luxuriant curls and sighed. 'The usual run around. Amtrust swears the cheque's in the post, but it's been there for three months now according to them.'

'Bastards,' grumbled Emma. 'The bloody film even won an award and nine months on we still haven't been paid for it. I'll talk to Tom – it may be time to get a solicitor on the case. Or I'll go and see them myself.'

'Let's hope they don't go bankrupt in the meantime – then we'll never get it,' said Rosa.

'Do you have any reason to think they might?'

'No more than any of the other clients who owe us money.'

Emma rose to her feet and stretched. 'I'd better get back to it, I suppose. See you later.'

It was still very warm in the early evening when Peregrine picked Rosa up in his BMW. He'd loosened his tie and rolled up the sleeves of his conservative blue and white striped shirt, but his usually pale skin was flushed, whether from the heat or from her earlier phone call she didn't know.

'Hello, darling,' he greeted her as she slid in beside him. He immediately kissed her passionately, fondling her breasts as he did so. 'Don't ever make another call like that to me again while I'm at work,' he warned her. 'I nearly came in my trousers.'

Rosa laughed throatily. 'You could have hung up on me.'

He didn't reply, merely put the car into gear and pulled out into the heavy traffic.

'Where are we going?' she asked a few moments later.

'My place.'

'Not yet. Let's go and get a drink and something to eat,' she said firmly.

'We can do that later. Right now all I can think about are all the things you promised to do to me,' he protested.

'And still will,' she assured him. 'But first I want to relax over a meal.'

She could tell Peregrine was unhappy about it, but his manners were too good for him to insist. Instead he found a parking space down an alleyway, just around the corner from several restaurants.

'What do you feel like eating?' he asked her, taking her hand as they walked back towards the busy road.

'I'm not sure – let's see what's on offer.'

After looking at the menus, Rosa eventually opted for an old-fashioned French restaurant with baroque decor and supercilious waiters. The *maître d'hôtel* managed, in typically Gallic fashion, to convey simultaneous disapproval and appreciation of Rosa's very short skirt and bare brown legs.

As they studied the heavy leather-bound menus she pressed her thigh against Peregrine's under cover of the starched white tablecloth.

He cleared his throat and asked, 'Do you know what you're having?'

'Other than you later? Melon and the noisettes of lamb with a green salad, I think. Have you decided?'

Despite the heat Peregrine opted for soup and *boeuf en croûte*, then sat and sipped his whisky, occasionally dabbing at his perspiring forehead with an immaculate white handkerchief. They chatted in a desultory way until the first course arrived.

Rosa spooned down icy chunks of fragrant melon steeped in Cointreau with great pleasure, wondering how Peregrine could bear to eat steaming soup on such a day.

Beneath the tablecloth she reached across and placed her hand on his knee. Bemused, he smiled at her and continued to drink his soup. Slowly she moved her hand up his leg, lightly stroking his thigh through the fine wool of his trousers.

When her hand smoothed over his groin he muttered, 'Steady on, old girl – plenty of time for that later.' She smiled at him serenely while she ran her fingers teasingly under the flap of his zip. He moved uneasily on his seat, then flushed as the waiter approached and removed their plates.

After giving his cock a gentle squeeze and feeling it swell in response, she removed her hand so she could concentrate on her main course.

Peregrine mopped his forehead again, then began to tell her about a particularly dull deal he was involved in. Rosa tuned him out and thought instead about what she had in store for him later that evening.

When she'd finished eating but Peregrine was only halfway through his rich, heavy pie, Rosa slipped her hand under the table and again stroked his cock.

'Darling – please don't,' he begged her, glancing furtively around the virtually empty restaurant to see if anyone had noticed anything.

'Relax and finish your meal,' she purred. 'I'm just getting your engine warmed up.'

'It doesn't need any warming up,' he told her in a strangled voice, 'not after your phone call this afternoon.'

Rosa ignored him and slowly drew his zip down. He gulped when her hand slipped inside his trousers and brought out his erect cock.

'For goodness' sake – someone might see!' he hissed, reaching under the table and trying to remove her hand. Her own tightened on his member and she gave the tip a warning pinch with her finger and thumb.

While Peregrine sat glassy eyed with terror and lust, Rosa stroked, squeezed and manipulated his cock into a state of eager, straining tumescence. He soon gave up any attempt to finish his meal.

When the waiter removed their plates he pulled himself together enough to request the bill, then as soon as it arrived he flung a wad of notes on the plate and said firmly to Rosa, 'We're leaving.'

He grabbed her wrist under the table and, with his other hand, managed with difficulty to stuff his cock back into his trousers. Then he strode from the restaurant pulling Rosa along behind him, holding his jacket over his arm so it hid his groin from view.

He didn't break stride until they reached the alleyway where he'd parked the car. Omitting his usual courtesy of opening the passenger door first, Peregrine wrenched open the driver's door and slid in.

He was taken aback to see Rosa swing herself sinuously

onto the bonnet then, while he watched open-mouthed, remove her cream silk panties.

'Rosa, what the hell are you playing at?' he demanded. In reply, Rosa opened her slim, bare legs and began to stroke her own silken skin. He caught a glimpse of the dark, secret place between her thighs and bounded out of the car. 'Rosa – for goodness' sake – we can be back at my place in ten minutes. Please get in the car.'

There was a note of desperation in his voice, and his head flicked swiftly from side to side to see if anyone was watching.

Rosa smiled seductively and ran a delicate forefinger over the soft curling hair of her bush, hoiking her skirt up as she did so, fully exposing the provocative pout of her labia.

Peregrine gulped, transfixed by the sight.

'Here – or nowhere,' she told him.

A low groan escaped from between his lips and he looked wildly around the alleyway.

There was no one in sight.

Yanking hard at his zip, he launched himself on Rosa and thrust deeply into her while she lay back on the sun-warmed bonnet of the gleaming BMW and wrapped her long legs around his waist.

As he thrust frenziedly away, Peregrine forgot where they were and was only dimly aware of the animal heat of Rosa's body, her exotic perfume and the slight pressure of her spike heels against his back. His hands clasped her breasts convulsively as he felt his approaching release.

When it came, it was with the force of a flood river roaring through a breach in its banks and pouring torrentially through the valley.

Sweating and shaken, Peregrine came slowly back to reality, horribly aware that he was bent over the bonnet of his car with his trousers around his ankles, still penetrating the warm, pliant body of his latest girlfriend.

He hastily withdrew, glancing furtively behind him as he zipped up his trousers.

He could say goodbye to his career in merchant banking if he was arrested on a charge of indecent exposure.

A swirl of dusty, exhaust fume-laden air wrapped a torn piece of newspaper around his ankles, and a skinny cat stalked by, intent on exploring the rubbish piled up around the dustbins behind the restaurants.

Rosa slid languidly down from the car bonnet and stuffed her discarded panties into her shoulder bag. She smiled to herself as Peregrine backed the car onto the main road.

A typical product of his conventional, middle-class upbringing, Peregrine was a man who did everything by the book.

Including making love.

Rosa knew she was nothing like his usual girlfriends, several of whom she'd met in the bars and restaurants he frequented. They all seemed to have names like Amanda and Lucy, and she would have put money on it that they'd all had ponies and been to boarding school.

Although not a bad lover, Peregrine always followed the same pattern, paying each breast a courteous amount of attention before moving gradually downwards. Rosa was certain that in asking her out Peregrine had moved as far away from his upbringing as he ever had, or was likely to.

To him, she represented a walk on the wild side.

Stretching out in the comfortable car seat, Rosa turned her head and studied his aquiline profile.

And this is just the beginning, she promised him mentally.

Chapter Three

'*Barbados*!' exclaimed Emma ecstatically, 'just how did you swing that? Or shouldn't I ask?'

Tom grinned at her smugly. 'The usual combination of charm, creative genius and sheer dumb luck.'

They were sitting in Emma's office the following morning. The hot spell had broken overnight, it was now raining torrentially and the air felt distinctly chilly.

After he'd been summoned to Brentwood's the previous afternoon, Tom had arrived to find that Sophia wanted his opinion on a new range of chocolates the company was bringing out. He'd dutifully tasted them and told Sophia what he thought.

She'd expressed dissatisfaction with the names the advertising agency had come up with. The last of the commercials they were going to make was for the new range, but the content hadn't yet been discussed.

Tom had tasted them all again then had said thoughtfully, 'Several of them have an almost Caribbean flavour – and they're the ones I like best. Why not ditch some of the fruit creams, add a few new ones based on coconut or rum and call it the Caribbean Collection?'

Sophia had gone for the idea in a big way, much to the annoyance of the advertising agency, who were already furious that she'd taken the unusual step of approaching film companies direct to pitch for the TV commercials, rather than letting them handle it.

Tom had spent the rest of the afternoon with her discussing the idea, and the upshot was that the first commercial was now going to feature the new chocolates. He'd managed to persuade Sophia that the shoot should be in the West Indies and Barbados had been settled on provisionally.

'I said we'd work on a treatment and get it to her as soon as possible,' smirked Tom complacently.

He had good reason to be pleased. A shoot in some exotic location was the ultimate perk in film production and with budgets cut there had been none on offer for the last couple of years.

Unless you counted the one in Morecambe – which he didn't.

He was also well aware that a hot climate caused Emma to become virtually insatiable. Some of their wildest sex had taken place while on location shoots under hot, tropical skies, and he had high hopes of becoming a permanent feature in her bed again on the island paradise of Barbados.

The downside of his meeting with Sophia was that she'd locked the door and embraced him passionately, making it quite clear that she wanted them to carry on where they'd left off early that morning.

Tom had felt forced to comply and couldn't deny that he'd enjoyed himself – she was a gorgeous, passionate woman who knew her way around a man's body – but he'd still been annoyed that it had been Sophia who'd instigated sex.

Why couldn't she wait for him to make the moves?

However attractive Sophia was, Tom was only interested

in women whose resistance he had to overcome. That was one of the things which had always fascinated him about Emma – a sort of shyness or reticence that she exhibited whenever sex was on the agenda.

He hoped Sophia didn't think that sex between them was going to be an ongoing situation – it could make things very awkward.

When he'd finished telling Emma the good news, she stood up and moved towards the door.

'I'll get Rosa started on the budget right away,' she said exultantly. Things were so tight that she hadn't even considered taking a holiday this year – now it looked like she was going to get one after all.

She looked at Tom speculatively as she left the room.

Was today going to be the day he wanted her to keep her part of the bargain they'd made? He hadn't mentioned it but she'd noticed him looking at her legs earlier. Trust him to make a meal out of it by keeping her in suspense.

Why didn't he just get it over with? The anticipation was killing her.

She passed Jake, who was just vanishing into the editing room and followed him in.

'Shall I make your day?' she asked him. He folded his arms behind his head and grinned at her.

'I wish somebody would.'

'We've got a shoot in Barbados.'

'Yeah? That's great.'

'Isn't it? Tom charmed Sophia Brentwood in a big way.'

They were interrupted by Rosa who put her head round the door to say, 'There's a woman in reception wants to see you Jake.'

'Yeah? Who is she?'

'Your favourite kind – she's breathing. Oh, and as an added bonus, she's wearing a uniform.'

Jake looked wary. 'What sort of uniform?' he asked suspiciously, but Rosa laughed and walked away. Reluctantly he went off to reception to be confronted by an attractive, but stern-faced traffic warden.

'Is that your Harley blocking the fire exit?' she demanded. She had a pretty face despite her stern expression, but Jake's eyes were immediately drawn to the pair of magnificent breasts which strained temptingly at the crisp white material of her blouse.

'It might be, I suppose,' he mumbled, pushing his hands through his tousled, light-brown hair and giving her the benefit of his most winning smile.

Behind him he heard Rosa snort derisively. Jake's habit of leaving his bike anywhere there was a space, regardless of 'no parking' signs, resulted in him paying an astronomical annual sum in parking fines.

'Well, move it!' she ordered him. 'I've given you a ticket but I want it moved right away.' She turned on her heel and stalked off.

As he followed her along the corridor Jake took in her shapely black-stockinged legs and large, well-rounded backside under the dark skirt of her uniform.

Great tits and a great arse – he wouldn't have minded getting her out of that uniform and giving her one, despite her abrupt manner, he thought lecherously as they emerged onto the street. He was in luck. A car had just pulled away from a meter so he was able to park the Harley legally for once. She stood in the doorway out of the rain with her arms folded, while he fed coins into the slot.

'I'll be back along here in a couple of hours, so no coming out and feeding the meter,' she warned him.

He looked injured in the extreme.

'I wouldn't dream of it sweetheart. I only left it there because I had an emergency to deal with. I was just about to move it – honest.'

'Don't bother telling me what it was,' she retorted, 'I've heard them all before.' She'd obviously noticed the name of the company because she asked curiously, 'Are you in films then?'

'Yeah – I'm a cameraman and occasional director on some of the low-budget stuff.'

Her eyes widened and her expression became more friendly.

'That must be really interesting. I always wanted to be an actress.'

'You've certainly got the looks for it,' he assured her.

She looked gratified then stared expectantly through the door as if she half expected Tom Cruise to come strolling out. Jake's eyes lingered on her knockout breasts.

'Would you like to come in and have a look around?' he invited her.

She hesitated a moment then said, 'Perhaps just for a few minutes.'

He ushered her past Rosa who raised her arched, dark brows heavenwards as he led his guest down the corridor into the editing room.

'With looks like yours you've got real potential, you know,' he told her, closing the door behind them.

'Do you really think so?' If you're just soft-soaping me in the hope I'll tear up the ticket, you can think again.'

'No, really. You've got a great face and a great body.'

'Do you think my backside's too big?' she asked anxiously. Jake was well aware that the camera added at least a stone, and she would, in fact, look fairly hefty on screen, but he wasn't about to tell her that.

'You've got a fantastic arse – it's just right,' he reassured her.

'Do you think you could get me into films?'

'Maybe – if you look as good out of your clothes as you do in them.'

He couldn't believe his luck when, without a moment's hesitation, she began to peel off her uniform. The jacket slid to the floor, followed a few seconds later by the starched white shirt.

Jake whistled silently when he saw the white lace half-cup bra which supported her staggering breasts, pushing them upwards and together in an intoxicating display of satiny female flesh.

The skirt was next. She stepped out of it with her back to him, revealing the glorious sight of her big, curvaceous backside, barely contained in a pair of white lace briefs. Her black stockings were held in place by a wisp of a suspender belt, which encircled a surprisingly small waist.

Jake gulped audibly and took a step towards her. She wound her arms around his neck and pressed her bosom against his chest.

'What do you think?' she breathed.

'Gorgeous,' he replied, freeing her heavy breasts from their lacy cradle and caressing them fervently. Her large, dark-brown nipples responded eagerly to his touch and he fastened his mouth over one, tugging at it with his lips as his tongue flickered wetly over it.

She reached for his zip just as he dragged her panties down around her thighs. A few seconds later they were banging away furiously against a cupboard door.

Tom walked past, paused for a moment, then continued on his way.

'What's going on in the editing room?' he asked Rosa.

'Jake and a traffic warden.'

'If he hasn't emerged by eleven, will you remind him that the rough cut of the Selex video has to be off by twelve?'

Tom helped himself to some coffee, feeling simultaneously envious and horny, then returned to Emma's office where they were working hard on the treatment for the Caribbean Collection commercial.

At around seven, after working all day without a break, Tom suggested a drink in a nearby bar.

'Why? Are you planning to collect your pound of flesh this evening and want to soften me up first?' enquired Emma sweetly.

'Is that what you're hoping?' he asked, moving to stand behind her as she sat at her desk.

'What I'm hoping is that you'll forget about it,' she told him untruthfully. 'Failing that, can we just get it over with? I'm already tired of this particular cat-and-mouse game, where I'm constantly wondering when you're going to pounce.'

Tom leant over her chair and began to massage her shoulders over her primrose silk blouse.

'You're very tense,' he commented.

'That's because you're touching me,' said Emma tartly, nevertheless allowing her head to drop back as he kneaded her knotted muscles with his thumbs.

'You used to like me touching you.'

'That was before I realised it was a pleasure I was sharing with half the female population of London.'

'We've been into all that – can't we just put it behind us?'

'We have. We split up. Remember?'

Tom slid his hands forward and began to massage her collar bones with featherlight strokes. Emma felt warm threads of lust uncurling from her groin and sighed. She sighed again when the tips of his fingers brushed the upper curves of her breasts.

She was aware that her nipples had formed hard points and that Tom couldn't have failed to notice, as he stroked her breasts seductively. A few seconds later he slipped his hands inside her blouse and under her silk slip. She gasped as he cupped her breasts, then bent down to kiss her neck.

Her stomach turned to liquid and she had trouble catching her breath as her body went into erotic overdrive in response to his caresses. The warm threads of lust in her groin became licking flames as she felt her desire mounting to a fever pitch.

It had been over a year since she'd last felt that intensity of arousal, and she was deeply relieved that Tom wasn't going to keep her waiting any longer before holding her to the bargain they'd made. She was too aroused even to put up the token resistance that she knew always turned him on.

She was taken aback when he stepped away from her saying, 'Tempted though I am, this isn't the right moment.'

'You must be joking!' she exclaimed. 'What the *hell* are you playing at Tom?'

He looked at her with some regret. 'This isn't the way I want it to be – that's all. It's been over a year and I'm not about to settle for a quickie in the office. Look upon this as an appetiser.'

Practically squirming in her chair from a combination of frustration and rage, Emma glared at him.

'Of course ... I've no objection to doing it now if it doesn't count as the one you owe me,' he offered.

So that was his game.

Getting her so worked up that she'd let him screw her now, as well as tomorrow, or whenever he decided to extract his pound of flesh.

Summoning up every iota of self-control Emma said coolly, 'In that case, I'll get off home. Let me know when you do want to do it – I'll set ten minutes aside.'

She stalked out of the office and hailed a cab. One of her casual lovers was going to strike lucky tonight – the question was, which one?

She was still trying to decide, when she opened the door of her flat, then stood stock still in horror at the sight which met her eyes. It looked as if someone had taken every one of her possessions, thrown them on the floor and stirred them with a big stick.

Her heart thudding with fright, she clutched the door knob and listened hard. Had the intruders gone or were they still in there? She couldn't hear anything so she stepped into the hallway, leaving the door wide open and quickly phoned the police.

They arrived within ten minutes and seemed more concerned with whether she was going to make tea for them than with what was missing.

A quick look around indicated that not much real damage had been done – it looked worse than it was. The video and sound system had gone, together with most of her CDs. A gold watch had vanished from her bedside table and about thirty pounds in cash which she kept in her dressing-table drawer for emergencies.

'Could be worse, love,' said the older of the two policemen, a beefy individual, who looked as if he'd be more comfortable in a larger size of uniform. 'I've seen places left in such a state that the owners moved out rather than try to put it right. Got any biscuits?'

The younger policeman, who looked about sixteen, stared fixedly at Emma's breasts. 'Are you a model?' he asked.

'Shouldn't you be dusting for fingerprints or something?' she enquired pointedly, as the two of them tucked into the packet of lemon puffs she produced.

'That's CID,' the beefy one informed her authoritatively.

'When will they get here?'

'Dunno, love. A law unto themselves the CID.' Both men guffawed at what was obviously a regularly aired joke, spraying copious amounts of lemon-puff crumbs around the room. Emma began to pick things out of the mess on the floor, thinking she might as well start tidying up.

'Don't touch anything,' beefy warned her. 'You might disturb something that would give us a clue.'

Biting back the acid rejoinder which sprang to her lips, Emma was relieved to hear the doorbell.

'Adam Losely, CID,' said the man lounging outside the door. He flashed his identification card at her, but Emma was too busy taking in his devastatingly attractive smile and lean, muscular body to look at it properly.

He seemed as struck by her as she was by him, and they stood in silent mutual appraisal for several moments, before Emma remembered why he was there.

'Yes . . . come in,' she invited him.

He really was attractive. Tall and dark, with an animal grace and athleticism that indicated the sort of sexual potential she was *very* interested in. He was wearing jeans and a tee-shirt with a light-coloured jacket, and he prowled restlessly around the flat as he asked her questions.

The two policemen soon left, much to Emma's relief. She went into the kitchen and took a bottle of white wine out of the fridge.

'I suppose I shouldn't offer you a glass of this while you're on duty?'

Adam glanced at his watch. 'That's right. Luckily I came off duty five minutes ago, so pour away.'

Emma opened the wine, then started to pick her clothes up off the floor. Adam looked with great interest at the lace teddy in her hand and said, 'Sorry, but would you mind leaving everything as it is until we've dusted for finger-prints?'

'When will you do that?'

'Tomorrow morning.'

She looked around in despair at the mess, then collapsed onto the sofa and kicked off her shoes. 'I suppose I'd better get someone to come and fix that.' She indicated the window, which had been forced and now hung open at a drunken angle.

Adam went over to it and glanced at it briefly. 'I can do a temporary job on it, if you like. You can get it fixed properly after it's been dusted.'

'Would you?' she smiled at him gratefully. It was at times like this she missed Tom. She knew she could phone him and he'd come round right away, but she'd spent the last year making it very plain that he now had no place in her life, other than as a business partner.

Ringing him while she was upset and vulnerable would be a bad idea. He'd no doubt end up staying the night, then assume they were permanently back together.

She drank her wine appreciatively while Adam went out

to his car and came back with a toolbox. The day had started out so well with the prospect of a trip to Barbados. Now she felt frustrated and cross, after first having had to suffer Tom playing his manipulative little games, then finding her flat had been burgled.

And it was getting a bit late to give one of her casual lovers a ring to come and spend the night with her.

Adam stood back and dropped his tools into their box, then he glanced at her. 'Have you eaten?' he demanded suddenly.

'No,' she replied, startled by his question.

'I'll take you out for something then. You won't want to sit around looking at this mess all night.'

The evening suddenly seemed more promising.

They went to a quiet Turkish restaurant about a mile away. Instead of touring the area and looking for a parking space, Adam merely drove onto the pavement and parked right outside the door.

'You'll get clamped,' she warned him. 'They're red hot on illegal parking around here.'

'No I won't,' he assured her cheerfully. 'Perk of the job.' He took her hand and led her into the restaurant.

Over couscous and a bottle of red wine, Emma started to feel a lot better. People were burgled every day, there was no point in worrying about it too much. Tomorrow would be boring, dealing with the insurance company and getting her flat made more secure, but that was no reason not to enjoy tonight.

Particularly since she was having dinner with one of the sexiest men she'd met in ages – he could take down her particulars any time.

'So, what do you do then?' he asked her, as he demolished his meal with the appetite of a starving man.

'I work for a film and video production company – I write and produce.'

'What sort of films?'

'Commercials, corporate videos, training films – that kind of thing.'

'Not porn then?' he asked, grinning.

'Certainly not,' said Emma, 'unless you count an ad for stockings – the client certainly seemed to think it was hot stuff – we couldn't prise him off the set at the end of the shoot.'

'Where are you based?' He emptied the last of the wine into her glass and signalled to the waiter to bring them another bottle.

'Soho. But I don't know for how much longer – the rents are prohibitive and the company's struggling at the moment.' Emma tossed back another glass of wine and felt the unmistakable pressure of Adam's knee under the table. She couldn't decide whether to return the pressure or withdraw her own knee, so settled for not doing anything.

'What about you?' she asked. 'Have you been with the CID long?'

'About ten years.'

'Do you enjoy your work?'

'Only when I get to do body searches of attractive female suspects.'

'Is that often?'

'Never, unfortunately.'

Emma finished her couscous and pushed her plate to one side. It was warm and cosy in the restaurant and she was filled with a sense of well-being, laced with erotic anticipation. Adam reached across the table and took her hand, then began to knead her palm with the pad of his thumb.

She knew she was becoming aroused again and heard herself say, 'Shall we have coffee at my place?'

'Only if I can continue with my investigation.'

'That depends on what you want to investigate.'

'Your underwear mostly.'

'Sure. It's in a big pile in the middle of the floor.'

Back at her flat, he reached out for her and kissed her lengthily, holding her close to his tall, hard body. Breathless she pulled away after a couple of minutes, murmuring, 'I'll put some music on, shall I?'

He looked ironically at the empty space where the sound system had been and where now there was only a rectangle of dust.

'I'd forgotten for a moment,' she admitted.

'Crime's on the up,' he told her, pulling her close again.

'Well something certainly is,' she agreed, feeling the hard bulge in his groin pressing into her stomach. 'Unless you carry a gun.'

'Nope. Just handcuffs.'

'Really?' she breathed. 'That opens up some interesting possibilities.'

He picked her up and carried her into the bedroom, depositing her firmly on the bed. She sat still while he removed her primrose-yellow silk blouse and black skirt, revealing an ivory silk slip, suspender belt and panties. She made a move to kick her high-heeled shoes off, but he stopped her.

'No – leave them on.'

She subsided obediently back onto the bed and watched, fascinated, as he produced a set of lightweight handcuffs from his back pocket.

'I . . . I was joking about the handcuffs,' she stammered.

'Never joke with a member of the police force,' he cautioned her sternly. 'We're not renowned for our sense of humour.'

He fastened her wrists to the headboard, laid her down on the bed with a pillow pushed under her hips, then threw the quilt over her.

'The first thing I like to do,' he told her as he stripped down to his briefs, 'is an undercover investigation.'

He dived under the quilt and Emma felt his warm mouth begin to trail up her thighs, pushing her slip up as he did so. She sighed and relaxed as he kissed and nibbled his way over her smooth flesh.

'I should warn you . . .' he began, his voice muffled by the quilt, '. . . that anything you're wearing can be taken down . . .' He drew her panties slowly down over her hips and Emma raised her backside to help him as he continued, '. . . and used in evidence against you.'

He emerged from the quilt holding her panties and dropped them on the floor. 'Exhibit A,' he announced. He threw the quilt to one side, parted her legs and knelt between them.

Emma gasped as his tongue invaded her private parts, lapping and tasting her moist female flesh, flickering erotically against her clit, then plunging into her over-heated pussy.

If he was as good with his cock as he was with his tongue she was in for quite a night. He licked away at her until she was squirming with lust and straining at the handcuffs that bound her to the headboard.

A sudden spasm of pleasure as he sucked delicately at her clit indicated that she was about to climax. It hit her with a jolt like an electric shock and she cried out, her head falling back and her breasts heaving.

He moved up her body and began to caress her breasts, first through the fine silk of her slip, then her naked skin. He took one hard, tingling nipple between his lips and teased it with his tongue as she groaned with abandoned pleasure.

'Now for that intimate body search,' he warned her, dragging off his briefs.

Emma opened her eyes and saw that his cock was exceptionally long and a few drops of pearly moisture were already glistening on the end.

'I see it isn't just the arm of the law which is long,' she commented. 'I think this means I'm in for a stiff sentence.'

'Very long and very stiff,' he assured her, opening her legs wide and pushing two fingers inside her. He explored the velvety contours of her honeypot for a long, and as far as Emma was concerned, pleasurable time.

At last he withdrew and muttering, 'All right, let's be having you,' poised himself above her then slid smoothly inside.

His cock was so long that it took a while before he penetrated her to the very hilt. He had to withdraw slightly then forge upwards again a couple of times, gaining more ground each time he did so.

Emma gasped and rotated her backside on the pillow, clutching at him with her internal muscles as he shafted her with firm, fluid strokes.

As the tempo of their love-making increased, she raised her hips to meet each thrust, pulling in vain at the handcuffs which restricted her movements.

She came again as the pressure on her clit intensified, arching her back and moaning as the shudders of satisfaction racked her slender body. After several more convulsive thrusts, Adam reached his own climax and erupted in a boiling flood of orgasmic release.

* * *

Emma awoke early the next morning and had to think for a few moments before she remembered who was lying beside her. Moving stealthily, she climbed out of bed and padded over to the heap of clothes Adam had thrown carelessly on the floor when he undressed.

After he'd released her from the handcuffs, she'd suggested doing the same to him, but he hadn't liked the idea.

'Policemen don't like wearing cuffs – it's a reversal of the natural order of things,' he'd protested, and tossed them onto his pile of clothes.

Adam might not like the idea, but Emma did.

She picked them up and returned to the bed. It was the work of a few moments to secure his wrists to the headboard. He woke up as she clicked the lock home and stared at her in confusion.

'What's going on?' he demanded.

'In some circles it's known as sauce for the gander,' she returned sweetly, dragging the quilt from his naked body. 'Well now, what have we here?' she purred when she saw his early morning erection.

'If you'll let me go, I'll do something meaningful with it,' he promised.

'You're going to do that anyway,' she assured him.

'Please, Emma – unlock them, this is sending me into trauma,' he begged.

Emma ignored him and sat astride his thighs, still in her ivory suspender belt and pale stockings from the night before.

'That hard-on isn't going to be around much longer if you don't let me go.' He jerked frantically at the cuffs, but only succeeded in chafing his wrists.

'Is that right?' she murmured, taking his cock in both hands and squeezing it gently. It immediately responded by burgeoning into an even more impressive size. 'Seems okay to me,' she commented.

He groaned and closed his eyes. 'You're doing untold damage to my psyche.'

'Your dick doesn't agree with you.'

Emma positioned herself over his treacherous member and lowered herself until the glans was nudging at the entrance to her honeypot, still swollen after their hectic screwing of the night before. Grasping his shaft firmly, she rubbed the head backwards and forwards against her clit, until a renewed surge of female juices bubbled inside her.

Slowly, tantalisingly, she sank downwards until his cock was completely encased; then, without moving, she began to caress her own breasts. Adam was watching like a hare trapped in the beam of a car's headlights, as she brushed her fingertips over her nipples until they jutted out like small chunks of rose quartz.

She knew she had him when he began to thrust upwards with his hips, and she responded with an answering downward movement of her own.

She rode him slowly at first, refusing to be rushed, but his determined movements beneath her soon had her bouncing up and down on his cock at a frenzied pace.

He came quickly – she suspected he hadn't made any attempt to hold back and wait for her, because he was unhappy about her dominating the situation.

'Let me go!' he ordered, almost before the last of his hot juices had spurted inside her. Still sitting astride him she reached for his keys and leant forward to release him.

He rubbed his wrists briefly before seizing her by the

arms and rolling her beneath him, his cock still resting within the velvet tunnel of her honeypot.

'Keeping a police officer prisoner against his will is a serious offence,' he admonished, holding her down by the shoulders. Emma smiled provocatively and wriggled her hips against him, feeling him grow hard within her again.

'How serious?' she whispered.

'Serious enough to warrant the use of my special, CID-issue truncheon,' he grinned, and began to thrust slowly in and out of her once more.

Chapter Four

Tom barred Emma's way in the corridor and stood very close to her.

'Tonight,' he stated.

She smiled at him sweetly, an expression of polite interest on her face.

'What is?' she enquired.

'You and me. Tonight's the night. I thought we'd start with a quiet dinner for two, then go back to your place.'

Emma knew that Tom wanted to see where she was living now, presumably in the hope of ascertaining whether there was any other man in her life, or how permanent a home her new flat was.

She'd steadfastly resisted all his attempts to visit her there, despite the various ruses he'd used. He'd even tried turning up on her doorstep without warning, but there was a spyhole in the door so she simply hadn't opened it.

'I'm sorry – I'm already doing something,' she told him firmly.

'We have an agreement. Cancel whatever it is.'

'We have an agreement that I'll have sex with you sometime before the week's out. That doesn't mean I have to drop everything just because tonight happens to suit you.'

Tom reached out and wound a strand of her shining

blonde hair around his finger, then gently stroked her neck. Emma suppressed a shiver of excitement but was determined to stand her ground.

'Are you seeing another man?' he demanded suddenly.

'That's none of your business.'

She folded her arms protectively in front of her and wished that even the faintest whiff of his cologne didn't set her groin tingling.

'When then? The deadline's in three days' time.'

'I'll check my diary and see when I can fit you in.' Emma turned on her heel and retraced her steps into her office.

'I could manage eleven to eleven-thirty tomorrow morning,' she offered.

Tom shook his head. 'I want a full night.'

'That wasn't part of the agreement.'

'It is now.'

'I could spare you about forty minutes right away – will that do?'

He shook his head again.

Emma decided to play him at his own game. 'Are you sure?' she asked softly and slowly began to unbutton her blouse.

His eyes never left her as the thin silk top fell open, revealing her high, luscious breasts. She let it fall to the floor, then naked to the waist stroked one raspberry-hued nipple. His gulp was audible.

'Are you sure?' she repeated, gently tweaking the other nipple between her finger and thumb. When he didn't reply, she drew her skirt up her thighs until the pale flesh between her stocking tops and panties was visible.

When she touched herself delicately between the legs he took a step towards her, to be brought up short by the telephone ringing.

Their eyes locked, then Emma reluctantly stretched out hand to pick it up. She knew that if she didn't, Rosa would come to see where she was.

It was one of their clients wanting further copies of a video they'd made for him, and he kept her on the line for several minutes.

By the time she'd finished Tom had got a grip on himself, though that didn't stop him from staring lecherously at her breasts.

'Tomorrow night then?'

'I suppose so,' said Emma ungraciously, 'but I won't be able to make it until around nine-thirty because I'm meeting someone for a drink at eight, so we'll have to skip dinner.'

He looked disappointed. 'I want to take you out for a meal.'

'Too bad – that wasn't part of the deal,' retorted Emma, slipping her arms back into her silk top. 'It's up to you, Tom – tomorrow evening at nine-thirty or tomorrow morning at eleven. Oh, and not at my flat – I'll come to the house.'

He looked as if he was about to argue, then obviously thought better of it.

'I'll get some food in and we'll have a picnic then,' he suggested.

'Whatever you like.'

Why, oh why did I agree to this? she asked herself in a cab heading towards Highgate the following evening. Tom had been out of the office all day, but he'd phoned her in the late afternoon to remind her of their date – as if she needed any reminding.

She'd met a friend of hers for a drink earlier, but had found herself unable to give Deena her undivided attention

– or in fact much attention at all – she'd been too busy thinking about her forthcoming rendezvous with her ex-husband.

She'd gone home after work to shower and change and had been annoyed with herself because she couldn't decide what to wear.

Something sexy?

Something severe?

She didn't want to look like she'd dressed up specially, but neither did she want to dress down too much. In the end she'd settled for a jade-green silk suit with a figure-moulding jacket and a short, tight skirt.

As the cab careered towards Highgate she tried to tune out the driver's rambling monologue about the decline-of-civilisation-as-he-knew-it. She wished he'd keep his eyes on the road and stop looking at her in the rear view mirror.

Why did cab drivers always think it was okay for them to hold forth on any subject they liked, regardless of the response from their passengers? The only other job she could think of that provided such a captive audience was that of a dentist. Or possibly a mortician.

She was half looking forward to the evening with a sense of stomach-churning, erotic anticipation, and half dreading it. She must be crazy to be going through with it. The last thing she needed now was to be caught up in a renewed sexual relationship with Tom and his ever-ready dick.

The cab drew up outside the house and she fumbled in her bag for some money. She was very tempted to omit a tip, but she couldn't face the tirade of abuse she suspected the driver would hurl at her.

The front door opened before she reached it and Tom stood there smiling at her wolfishly.

'You needn't look so pleased with yourself,' she said crossly as she entered the house. 'I want it on record that

Yawning, Emma rinsed her cup out and decided to try to get a few more hours' sleep.

'No problem, Rosa, you and me can share a room,' suggested Jake lasciviously.

Rosa tossed her head so that her silver hoop earrings danced, and glanced at him dismissively.

'No thanks – I have it on good authority that you snore.'

Jake was obviously outraged by the slur on his character.

'No I don't!' he protested. 'Who said I did?'

'I forget her name. One of the girls who came here looking for you last year. The one with the long red hair. Davina or Diana or something.'

Rosa was in the middle of making the arrangements for the shoot in Barbados. No easy matter. She'd just discovered that the hotel was a room short of the number they needed, which had prompted Jake to make his suggestion.

It was a source of some frustration to him that he'd never managed to add Rosa to the long list of women he'd shagged. It wasn't for the want of trying but, for some reason he could never fathom, she appeared to find him wholly resistible.

Jake knew that it was generally a bad idea to get involved with anyone he worked with – it meant that when it was over he would still have to see them every day. But he was quite incapable of resisting the pull of his dick – whichever way it drew him.

And it drew him towards Rosa with unfailing frequency.

He fancied Emma too – what man with functioning hormones wouldn't? But he found Emma's cool reserve off-putting – and she was his boss, which was even more off-putting.

He was also well aware that if Tom spotted him even looking at Emma too appreciatively, he'd be out of a job. No, Emma was definitely off limits.

But Rosa was another matter.

She was just so fucking *hot* that it was impossible to spend any time in the same room without trying to put the make on her. Every time he made a play for her and she turned him down flat, he swore to himself it was the last time.

There were plenty of women out there who were more than willing – why waste his time on one who wasn't?

Then he'd watch her bending over to get something out of a filing cabinet, her long legs on display almost up to her crotch, or he'd walk down the corridor behind her, mesmerised by the sway of her voluptuous arse, and his dick would express its appreciation of her charms in its customary manner. She made him feel like a dog on heat, always sniffing around her.

She was a permanent itch he couldn't scratch.

He wanted to pull her fantastic tits out of her tight tee-shirt and cover them with his large hands. He wanted to back her up against the wall and grind his hard-on into her groin, then drag her skirt up, pull her knickers down and give her a seeing-to that would have her moaning with pleasure and panting for more.

But she wouldn't let him.

It had cheered him up a bit to overhear Tom trying his luck and being practically blasted into orbit by the vehemence of Rosa's response.

She'd told him in no uncertain terms that as far as she was concerned, he was a complete shit for making a pass at her when he was married to Emma.

Jake didn't know whether Tom had ever tried again after

Emma had left him, but if he had it was odds on he'd still got nowhere.

Tom came wandering into the office at that moment.

'What's the problem?' he asked Rosa.

'The hotel has one room fewer than we need, and Jake was just selflessly offering to share with me. Don't worry about it – I'll find a hotel that can fit us all in.'

Tom looked thoughtful for a moment. 'You don't need to do that – Emma and I will be sharing a room, so problem solved.'

'Does Emma know that?' asked Rosa sceptically.

'Haven't you heard? We had a big reunion last night, so you can go ahead and make the booking.'

Tom smirked at her, looking so pleased with himself that Rosa almost believed him. 'Oh, and, Rosa . . .'

'What?'

'No need to mention it to Emma just yet. It's all part of a surprise I'm planning for her.' He sauntered out of the office with his hands in his pockets, whistling tunelessly.

Jake and Rosa exchanged glances.

'Do you think it's true?' she asked him, 'or do you think Emma would tell a different story?'

'Hard to tell. But if Emma won't share a room with him, my offer to you still stands, sweetheart.'

Chapter Five

The heat hit them the moment they stepped from the plane in the early hours of the morning. It was like being inside a conservatory – hot, damp and carrying the odours of a dozen different types of tropical vegetation.

The wait in the customs hall seemed endless and, although theirs was the only plane to land in the last couple of hours, they still had to queue for quite a while to clear customs with all their equipment and other luggage.

It would have been longer but Rosa, hips swaying, went over to talk to a couple of customs officers who were lounging indolently against the wall. After a couple of minutes' conversation they opened another desk and, after that, things moved much faster.

Rosa oversaw all the travel arrangements, and she'd booked a minibus and driver for the duration of their stay. The drive through the dark, humid night had a surreal quality. They all had that dazed feeling inevitable after the plane journey, a change of time zones and, in the case of Tom and Jake, a lot of alcohol.

A hot wind blew in through the open windows of the bus, tangling Emma's hair. She peered out into the gloom but the only thing she could see clearly was her reflection in the window. She was tired and hoped they'd be able to check into the hotel with a minimum of fuss so that she could get some sleep.

Rosa took the room keys from the receptionist and the sleepy-looking porter began loading their bags onto a trolley.

'Here's yours Emma,' Rosa told her, passing her a key with a brass tag the size of a saucer attached to it. Tom reached out and took it from her, looking rather sheepish.

Sometime on the journey out he'd meant to tell Emma that they'd be sharing a room, but somehow the right moment had never presented itself. He drew her to one side.

'Emma, there was a bit of a problem with the number of rooms – we were one short, so I told Rosa we'd share.'

Emma drew the key firmly from his grasp.

'That was very noble of you, Tom. I'm glad you don't mind sharing because you and Jake are in the same room.'

Rosa came up at that moment, her eyes gleaming with amusement at Tom's discomfiture, and handed him another key. Jake followed her looking annoyed.

'What do you mean?' demanded Jake. 'I need a room of my own, or it'll cramp my style.'

'Can't be helped,' Rosa told him, hiding her laughter with difficulty. 'You two will just have to work out a rota. I asked for a twin, but I think a double was all they had left – I hope that's not a problem.'

Tom was obviously very put out by this unexpected turn of events.

'Come on, Em,' he pleaded. 'You can't expect me to share with Jake.'

The porter picked up Emma's bags, threw them on his overflowing trolley and set off.

'I'm sure you'll sort something out,' retorted Emma sweetly.

They followed the porter out of the reception area and along a path which wound through fragrant banks of scented flowers, with Tom and Jake complaining all the way. It was too dark to see much but the path itself, though over to the right Emma could hear the sound of the waves crashing on the beach and smell the salt in the air.

Their accommodation was in small beach cottages dotted around the grounds of the hotel. Emma was so tired by the time the porter deposited her bags that she didn't really take anything in.

She stripped off, had a brief shower, then fell into the massive king-sized bed and was asleep within seconds of her head hitting the starched pillowcase.

When she woke up, the bright sunlight was flooding in through the thin curtains and she could hear the sound of birds cheeping on the roof. She stretched sleepily and wondered whether Tom and Jake had slept as soundly in their shared accommodation.

She smiled to herself as she remembered the look on Tom's face when he realised his scheme had backfired on him. Since their night of, admittedly fantastic, sex, she knew he'd had renewed hopes that she'd go back to him. Rosa had told her that he'd claimed they were together again and about his 'surprise' that they'd be sharing a room.

The sex had been great, but as far as she was concerned it didn't change anything. Her problem now was going to be keeping Tom at arm's length throughout their stay. She was uncomfortably aware that hot climates always made her unbearably randy, so it wasn't going to be easy.

In fact, she felt randy right now.

Determined not to give in to it, Emma slid out of bed, wrapped herself in the bedspread and stepped outside onto the veranda.

The view was breathtaking.

A hundred yards away a white sand beach and a turquoise sea reflected the intense sunlight back at her so intensely that she had to close her eyes for a few moments.

The wooden floor of the veranda felt warm beneath her bare feet. There was a thatched roof overhead and a chaotic mass of brightly coloured flowers growing up the sides, screening it from other nearby cottages.

It was paradise.

Inside, there was a spacious bedroom tastefully furnished with bamboo furniture and floral chintz. The bathroom had a bath big enough to hold a party in, as well as a large shower cubicle.

Going back inside, Emma opened her suitcases and made short work of the unpacking she'd been too tired to do the night before.

Her rumbling stomach was telling her she was hungry, so after a quick shower she pulled on a pale-blue tee-shirt with a pair of white shorts and with her blonde hair blowing in the humid breeze, she went off to find the restaurant.

Only Tom and Jake had surfaced and were tucking into a large cooked breakfast. Like the cottages, the restaurant had a thatched roof, but was open at the sides, and located right next to the beach. Tiny, brightly coloured birds flew around, engagingly, if not very hygienically, diving down for crumbs from the tables.

'Morning boys,' she greeted her ex-husband and their

cameraman, ignoring the admiring glances she was attracting from the other men in the vicinity. Neither Tom nor Jake looked particularly cheerful. 'Sleep well?' she enquired.

'Not particularly,' returned Tom, spreading a piece of banana bread lavishly with butter. 'That girl was right – he does snore.'

'At least I kept to my side of the bed,' said Jake grumpily. 'I had to elbow him in the ribs half a dozen times. It's not on, Emma, either get me a cottage of my own here, or I'll move to another hotel. It's off season, there must be somewhere with vacancies nearby.'

'Speak to Rosa,' said Emma firmly, pouring herself a cup of coffee.

The four of them had flown out early to scout for locations. The rest of the film crew and the actors and actresses who would appear in the commercial would arrive in a couple of days.

As she sipped her coffee, Emma cast a sidelong look at Tom. Even unshaven and rumpled – he'd never been any good at packing so his clothes were creased – he set her juices stirring in the morning's heat. She shifted uneasily on her chair.

Get a grip, Emma, she admonished herself silently. Pick up a tourist if you must, but *don't* let Tom coax his way into your bed again – however tempted you are.

She must have put on a couple of pounds since she last wore her shorts, because they fitted very tightly around the crotch and made her very aware of the insistent throbbing of her private parts.

Rosa chose that moment to put in an appearance, causing a quite a stir among the male guests. She was wearing a sleeveless, scarlet-and-white striped tee-shirt which clung to her full breasts so tightly that every crinkle in her nipples seemed to be outlined. She was barefoot and her tiny red shorts made her long legs look endless.

'Bloody hell, Rosa,' muttered Jake, 'how can I eat my breakfast with you looking like that? Get some clothes on sweetheart – or take the consequences.'

As a concession to the heat he'd shed his leather jacket and boots and was wearing jeans and a white tee-shirt, with a pair of battered trainers.

Rosa smiled serenely and looked around her.

'This is what I call a location shoot,' she said contentedly. 'I can't wait to have my first swim. It was only hunger that stopped me from diving straight in when I woke up.'

'And another thing,' continued Jake, 'I'm not sharing with him for another night. If you haven't found me my own room by this evening, I'm moving into your cottage whether you like it or not.'

'How can you be so grouchy in such beautiful surroundings?' asked Rosa. 'Are you already missing the litter, noise and petrol fumes that characterise our great metropolis?'

'No – I'm missing a bed to myself. I don't mind sharing it with any halfway-fit female who comes along, but not another bloke.'

'See what you can sort out after breakfast will you, Rosa?' interjected Tom mildly. 'Even if it means us all moving to another hotel.'

'Okay. What's on the agenda today? Other than my swim, that is?'

'We all pile into the minibus and go and search out locations,' said Emma. 'At some stage we break for lunch and, later on, we'll knock off for a swim. No point in overdoing it until we've all adjusted to the climate. How does that sound?'

'I need to check in at the police station about the permits, get a local driving licence and pick up a mini-moke,' said Rosa. 'I'm not sure how long all that will take, so if you like I could meet you somewhere for lunch.'

Emma studied a map of the island and a guide book and they arranged to meet at a hotel a few miles down the coast.

After breakfast, Rosa went to see the assistant manager, and arranged a separate cottage for Jake, even though the female receptionist had assured her that the hotel was full. The assistant manager, who could barely take his eyes off her breasts, was extremely helpful and she promised to have a drink with him one evening. She then packed a beach bag and had the minibus drop her at the police station.

Everything took much less time than she'd expected, so she set off in the mini-moke to do some exploring of her own until it was time to meet the others.

She parked at the edge of a deserted, palm-fringed beach and walked along the fine white sand with the waves lapping at her bare feet. The sun beat down on her slender brown limbs as she savoured being alone. Most of her time on Barbados would be spent working hard from early in the morning until late at night, so it was good to have a couple of days recovering from the flight and taking it relatively easy.

She walked for about a mile, then was about to retrace her steps when the sun went behind a cloud. A few minutes later she was caught in a sudden tropical downpour, which drenched her within seconds. Rosa looked around her and could see no sign of anyone else.

Impulsively, she stripped off her clothes, left them on a

75

rocky headland, which jutted out into the sea, and dived exuberantly in. For about twenty minutes she swam around in the clear aquamarine water, as the rain poured down from the sky. As suddenly as it had started, the downpour stopped and the sun came out again.

Reluctantly, Rosa left the water and wandered back along the beach towards the rocks, squeezing her dripping hair, which fell in a tangled mass to her shoulders.

She stopped dead in her tracks when she saw the man lounging a couple of yards from her clothes, a pair of faded denim shorts his only covering. He was fishing, but took his eyes off his line to run them appreciatively over her naked body.

'G'day,' he greeted her.

Automatically, one hand went to shield her bush and the other as much of her breasts as it would cover – which wasn't much.

'Don't worry – I'm not the local rapist,' he continued, in an unmistakable Australian accent. 'Incidentally, the local police take a dim view of skinny-dipping, topless sunbathing or fornicating in public places.'

'Do they really?' asked Rosa, grabbing her bag and retreating behind a rock. She swiftly pulled on a scarlet bikini and emerged again, then laid her wet clothes out on a rock to dry. 'How do they feel about Peeping Toms?'

'How was I to know you were skinny-dipping? All I could see was your head. Besides, I catch my lunch here every day.'

He looked to be in his early thirties and had a deep tan and sun-bleached blond hair. A broken nose added character to an otherwise pleasant, but unremarkable face.

'Want a beer?' He nodded invitingly towards a coolbox just next to him.

'A beer would be great.'

He extracted one and tossed it to her. Rosa spread her towel out on the rocks and sat on it, sipping her cold beer gratefully, and wondered how long it would take for her clothes to dry – not long in this heat presumably. 'Are you local?' she asked idly, 'or just on holiday?'

'I've been here about six months – I've got a cabin just over there.' He nodded behind him to where the beach finished and a wilderness of luxuriant tropical foliage began. He ran his eyes over her body again and said, 'You got any suntan cream in that bag of yours?'

'Yes – do you want some?'

'No, but you do. It's coming up to noon and you'll fry if you sit there much longer.'

Rosa had applied some to her exposed limbs before leaving the hotel, but had neglected to re-apply it after swimming. She found it in her bag and began to massage a dollop into her shoulders.

'Thanks – I'd forgotten.'

'You on holiday?' he asked, watching her.

'Working. We're shooting a commercial for chocolates.'

'You're an actress – right?'

'No – general dogsbody.'

There was a pause. His eyes were following every movement as she rubbed cream into her smooth, tanned skin.

'I don't suppose you need any help with that?' He grinned at her engagingly, showing very white teeth. Rosa looked at him through her thick, dark lashes appraising him speculatively. His eyes were the same shade of blue as his faded denim shorts, and his body looked lean, hard and fit.

'Sure. You can do my back.' She tossed him the tube and rolled onto her stomach. He wedged his fishing rod between two rocks and knelt by her side. She felt him undoing the clasp of her bikini, then he squeezed a generous amount of cream onto her shoulder blades and began to massage it in.

As his hands moved over her back, Rosa closed her eyes and made a small murmur of appreciation deep in her throat. From high overhead, the sun beat strongly down on them and she could hear the rhythmic sound of the waves breaking on the beach below.

A slow heat began to build in the pit of her stomach as he massaged the small of her back. Beads of perspiration broke out on her brow as her excitement grew and she found herself pushing her groin unobtrusively against the unyielding hardness of the rock below.

He turned his attention to her legs, slathering lotion on them and paying particular attention to the tops of her thighs. It was no good, she couldn't keep still any longer – she was practically squirming in her bikini bottoms. Of their own volition her thighs parted and she wriggled her bottom voluptuously.

He paused in his ministrations. 'Some men might take that as an invitation,' he remarked.

Rosa turned her head and looked at him seductively over her shoulder. 'And how would "some men" feel if it was?'

'Like all their birthdays had come at once, I reckon.'

'Happy birthday.'

Rosa lay back on her stomach and a few seconds later felt the Australian's hands sliding under her bikini briefs and caressing the smooth globes of her backside. His thumbs slid into the crease between her buttocks, then downwards until they found the warm, moist entrance to her pussy.

She opened her legs wider and gasped as he stimulated

her clit with his thumb, causing a renewed surge of honeyed juices.

'You want to come back to my cabin?' he asked her.

'What's wrong with here?' she murmured.

'Nothing, as long as no one sees us. Better be careful – we can't risk stripping off.'

He joined her on the towel and she turned onto her side to face him. He stroked her breasts through her bikini top, then slipped his hand under the thin fabric to fondle them more intimately. His other hand was busy inside her bikini pants, exploring the soft wetness he found there.

Rosa reached out and unzipped his denim shorts. He was naked beneath them and his heavily knobbed cock was big, hard and obviously more than ready for action.

'That's some boomerang you've got there,' she breathed admiringly. She grasped it firmly and squeezed, rubbing her thumb over the glans to spread the drops of fluid which were oozing out.

He groaned, pulled her closer, then pushed his cock inside the leg of her briefs. It took a few moments of frustrating manoeuvring to get the right angle for penetration without either of them having to remove their clothes.

'Don't worry – where there's a willy, there's a way,' murmured Rosa huskily as, with a triumphant grunt, he managed it at last. She tightened her internal muscles to grip his cock tightly as he began to move against her.

Their bodies were already slippery with a combination of sweat and suntan cream as they humped each other breathlessly under the sweltering midday sun.

It didn't last long.

The possibility of discovery, together with the feel of his huge cock moving deep inside her, was almost enough to make Rosa come right away.

After a few glorious minutes the Australian climaxed, emitting a string of disjointed and colourful expletives as he did so. They separated and she rose shakily to her feet and adjusted her bikini.

'Now I need another swim,' she announced weakly. She dived off the rocks again and a few seconds later he followed her. They splashed around for a while, fondling each other insatiably under water. Eventually Rosa clambered reluctantly out again and dried herself off.

After scrambling back into her shorts and tee-shirt she glanced at her watch and said, 'Got to go . . . What *is* your name?'

'Kenny. What's yours?'

'Rosa.'

'Well, Rosa, d'you want to come back to my cabin for something to eat? I can offer you the freshest fish on the island. It's so fresh I haven't even caught it yet.'

'Thanks, but no thanks. I've got to meet the others at a hotel down the coast and I'm already late.'

'Okay, but if you fancy getting together again while you're here, turn off the road by Danny's pizzeria and my cabin's along there at the end of the track.'

'I'll remember. See you, Kenny.'

'You've been swimming!' Jake accused her, after taking in her damp, tousled hair when she joined the others on the terrace of the hotel fifteen minutes later. They were all already onto their second beer.

'That's right. And believe me, the water's lovely.'

They all accepted menus from the waitress. Tom whistled when he saw the prices.

'Not exactly cheap is it?' he commented cheerfully. 'But it's all on Sophia thank goodness.'

They ate an excellent lunch overlooking the calm, turquoise sea. A huge cheese plant grew up against the side of the terrace next to a giant mother-in-law's-tongue, making Emma feel as if she'd shrunk like Alice in Wonderland and been transported to a land where house plants were the size of trees.

Tom kept pressing his thigh meaningfully against her own bare one, making her stomach lurch with lust. She contemplated jabbing her fork into him, but decided it was too beautiful a day for naked aggression.

Naked screwing would be much better.

Or partially naked screwing.

But not with Tom.

After lunch, they explored more of the island and eventually, in the late afternoon, decided that they'd earned a break. They spread out their towels on a white crescent of sand near a small beach bar and stretched out in the sun. They became immediate targets for the vendors patrolling the beach and selling clothes, jewellery, hand-made ornaments and dope.

The vendors were good humoured but determined, prompting all four of them to take a swim in the lukewarm waters of the Caribbean in the hope that they'd have gone away by the time they came out.

Later, as she lay sunbathing, Emma was uncomfortably aware of Tom's close proximity and the demanding heat throbbing in her groin. She wished hot climates didn't make her so unbearably randy – it would be hard to concentrate on the job if she didn't find an outlet for her sexual energy.

When they returned to the hotel, Jake went to move his belongings into the other cottage which had been found for him and Tom followed Emma onto her veranda.

'How about inviting me in?' he suggested, his hand slipping down over the curve of her hip and onto her naked thigh.

'I don't think so,' she said, moving away.

He followed her, this time trailing his fingers over the cup of her bikini top, making her nipples push excitedly against the damp fabric.

'Why not? We both know what this sort of climate does for your libido – why waste it, when we could spend the next few days screwing each other's brains out? That's what you'd really like to do, isn't it?'

He slid his hand inside her bikini top and cupped her breast. Emma felt her breath coming in little gasps and tried to back away, but his other arm snaked around her and he pushed his hand down the back of her bikini briefs and pulled her close to him so she could feel the size of his hard-on under his shorts.

She knew that in another minute he'd have wriggled his fingers between her legs and felt for himself how wet she was. Emma hesitated, torn between a desire to knee him in the balls for pursuing her after she'd told him it was over; and dropping to her knees, freeing his cock and taking it in her mouth.

At that moment Rosa came into view and walked towards them. Swearing under his breath, Tom released her.

'Am I interrupting anything?' Rosa asked cheerfully, stopping at the bottom of the steps.

'No,' said Emma, furtively adjusting her bikini, 'Tom was just going – which one of us did you want?'

'You.'

'Come on in then.'

Tom reluctantly left and Rosa followed Emma inside.

'I just wondered if you felt like hitting the town tonight – just the two of us?'

'Great idea!' said Emma fervently. 'Otherwise Tom will spend the evening trying to persuade me into bed – and I'm frightened I might succumb.'

'That's what I thought. Jake's like a dog on heat too.'

'Why don't we just slip off in the mini-moke when we're ready,' suggested Emma, 'or they'll want to come along. I can tell that Tom doesn't intend to let me out of his sight if he can help it – he doesn't want some other bloke taking advantage of the fact that this heat is making me horny as hell.'

'You too? The moke's under the trees just to the left of reception. Shall I meet you there at eight?'

'Eight will be fine. See you later.'

Chapter Six

Driving through the warm, humid night in the mini-moke made Emma's freshly washed, normally sleek hair turn into a wavy golden mane, and caused Rosa's dark curls to riot uncontrollably around her wanton, high-cheekboned face.

The two women attracted a lot of attention when they walked into the beachside restaurant and perched on high rattan barstools at the bar, both showing a lot of bare leg.

Emma's ice-queen beauty was set off by a tight-fitting, pale green silk dress, which left most of her shoulders bare and stopped at mid-thigh. Rosa's more exotic appearance was heightened by a canary-yellow silk vest tucked into a tight black mini-skirt.

They were immediately joined by two middle-aged men whose Hawaiian shirts and baggy shorts did nothing to disguise their paunches.

''Ello, darling', where you from then?' one of them asked Rosa, his eyes riveted on her jutting nipples. The other leaned against Emma, breathing beer and garlic fumes into her face.

'Tell you what, love, I'll bet you aren't local.'

The men were difficult to dislodge and it was only the appearance of their wives which eventually prised them away from the bar. Thankfully alone again, Emma and Rosa had another drink, and enjoyed the sensation of the warm breeze playing over their bare limbs.

'Shall we eat here?' asked Rosa. 'The food looks great.' The restaurant specialised in local cuisine and the smells drifting out of the kitchen were making her mouth water.

'Sounds good to me,' said Emma absently, eyeing two men who'd just come in.

This was more like it.

The men who'd just left to join their wives were not what she'd had in mind to distract her from tantalising thoughts of sex with Tom. An evening of their company and she'd be banging on Tom's door, begging him to screw her.

Rosa followed her gaze and Emma was amused to see the tip of her colleague's tongue flicker over her red lips as she appraised the newcomers briefly. The two women exchanged a meaningful look, then continued with their conversation.

They'd just been seated at their table in the dining area, when one of the men came over to speak to them.

'Excuse me, my friend and I are doing a survey to see how many attractive women will let a couple of total strangers buy them dinner.'

'What do the results of the survey indicate so far?' asked Emma.

'Nothing yet. You're in the enviable position of being the first ladies invited to take part.'

He had reddish hair, a fair skin, dark-brown eyes and a Canadian accent. His friend appeared and hovered behind him, smiling hopefully. Emma looked across at Rosa.

'What do you think?'

Rosa had already decided to do a survey of her own later – a very thorough survey.

'I think we ought to give them every possible assistance with their research,' she said slowly and meaningfully.

'In that case, won't you join us?' Emma invited them. A waiter brought two more chairs and the men introduced themselves as Donald and Steve, both airline pilots from Toronto on a one-night stopover.

Emma watched them from beneath her lashes while they all chatted. She found them both attractive, but she could see that Steve had his eye on Rosa, so she turned her attention to Donald.

After dinner, Rosa and Steve decided to visit a neighbouring nightclub, and Emma and Donald strolled down to a nearby beach bar.

Donald took Emma's hand as they wandered along the sand. She walked barefoot, carrying her high-heeled shoes and allowing the occasional wave to wash over her feet. There was a three-quarter moon rising above them, casting a silvery light over the sea, but Emma was in the grip of such strong sexual excitement that she barely noticed the beauty of their surroundings.

She'd been contemplating the wisdom of inviting Donald back to her cottage, but regretfully decided it was too much of a risk. There was no guarantee that Tom wouldn't turn up at some stage in the proceedings and take unreasonable, but heated exception to his ex-wife sleeping with another man.

'Which hotel are you staying at?' she asked Donald when he'd ordered their drinks.

'The Trade Winds – it's about a mile down the coast. How about you?'

'I'm in a cottage at the Silver Reef.' She picked up a paper napkin and fanned herself with it. Even the short walk down the beach had made her feel hot. Or maybe it was the close proximity of such a sexy man. 'Isn't this heat wonderful? I spend most of the year back home shivering.'

'I find it a bit much myself – I prefer it cooler. And I rarely stay anywhere long enough to acclimatise.'

A few yards from where they sat, the sea was making sexy lapping, slurping noises, which were driving Emma into a frenzy. She was sure that Donald would get round to suggesting they go back to his hotel sooner or later, but she didn't want to wait.

In the shadows she slipped her hand along his thigh, feeling at the hard muscles under his cotton trousers.

'Do you work out?' she asked him. 'It certainly feels like it.'

'I go to the gym, play a little soccer. How about you? You're certainly in great shape.' He glanced down to where her breasts pressed against the thin green silk of her dress and let his gaze move slowly down over the curve of her hip.

'I'm a member of a health club, but I don't get there as often as I should – I think I'm getting flabby. What do you think?'

She took his hand and placed it on her own thigh, then heard him catch his breath as he ran his hand up it. She could feel the heat from his palm burning her bare flesh and electric shocks of pure carnal sensation leapt up to her groin.

'You . . . you don't feel flabby to me,' he assured her.

Emma didn't usually come on so strongly with a man she'd just met, but the combination of the heat and Tom's behaviour earlier in the day were too much for her.

She put her hand over his and moved it further upwards.

They had only today to cover the rest of the island before the others arrived and Emma decided that for maximum efficiency they needed to split up.

'Rosa and I could take the Atlantic side, and you and Jake could cover the rest of the west coast and the far north,' she suggested to Tom – the last thing she wanted was having him glower at her suspiciously all day.

'We need to stay together, Em,' he said immediately. 'There are a couple of shots I want to work in, which will mean a change in the script.'

'We could discuss that tonight,' she suggested brightly.

'Over dinner? Just the two of us?'

Emma's heart sank as she swiftly tried to decide which would be worse: a full day in Tom's company, or a long, hot, tropical evening.

Followed no doubt, if he had his way, by a long, hot, tropical night.

'Maybe it would be better if we scouted locations together today,' she said eventually.

'Fine,' he said, cheering up perceptibly. 'Rosa – we'll take the moke. You and Jake take the minibus.'

Emma felt gloomy as she packed a bag for the day. A shoot in Barbados had seemed like a great idea when Tom had told her about it, but it was the first time they'd been on location together since they'd split up.

Back in London, when work was over for the day, she simply returned to her own flat and her separate life. Here it was more complicated.

Particularly with her juices constantly on the boil like a permanently simmering cauldron.

The Atlantic coast was very different from the serene, turquoise sea which lapped the white-sand beaches on the

Caribbean coast. On this side of the island the landscape was bleak and windswept. Great white-crested waves crashed ferociously onto the deserted beaches, where only strange phallic rock formations and a few leafless trees broke up the otherwise barren landscape.

It was another hot day, but Emma shivered when Tom brought the mini-moke to a halt on a cliff overlooking the boiling sea.

'It's hard to believe it's the same island,' she commented. 'This side never features in the travel brochures – and it's easy to see why.'

'We can shoot some great footage though,' said Tom enthusiastically. 'The more contrasts, the better.'

The commercial was going to highlight the contrasting aspects of Caribbean life and then draw a parallel between that and the different chocolates in the Caribbean Collection. As a concept, they were both well aware it hardly broke new ground, but under Tom's direction it would be an attractive, stylish commercial, which would undoubtedly sell chocolates.

And possibly win an award or two.

If they were lucky.

They drove slowly along the coast road with Emma making notes. As producer, it was her job to keep everything together and she was good at it.

'Time for a beer,' said Tom eventually, and pulled to a halt above a small cove, which was backed by a cliff-face honeycombed with caves. He pulled two beers out of the coolbox and they scrambled down the steep path to the beach. They had some protection from the wind down there, but it still howled around above them so noisily that they virtually had to shout to hear each other.

They drank their beers then explored a couple of the

caves, where it was at least quieter, though Emma didn't like caves and went in very reluctantly. But they needed to shoot some footage in one, so she didn't have much choice.

'Fancy a swim?' asked Tom when they discovered a deep, still pool several hundred yards into a cave. They'd walked so far in, that only a pinprick of light a long way behind them showed the entrance.

Emma kept glancing nervously behind her to make sure it was still in sight. She'd no intention of going in so far that they wouldn't be able to see the way out. A limited amount of light shone in from holes directly overhead, but, even so, she found the whole place distinctly spooky.

'No thanks,' she said firmly. 'Tom, I don't think we ought to hang around here – we don't know what time the tide comes in, or how fast. If you think we might shoot some footage, we'd better go and talk to some of the locals and find out.'

'It was way out half an hour ago,' he said cheerfully. 'I think I will just take a dip – the sea's much too rough to swim in and I'm melting. Sure I can't tempt you?'

She shook her head, so he stripped off his clothes and stood naked in front of her, poised on top of a rock jutting out over the pool. 'Come on, Em.' he said invitingly, 'just for a few minutes.'

The sight of Tom's naked body was having its usual effect on her. He was semi-erect and she suspected that the thought of them swimming naked together was responsible. But he'd miscalculated this time – the place gave her the creeps and wasn't somewhere she'd ever choose for an erotic interlude.

'I'll wait for you on the beach,' she told him. 'Then I can let you know if the tide's coming in.'

Without waiting for a reply she set off and, a few seconds

later, heard a splash as he dived in. Even the windswept beach seemed desirable after the gloom of the cave and Emma sat on a rock warming herself in the hot sunshine.

It wasn't long before he joined her, naked and dripping.

'It was freezing,' he complained. 'Pass me a towel, will you please?'

'Mine's in the mini-moke,' she said, 'where's yours?'

'In the mini-moke. Oh well, I'll soon dry off in the sun.'

He sat down beside her on the rock, his erection vanquished, at least temporarily, by the icy water. But Emma knew that she only had to stretch out her hand and squeeze his limp cock for it to grow swiftly into the huge instrument of pleasure she'd known so intimately for so many years.

Once she'd caressed it into tumescence she could . . .

For *goodness' sake*, Emma! she castigated herself. That's just the sort of thing he's hoping you'll think. Go out again tonight and find yourself another man if you must – but forget about this one.

But that was easier said than done, particularly with her private parts throbbing a hot, urgent message. They might as well have been chanting, 'Fuck me, fuck me,' because it was the only thing she could think about. She knew damn well that if Tom as much as put his hand on her knee she'd melt into his arms.

'How about lunch?' she said brightly, thinking it would be as well if they went where there would be other people as soon as possible. Otherwise she might just be fool enough to bury her head in his groin and lick her way over his balls, up his cock and . . .

Leaping to her feet, Emma set off up the cliff path saying, 'I need another beer.'

Tom pulled on his clothes and followed her.

'Where's the best place for lunch do you think?' he asked, starting the engine. Emma consulted her guide-book.

'There's a place a few miles up the coast.'

The restaurant was in a flower-filled garden behind a single-storey wooden building set back from the road. They sat at a table under a parasol and talked about the shooting sequence while they waited for their food.

They had a long wait.

Delicious smells kept wafting out of the kitchen, but no food seemed to be forthcoming. Two other couples were also waiting patiently, but service was slow even by Caribbean standards.

'I'm getting pissed,' complained Emma, after three more beers. 'I'll probably fall asleep this afternoon and there's loads to do yet.'

'I like you pissed,' said Tom amiably. 'After lunch we can go and find a deserted spot in the sun and have a siesta if you like.'

The look he gave her as his eyes lingered on her firm breasts under her sleeveless, pale-mauve tee-shirt, made her press her bare thighs together.

'Here's our food,' she said thankfully, as the waitress emerged from the kitchen carrying huge platefuls of spicy bean casserole and rice.

It was mid-afternoon by the time they climbed back into the mini-moke and continued on their way. The combination of the beer, the food and the hot sun made the rest of the afternoon pass in a haze, and by the time they returned to the Caribbean side of the island Emma could barely stay awake.

'How about half an hour in the sun, then a swim?' proposed Tom. 'We've earned it.'

'Okay,' agreed Emma. 'Just half an hour.'

They found a thin strip of powdery white sand fringed by palm trees and spread out their towels. There was no one else in sight but Emma ducked into the undergrowth to change into her emerald-green bikini.

She refused Tom's offer to rub her with sun oil and applied a liberal coating herself, then stretched out on her back and immediately dozed off.

She had a vivid erotic dream.

She was standing naked and blindfolded on a ledge near a waterfall. Spray from the water ran down her body, trickling over her curves, stimulating and arousing her.

Her hands began to follow the tiny streams of water and she smoothed over her breasts, pausing to tease the crinkled nub of one nipple, cupping the other in the palm of her hand. She knew someone was watching her but she couldn't see who it was – but knowing she was being observed was unbearably exciting.

She turned her back on the hidden watcher and stroked her own buttocks, before bending forward from the waist so the water could trickle into the cleft between the satin-skinned globes of her backside.

It felt wonderful.

She lay down on the ledge on her back and opened her legs so the spray could spatter down onto her heated honeypot and stimulate the tiny bud of her clit. She began to rotate her backside on the smooth, cool stone of the ledge, then with both her hands she parted her labia, exposing the inner folds of her pussy.

It felt good.

So good that she began to rub her clit, feeling it grow from a tiny bump of pliable flesh to a swollen, urgently pulsating centre of pleasure.

Emma's dream became very confused. Now, whoever had been watching her had joined her on the ledge, but she was still wearing the blindfold so she couldn't see him. He began to touch her breasts, kissing and stroking them, with the spray cascading over both their bodies and cooling the heat which consumed them.

She felt his fingers between her legs and he brushed aside her hand, taking over the rhythmic caressing of her clit. She heard her own moans, and then she opened her eyes to see Tom bending over her, one hand stroking her exposed breasts and the other buried in the skimpy briefs of her bikini.

He smiled at her when he saw her eyes flutter open, but didn't cease his erotic exertions. Still only half awake, she felt her climax building and was unable to do anything except go with it.

Tom had always been terrifyingly adept at bringing her to a climax manually. Even starting from stone cold, he could do it in three minutes flat – or spin it out indefinitely until she began thrashing about and begging him to finish it.

She could tell by the depth of her arousal that he'd been touching her for a while, then everything was blotted out as she exploded into an orgasm, which left her drenched in perspiration and shaking weakly.

His fingers stopped moving but he kept his hand where it was.

'What ... what happened?' she managed to say at last.

'The heat gets you every time, doesn't it, my sweet? I was just lying here blamelessly by your side, when you started moaning and the next thing I knew you were fondling your own boobs. Not being slow on the uptake I realised you were having a naughty dream and I thought you might enjoy it even more if I joined in.'

Emma was about to protest when he began to rub her clit

again with a tiny, arousing, tickling movement. The blood pounding away in her groin made it difficult for her to think straight.

'I wasn't wrong was I?' he demanded softly. 'By the way, you might want to do up your bikini top – there's a party of tourists coming this way and my hands are otherwise occupied. Or at least one of them is. Don't worry, they can't see what I'm doing.'

With fumbling hands, Emma fastened the tie which held her bikini closed.

'Oh good,' continued Tom. 'They're laying out their towels about fifty yards away – and with all this beach to choose from too. Try not to moan too loudly, darling – I know it's difficult because I'm very good at this.'

He looked so smug that if Emma hadn't been concentrating on the expanding circles of pleasure pulsing out from her pussy, she'd have been tempted to slap him. As it was, she closed her mouth, opened her legs a little wider and let him bring her to another slippery, gasping climax.

When it was over he withdrew his hand and licked his own fingers appreciatively.

'I'd have my head between your legs if it wasn't for our audience,' he said conversationally, 'but this will have to do for now.'

The thought of Tom's large, muscular tongue delicately probing her private parts made Emma squirm with a renewed flood of lust.

'I don't suppose there's any chance of your returning the favour?' he asked. 'If I sit with my back to them and you sit facing me so I'm blocking you from their view, I don't think they'll notice anything, do you?'

They rearranged themselves and Emma freed Tom's cock from where it had been straining painfully at his swimming trunks. After warming a palmful of sun oil, she began to massage it skilfully, kneading and stroking it into even greater tumescence.

She kept glancing nervously over his shoulder, but the two other couples were either reading or dozing and no one was looking their way.

When the whole of his member was glistening with a thick coating of oil, she closed her hand around it and began the rhythmic motions that would soon bring about his release.

When he came, it was in a great series of spurts, which leapt skywards before descending to land on the top slopes of Emma's breasts, then trickled down into her bikini.

She rubbed it in, coating her cleavage with the thick, creamy liquid.

'How about a swim? Then we'll go back to the hotel and screw each other's brains out. Possibly stopping briefly for dinner, or possibly not. We could always have room service.'

Emma knew she should say no, but it was difficult when it was exactly what she felt like doing.

They ran into the sea and swam around in the tepid water, then returned to their towels to get dressed. Emma dived into the undergrowth again, stripped off her bikini and pulled on her shorts and tee-shirt.

They walked to their mini-moke and set off back towards the hotel. As soon as they were driving along the deserted coast road, Tom reached across and slipped his hand between her legs.

'I was hoping that was the case,' he said when he discovered that she'd dispensed with her knickers, and he could easily get his hand up the loose leg of her shorts.

He kept her in a state of red-hot arousal on the short

drive back, until she was literally squirming on the hard seat of the car. She knew quite well he was doing it deliberately to stop her having second thoughts. He touched her intimately again as they approached his cottage on the shrub-shaded path.

Emma could barely breathe, she was so hot to have his cock inside her, filling her up and . . .

They emerged in front of his cottage to be met by the sight of Sophia Brentwood reclining in one of the chairs, sipping a cocktail and looking remarkably at home.

'There you are!' she greeted them. 'Did you find all the locations you need?'

'Sophia!' Tom managed to say. 'What . . . what are you doing here?'

'You didn't think I was going to let you have all the fun out here alone did you? I've come to watch the shoot. Oh, and Tom . . . they didn't have a spare cottage, so I've moved into yours. That bed's far too big for just one person.'

Chapter Seven

Emma couldn't stop laughing as she stood under the stinging needles of a cool shower. Tom had looked so appalled for a few brief seconds before he'd pulled himself together, that she'd felt almost sorry for him.

She herself was half relieved, half annoyed. Sophia's unexpected arrival had saved her from finding herself back in Tom's bed, a victim of her own uncontrollable urges. But having the client hanging around while they were shooting a commercial would make life difficult.

Although she knew it was Tom who would suffer most because he was the director, it would fall to her unhappy lot as producer to keep Sophia away from him during the shoot. Their client would undoubtedly want to hang around him, making unwelcome suggestions and trying to tell him how to do his job.

If the commercial was going to be any good, Tom needed to be left alone to direct it, so Emma could foresee problems ahead.

But at least with Sophia around he would be forced to stop trying to get his ex-wife back into bed. It was obvious from the gleam in Sophia's eye that all Tom's considerable sexual energies were going to be needed to keep her happy.

The five of them ate dinner together. Emma, Rosa and Jake had to wait for ages before Tom and Sophia emerged from his cottage, and when they did Tom looked absolutely knackered.

Emma found it difficult to hide her amusement over dinner. Sophia, resplendent in a low-cut white dress and an alarming amount of jewellery, kept touching Tom, stroking his dark hair back from his brow, and squeezing his thigh. She insisted on feeding him titbits from her plate, and generally treated him as if he were some kind of favoured pet.

Tom drank much more than he usually did and became increasingly withdrawn. Emma could see he was having trouble being pleasant and hoped he would remember that, however annoying Sophia's behaviour was, she was still the client.

After dinner, Rosa left to have a drink with the assistant manager and Jake announced that he was off to the disco of a neighbouring hotel to see Shelley, the tour rep he'd met the night before. Sophia clapped her hands together girlishly.

'Let's all go! What do you think, Tom?'

Tom looked as if it were the last thing he wanted to do but, as he suspected that the alternative was to return to his cottage and fuck Sophia again, he tried to sound enthusiastic as he said, 'Sure. Let's go.'

He was completely pissed off at this latest turn of events. Sophia appearing out of the blue had completely ruined his plans regarding Emma – instead of screwing his ex-wife he'd been forced to screw Sophia.

As soon as Emma had vanished in the direction of her own cottage, Sophia had dragged him into the bedroom and had his clothes off within thirty seconds. She'd taken his enormous erection as a compliment, unaware that it hadn't been intended for her.

He'd fucked her long and hard, taking out the frustrations she was causing on her compliant, willing body. It galled him that she'd just moved into his cottage without waiting for an invitation. The sight of her clutter of cosmetics in the bathroom irritated him intensely, though he'd never felt like that when he was living with Emma.

He couldn't stand the way Sophia kept touching him, and the thought of having to spend a good proportion of his time for the rest of their stay servicing her, whether he felt like it or not, made him furious.

And he knew himself too well to think that he might be able to say no. He'd never been able to turn down sex with an attractive woman, even if being the pursued, rather than the pursuer, pretty well ruined it for him.

Shortly after they all arrived at the disco, Tom was struck by an idea. Leaving Sophia with Emma, he went over to where Jake was nuzzling the ear of his extremely pretty travel rep and asked if he could have a word with him.

'What's up?' asked Jake, clearly reluctant to leave Shelley on her own for long. Several unattached men were already eyeing her lasciviously.

'Jake, I'm in a bit of a spot,' began Tom uncomfortably, drawing him to one side. 'Can you help me out, mate?'

'How?' asked Jake suspiciously.

'It's Emma – she's not happy about Sophia moving in on me. We're pretty much back together again and Sophia turning up has made it all a bit awkward. Can you take Sophia off my hands while she's here? It shouldn't be too difficult with your way with women.'

'You *must* be bleeding well joking!' protested Jake. 'It's you she's got hot knickers for – not me. And I'm just the cameraman, not the boss – she wants the head honcho, not the hired help.'

He turned on his heel and was about to walk off.

'I'll let you direct one of the Brentwood commercials,' offered Tom desperately.

Jake paused for a moment and considered. He was keen to direct, but only got the opportunity when Tom had too much on – which was almost never these days.

'But only if you manage to get her out of my cottage and into yours tonight and for the rest of the shoot,' Tom added hurriedly.

'It won't work,' said Jake reluctantly. 'She won't go for it. Not in the space of one evening. I'd just be wasting my time.'

It wasn't that he wouldn't like to shag Sophia – he definitely would. Her found her ripe, voluptuous body a real turn-on and would have welcomed the chance to get his hands on it. But Shelley was a dead cert and Sophia only a remote possibility.

Which made it an easy decision.

At that moment one of the unattached men moved in on Shelley and Jake left Tom's side without another word.

Gloomily, Tom returned to Sophia and ordered another rum. He was further enraged to see Emma dancing with a man and appearing to have a wonderful time.

It should be him she was dancing with, not some other bloke who would undoubtedly only be after one thing.

Sophia insisted that they dance too, and proceeded to press her heavy breasts into his chest and grind her ample hips against his groin. His cock responded in the usual manner but it was the only part of him that did.

He steered Sophia until they were dancing next to Emma and her partner and tried to hear what he was saying to her. When he saw that the man had his hand on Emma's bum, Tom almost ground his teeth together in a fury of jealousy.

'I just need to speak to Emma about something,' he told Sophia through gritted teeth.

'Don't be a spoilsport, Tom,' cooed Sophia, giving his hard-on a furtive feel in the dim light. 'Can't you see she's busy? Surely whatever it is can wait until tomorrow?'

She dragged him back to their table and began to kiss him passionately. He responded mechanically, still trying to see what Emma was doing. When he saw her heading towards the exit, with the man's arm around her, he broke free of Sophia and hurried after them.

He stood in the doorway, but they were nowhere in sight. The thought of what they might be going to do made the blood pound through his body at an alarming rate. Sophia came up behind him and caught his arm.

'What on earth are you doing?' she demanded.

'I . . . I forgot to tell Emma something,' he replied lamely.

'Forget about work!' she said exasperatedly. 'I know you workaholics – you just don't know how to relax. Well, I'm going to teach you.'

Taking his hand, she led him back to the cottage and sat him on a sun-lounger on the veranda. A moment later she was on her knees with his cock in her mouth, hidden from view by the low fence. She sucked his cock hungrily, winding her tongue around it in a series of oral contortions which took his breath away.

He ripped open the front of her low-cut dress and released her breasts from her underwired, ivory satin bra. He squeezed and kneaded them roughly, letting them fill the palms of his hands, circling her prominent caramel-coloured nipples, then rubbing them with his thumbs.

If Sophia wanted him so badly she could have him – but they were going to do it his way.

He would punish her for not being Emma.

Getting to his feet so abruptly that his cock sprang out of her mouth with a wet, slurping sound, he pushed her so that she was bent over the veranda rail, her breasts hanging out of her bra for anyone passing to see.

He dragged up the tight skirt of her dress, exposing her plump buttocks and strong thighs. She was wearing a pair of ivory satin camiknickers and he yanked them down to her knees, shoving his own knee between her legs to open them wider.

She gasped in shock and turned her head to say, 'Tom – not here, anyone could . . .'

He ignored her, thrusting into her with no preliminary caresses, burying his cock deep in her syrupy wetness with such force that she gasped again and her buttocks quivered against his groin.

Holding her by the hips, he proceeded to shaft her vigorously. He wasn't by nature a violent man and, even angry as he was, if she'd indicated that he was hurting her, he would have paused and moderated his movements.

But far from finding his roughness unacceptable, Sophia began to moan and thrust forcefully back at him, her buttocks making slapping noises against his thighs, bouncing around like a couple of erotic, spherical jellies between each thrust.

He leant over her and grasped her breasts, clamping his hands around them as they worked each other towards a sweating, gasping climax. Tom came first, with a low-pitched, long drawn-out moan, then slumped over her briefly as he tried to catch his breath.

With a strong contraction of her internal muscles, which squeezed the last few drops of fluid from Tom's dick, Sophia reached her own climax a few seconds later.

He withdrew abruptly and lay down on a sun-lounger, wiping his dripping forehead on his shirt sleeve. Sophia pulled her camiknickers up over her ample backside and sank down next to him, her dress was by now badly crumpled. She began to tuck her breasts back into her bra, but Tom stopped her.

'Leave them,' he ordered her, 'I want to look at you.'

She lay obediently back with her breasts exposed, while Tom stretched out thoughtfully.

If Sophia insisted on having him as a lover as the price he had to pay for making the Brentwood commercials, there would be a price for her to pay in return.

They were going to do it his way.

He was going to be the one to call the sexual shots.

It would be interesting to see how far he could go.

The following day, the cast and the rest of the production team arrived, and work began in earnest. Sophia, as both Tom and Emma had anticipated, made a complete nuisance of herself.

By lunchtime Tom, usually easy-going and unruffled, was in a foul mood. He'd been unable to get a moment alone with Emma because Sophia literally wouldn't let him out of her sight.

They'd only managed to cover a third of the ground they needed to at the production meeting in the morning, because Sophia kept interrupting; either to have something explained to her, or to volunteer her views on whatever was under discussion.

After lunch she dragged Tom back to the cottage and pulled him down on the bed. They'd already done it twice that morning, but Sophia was insatiable. Tom didn't really want to fuck her again, but, unfortunately, his cock did.

He made her masturbate herself to a climax, standing on the coffee table wearing only her high-heeled shoes, stockings and a suspender belt while he watched, aroused despite himself.

She didn't want to do it, but he insisted.

When she'd come, and her voluptuous body was suffused with a pink flush, she stood mutely on the table awaiting his further instructions, a thin trickle of clear, female secretions creeping down her thigh.

Tom was struck by an idea and told her to lie on her back on the bed. With his belt he lashed her wrists to the headboard, then spreadeagled her legs and began to secure her left ankle to one corner.

'Tom – I'm not into bondage,' she protested, but he could tell by the feverish glitter in her eyes that she found the prospect exciting.

'You soon will be,' he assured her, securing her other ankle, then pushing a pillow under her ample hips. She lay there helplessly, her private parts a dark glistening pink, surrounded by a reddish thatch of pubic hair. Tom was overcome by an uncontrollable sexual excitement of his own as he looked at her, completely in his power.

He knelt on the bed and massaged the quivering lips of her pussy with the palm of his hand, feeling how hot and wet she was.

'You like being tied up don't you?' he asked her softly.

'It's making me ... ner ... nervous,' she gasped as he pushed two fingers deep inside her.

'It's making you as hot as a cat on heat, you mean,' he corrected her, rubbing her swollen clit. 'Isn't it?'

'Yes ... yes,' she moaned, as he explored the furthermost depths of her dripping cavern. As he did so, he told her in explicit detail what he was going to do next, while she writhed and pulled at her bonds, her head thrashing wildly from side to side.

She climaxed again, her whole body shuddering, and her head fell back as he intensified the pressure on her clit. While she was still gasping, he unzipped his trousers and entered her, shafting her with long, unhurried strokes and resisting all her attempts to get him to speed up.

She kept bucking her hips upwards, wanting more than he was giving her, until he suddenly withdrew and casually poured himself a beer.

'Tom!' she pleaded. 'Don't stop!'

He sat on the edge of the bed, fondling her breasts for a while as he sipped his drink, then suddenly splashed some of the icy liquid over her chest and stomach. She cried out in shock, then moaned again as he began to lick it off, his tongue lingering on her nipples and navel.

When it had all gone, he played with her private parts, separating her soft lips and holding them open, before dousing them with the rest of the beer and burying his face between her legs. By the time he sat up, her head was flailing on the pillow, her mouth open, her eyes closed.

He thrust his cock into her again and fucked her relentlessly, keeping it going so long that even he wondered where he was finding the energy. He had his hands hooked into the back of her suspender belt, clasping her buttocks and holding her tightly against him as he fucked her into another dimension of sexual pleasure.

When he'd come, he climbed off her without a word and went into the bathroom for a much needed shower. When he emerged and began to pull on some fresh clothes, she murmured, 'Untie me.'

He ignored her until he'd finished dressing, then picked up the key with its heavy brass tag and headed for the door.

'*Tom*!' she cried after him, 'untie me!'

He paused in the doorway.

'But I haven't finished with you yet,' he told her. 'That was just the beginning – I'll be back in a while to take up where we left off.'

'*Tom*!' she screeched, wrenching at her bonds. 'Don't you *dare* leave me here like this!'

He found the others in the bar and took Emma to one side.

'Where's Sophia?' she asked, glancing behind him to see if she was following him.

'Having a siesta,' he said casually.

'Great. Let's finish the production meeting before she puts in an appearance. Poor Tom – you look exhausted,' she added mockingly.

He took her hand. 'Tell me you didn't let that bloke screw you last night,' he said urgently.

She stared at him for a moment. 'That's rich, with you still damp from the body of your latest girlfriend,' she said coldly, trying to withdraw her hand.

'Tell me, Emma – did you let him screw you?'

'For goodness' sake, Tom. Can we just get on with the meeting?'

'You know as well as I do, that if Sophia hadn't turned up yesterday evening we'd have spent all night shagging each other senseless. I don't want you going with other men, Em – say the word, and I'll tell Sophia to move out of my cottage and you can move in.'

'And risk saying goodbye to the rest of the commercials? She'd probably have to let us shoot this one as we're already here – but I'll bet we could whistle for the rest.'

'I really don't care.'

'Well *I* do! Get a grip on yourself, Tom, and let's get this meeting underway.'

She wrenched free and returned to the others who'd all been looking at them curiously. Without Sophia to interrupt, they covered all the business quickly and by mid-afternoon were ready to go off to the first location for a rehearsal of the dance routine.

Tom was tempted to leave Sophia tied up all afternoon, but it occurred to him that she might get dehydrated, or need a piss, so after arranging to meet at the minibus in half an hour when Jake had supervised the loading of the equipment, Tom returned to the cottage.

He found Sophia angry but still aroused, and freed her so she could go to the bathroom. When she flounced back into the room he silenced her protests by making her kneel down and take his dick in her mouth.

He let her perform fellatio on him until he was almost ready to come again, then pulled her onto his lap, with his cock embedded deep inside her.

She moved up and down on his ramrod-hard shaft, her large breasts bouncing rhythmically, while he encouraged her movements with his hands on her waist. When it was over and he'd zipped himself up, he walked towards the door again.

'Where are you going now?' she demanded.

'We're rehearsing the dance routine.'

'Wait for me – I want to come,' she said imperiously.

'You mean I haven't made you come enough for one afternoon?'

'You know very well what I mean.'

He returned to her side and sat down next to her on the bed, stroking her damp red hair.

'It's just a rehearsal. It'll be hot and tiring and we won't actually be shooting anything. Now what I want you to do is have a rest, then get ready for this evening, so when I get back you'll be waiting for me all cool and refreshed.'

She looked slightly mollified, but he knew that she would have insisted on coming if she hadn't been in such a sated state.

'All right,' she said, reluctantly. 'I suppose I could do with catching up on some sleep.'

When work was over for the day, everyone went to a restaurant down the beach for a long, boozy dinner. Although Jake enjoyed himself chatting up Melanie, the glamorous star of the commercial, he excused himself early because he had a date with Shelley.

She was waiting for him in her apartment and greeted him with a long, deep kiss.

'Do you want to go out?' he asked her after they'd separated to draw breath. 'Or shall we stay in and fuck?'

She caught her full upper lip between her small white teeth and pushed back a handful of tousled blonde hair.

'I thought it would be more fun to stay in,' she giggled. She was wearing a pale-blue baby-doll nightie in a gauzy cotton, which did little to conceal her gorgeous figure. Under it he could see she wore a tiny pair of matching panties.

She led him into the bedroom and pulled him hungrily down onto the bed.

An hour later, the two of them lay side by side while a warm breeze from the open window played over their perspiration-soaked bodies.

There was a sudden sound from the doorway and Jake was alarmed to see the door swing slowly open. Half expecting it to be an intruder, he was relieved to recognize

Anthea, Shelley's flatmate, whom he'd met briefly in passing.

He pulled the sheet hastily over his detumescent dick, while she stood there with her ebony skin gleaming in the light, wearing a diaphanous cream nightdress which was so short it only half covered the tight, black curls of her bush.

'Hi, guys,' she greeted them.

Shelley's eyes fluttered open, and she turned her head to look at her flatmate, but made no attempt to cover her own body, naked except for her nightie bunched around her waist.

'Hi, Anthea – what's up?'

'I was feeling lonesome on my own – can I come and join you?'

Jake's gently slumbering manhood leapt into immediate and expectant life.

What was going on?

Did she mean join them in bed, or come in for a chat?

He fervently hoped it was the first option.

'Is that okay with you, Jake?' asked Shelley, turning on her side and propping herself up on one elbow.

'Sure,' he croaked.

Anthea ran across the room and snuggled down on the other side of him, then looked across at her flatmate.

'Do you mind if I get in the middle?'

In reply, Shelley obligingly moved over so Anthea could scramble across Jake's recumbent form, brushing her large breasts pleasingly over his bare chest as she did so.

She was a beautiful girl with huge, liquid brown eyes, a petite, curvaceous body and the most fantastic arse he'd ever seen.

She cuddled down between them saying, 'That's better – I hate feeling left out.'

Jake was still unsure where this was heading, but he was quite prepared to follow their lead. He folded his arms behind his head and awaited developments.

He didn't have long to wait.

Anthea half turned towards Shelley and began to stroke her naked breasts, trailing her fingers down over the other girl's belly, then moving up to caress her breasts again.

Jake had been around, he'd taken part in three-in-a-bed scenarios before but, even so, he found he could hardly breathe, and his chest felt heavy and tight.

Shelley sighed languorously and stretched out like a cat, while Anthea continued with her languid exploration of her friend's body. Anthea's nightie had ridden up to expose the gorgeous thrust of her backside, which began to make erotic, circular movements.

Jake couldn't help himself, he stretched out a hand and ran it over the dark, silken skin of her bottom. In response, she turned completely on her side and pushed it back against his hand.

After that things hotted up fast.

Jake fondled Anthea's willing body, pushing his hand between her legs and discovering that she was wet and ready. While he did so, he watched her kissing and caressing Shelley, until he thought his dick was going to explode.

It reared up between his thighs like a volcano ready to erupt. He guided it between Anthea's gleaming buttocks and parted them, then moved it up and down in her sweat-slippery cleft.

She left off stroking Shelley's thighs for long enough to guide his cock downwards, then opened her legs and eased it into position at the dripping entrance to her honeypot.

One hard thrust and he was tightly sheathed in her pussy and moving against her like a man possessed.

'Slow down,' she murmured over her shoulder, then recommenced her delicate massaging of Shelley's clit. Jake managed to control himself and made his thrusts long and slow, so they echoed the languid mood the women were creating.

He saw the picture the three of them must make, as if he were watching through the lens of his camera, he only wished that he could record it on film to replay as often as he wanted.

Shelley was on her back, her full tits with their small, hard nipples pointing towards the ceiling, one arm outflung, and the other around Anthea. Her legs were widely parted, the blonde fuzz of her bush damp and softly curling, as Anthea stroked her towards a climax.

Anthea on her side facing her friend, her dark skin a pleasing contrast to Shelley's pale one, being shafted from behind with her nightie pushed up around her small waist.

Himself with one arm around Anthea, sometimes stroking her tits, and sometimes reaching further to stroke Shelley's, as he thrust smoothly in and out of her, wondering if he'd wake up and find it was a dream.

Shelley suddenly went rigid and then a series of shudders racked her body as she convulsed in orgasm.

'All change,' ordered Anthea happily.

'Here, I've not finished yet,' protested Jake, but they ignored him and Anthea moved away so that his cock jerked out of her with a wet, plopping sound.

This time Shelley knelt between Anthea's widely parted legs on her hands and knees and began to kiss her way up her friend's thighs. Rendered clumsy by the unexpected interruption to his own pleasure, Jake took a few moments to kneel behind her, and grasp her hips ready to push inside.

She gasped when he thrust into her for the second time that night. Her pussy felt hot and velvety, as if it were boiling over with juices, as he slid easily in, right up to the hilt.

He loved the way she squirmed her bottom back into his groin at each stroke, and the way the three of them moved together on the bed like a scene in a porno movie.

He wanted to keep it going longer but he couldn't – it was just too fucking exciting. With a strangled groan he erupted and flooded Shelley's overflowing honeypot with yet more hot juices, just as Anthea reached her own climax.

'All change again,' said Shelley a few minutes later.

Jake lay weakly back across the bottom of the bed.

'You two start without me,' he muttered.

Chapter Eight

'Okay – cut and print!' shouted Tom, and everyone heaved a sigh of relief. The dance routine on the rocks, then in the shallow waves where they broke on the glittering white sand, had been a nightmare to get on film.

The cast were exhausted. They'd done the routine innumerable times under the blistering heat of the afternoon sun and Melanie, the star, was trembling so hard from fatigue that her teeth were chattering.

Rosa handed round bottles of mineral water as they all collapsed in the shade of an awning erected under the palm trees at the edge of the beach.

'Thanks, Rosa,' said Dominic, the male star of the commercial. He was running with so much sweat that it was forming a puddle in the sand around him. 'Is he always so hard to please?' he asked, indicating Tom with a nod of his head. His eyes, however, were on the luscious orbs of Rosa's breasts.

'He is a perfectionist, but he's on a particularly short fuse at the moment because he's getting a lot of grief from the client.'

Rosa and Dominic had been exchanging burning looks all day, ever since she'd accidentally brushed against him going into the restaurant for breakfast. The jolt of sexual electricity between them had been unmistakable.

Unfortunately there'd been no time to do anything about it.

At least not yet.

Sophia was sitting on a canvas chair, well away from the others, looking sullen. A while earlier she'd gone up to Tom when he was in the middle of directing a scene and suggested he shoot it from another angle. As she'd just managed to walk in front of the camera for the second time that day, Tom had blown his stack.

Emma had hurried across and led her away, but not before Tom had unleashed a flood of invective which would have had most women – and a lot of men – in tears.

Sophia merely looked furious, which boded ill for later. Emma was deeply thankful that she wasn't the one sharing a cottage with their client.

The members of the cast who weren't wanted again that day either lay comatose in the shade or staggered down to the sea to immerse themselves in the tepid water while the next shot was being set up.

Rosa collected an armful of props and walked down to the minibus, which was parked in the shade a couple of hundred yards away. She was just loading them in the boot when Dominic, dripping seawater, came up behind her.

'Is there a spare towel anywhere, Rosa? I forgot to pack mine.'

The star of a recent mini-series and several West End productions, Dominic had the sort of blond, boyish good looks women found very appealing. In the heat of the afternoon he looked so sexy that Rosa could feel her nipples hardening under her tight khaki tee-shirt. His hair was slicked back with water and his slim, hard body was naked except for a pair of brief trunks.

'There are some inside – I'll get you one.'

Their eyes met as she brushed past him and, for an instant, he felt the heat emanating from her body, and caught a whiff of the fiercely sexual scent she exuded.

She climbed onto the bus while he stared at her long, tanned legs and the luscious curve of her backside outlined by a tight pair of khaki shorts.

Like a man in a trance he followed her. She turned around with a towel in her hand, and stopped short when she realised he was standing right behind her.

A movement in the region of his groin made her drop her eyes to where an enormous erection bulged beneath the inadequate covering of his trunks. It was growing bigger by the second, and just at that moment the swollen purple end thrust into view.

The ensuing silence was broken only by the sound of their ragged breathing, before Rosa completely forgot where they were and reached out a hand to grasp his throbbing cock.

They fell onto the floor in the aisle of the minibus, tearing at each other's clothes. Dominic usually prided himself on being a skilled and subtle lover, but there was nothing subtle about the way he wrenched Rosa's shorts down around her thighs and drove into her, with his trunks still twisted around his buttocks.

He felt her internal muscles clench around him like a moist fist, then they were rolling around the aisle, writhing wildly against each other. Rosa's nails were clawing at his bare back and he grabbed her hips, dragging her closer so he could thrust further into the tight, velvety confines of her pussy.

Her tee-shirt was up around her collar bones and he buried his wet face between her tanned, biscuit-brown breasts, rubbing it over the hard points of her flared nipples.

It was hot and stuffy inside the minibus, even with the windows open, and within minutes Dominic's body was dripping with sweat again as well as seawater. Rosa's lithe body was gleaming with a similar dew of perspiration, so that they slipped against each other as they humped their way down the aisle.

They ended up in a tangle of limbs against the back seat and, unable to go any further, Rosa rolled on top of him and gripped his hips between her thighs as she moved frantically above him.

It was almost more like fighting than fucking, as they grappled in a sweaty tangle of naked limbs, their groins grinding against each other as they sought satisfaction.

Rosa's dark curls were tangled around her face and she rode him as if he were a bucking bronco she'd mounted at a rodeo.

Dominic let out a strangled groan and his hands tightened on her breasts as he emptied himself into her. She felt the hot spurting high up inside her and bore down with one last cry, as she convulsed into a climax so strong that she practically blacked out.

When her trembling limbs had steadied themselves, Rosa tried, with only partial success, to repair the damage their abandoned fucking had done to her appearance. Her tee-shirt, arms and legs were streaked with dirt, there was a love-bite on her neck and the zip of her shorts had burst.

A sudden sound from the open door of the bus made her look round and she was nonplussed to see Emma standing there, looking cool and unruffled in a pair of white trousers and a deep-pink tee-shirt. Emma took in the scene while

Dominic tried unsuccessfully to haul his twisted trunks up over his buttocks.

Emma's expression didn't alter as she said, 'Tom's ready to do the pack shot and we don't seem to have the dummy boxes.'

'On the front seat,' said Rosa.

'Thanks.'

Emma picked up the boxes and got off the bus, leaving Rosa embarrassed by her own complete lack of professionalism in abandoning the shoot to satisfy her carnal lusts.

She stopped struggling with her zip, realising belatedly that her own clothes were unwearable, and after a quick look around, pulled on a spare swimming costume from a scene already shot and an oversized tee-shirt she found on one of the seats.

'I think I'll take another dip,' said Dominic. 'Will I see you later?'

'Oh, I should think so.' And with a provocative twitch of her hips, she set off back towards the shoot.

While the crew were packing up the equipment after they'd stopped work for the day, Tom took Emma to one side.

'I'm having second thoughts about tomorrow's location, Em – I don't think it's going to be right.'

'Why not?'

'I think the beach is too long. We need somewhere that curves around behind the action, otherwise there's just going to be too much sea.'

Emma folded her arms thoughtfully and they paced along by the water's edge, discussing the problem.

'What about the beach above Bridgetown – the one with the pizzeria?' she suggested.

Tom thought about it.

'Maybe,' he said eventually. He glanced at his watch then grabbed Emma's hand. 'Come on,' he urged her. 'Let's go and check it out before it gets dark.'

Emma glanced behind them to where Sophia still sat.

'What about Sophia?' she asked.

'She can go back with the others in the minibus. We'll take the moke.'

'She won't like it. Maybe we should ask her to come with us.'

'Over my dead body. I've had just about as much as I can stand of her for today.'

'I know. But the fact remains that she is the client and she's going to expect an apology at some stage.'

'If there's any apologising to be done, it isn't going to be me doing it. Why couldn't she stay in bloody England instead of following us out here?'

'I think it might be something to do with your sexual charisma,' teased Emma. 'You were obviously so good she can't get enough – so you've only yourself to blame.'

'It's not funny,' said Tom gloomily. 'How would you like having to fuck someone you didn't want to, on a daily basis? I only did it the first time because it seemed like a good way to get you back into bed. I didn't bargain for having to keep on performing.'

'You know you love it really. I'll just go and tell her where we're going,' said Emma, and walked over to their disgruntled client.

'Sophia, Tom and I are just going to check out a location. We'll see you back at the hotel.' She glanced around and beckoned to Toby, the assistant cameraman. 'Toby, will you look after Mrs Brentwood until Tom and I get back please?'

She hurried off before Sophia could protest.

* * *

They got caught in what passed for rush-hour traffic in Bridgetown, and the light was fading by the time they arrived at the beach.

'I think it will be okay,' said Tom eventually. 'What do you think?'

'It should work. Let's get set up early and try to get it in the can by lunchtime.'

On the way back to the mini-moke Tom suggested they stop for a drink at a nearby beach bar.

'We'd better get back,' Emma demurred. 'You need to make it up with Sophia. I mean it, Tom, she could still pull the plug.'

'Just one,' he assured her, ushering her up the steps and ordering two rum punches from the barman.

He settled back in his chair and surveyed her appreciatively.

'Isn't that the tee-shirt I bought you in Nice?'

'Probably,' returned Emma coolly, although she knew quite well it was.

'Weren't you wearing it when I screwed you over the balcony rail at the Negresco?'

A flush of pure sexual heat rose slowly through Emma's body at the memory.

They'd been in their room overlooking the *Promenade des Anglais*, when she'd heard a commotion outside. She'd been undressing prior to taking a shower and had wandered out onto the balcony wearing only the pink tee-shirt Tom had bought her that afternoon and a pair of frilly white panties.

She'd leaned over the balcony just in time to see the arrival of a famous film star and her entourage in a fleet of limousines.

125

'Tom!' she called over her shoulder, 'come and look at this.'

He came up behind her and she felt his hands on her hips, before he slowly drew her panties down her thighs.

'I'd rather look at this,' he told her, stepping back to admire the curves of her smooth, taut bottom.

While Emma watched what was going on below her, Tom slipped his fingers inside her and explored her honeypot, not stopping until she was dripping with erotic anticipation.

Then, while the photographers jostled for position and the film star struck various poses, Tom eased her legs apart and entered her.

His strokes were long and smooth, working her slowly up to mindless ecstasy, until she lost interest in what was going on below and was only aware of the salt breeze in her face and the feeling of Tom's huge cock pleasuring her.

She was pressed against the balcony rail, gripping it hard and trying not to cry out and attract any attention from the crowds below. She tried to open her legs even wider but was unable to do so because her panties were hobbling her around the thighs.

Tom ripped them off her in one swift movement, then speeded up his strokes, until she thought she was going to be sent flying off the balcony by the force of his thrusts.

Now, sitting in a beach bar in Barbados Emma pressed her thighs together and wished she didn't feel so randy.

Coming across Rosa and Dominic in their post-coital confusion earlier in the day, had turned her on – she wouldn't have minded a go with Dominic herself – and now here was Tom deliberately dredging up erotic memories that she'd rather had stayed dormant.

He leant across, placed his hand behind her neck and kissed her hard on the lips. Against her will, she found herself responding, a fire spreading upwards from her groin and raging through her body.

She managed to pull away at last and gasped, 'Save it for Sophia.'

'Let's go back to your cottage,' he said urgently.

Emma sprang to her feet and headed towards the mini-moke parked behind the beach bar. Just as she reached it, he caught her up and pulled her into his arms. He kissed her again, his hands roaming over her body, roughly caressing her backside through the thin cotton of her white trousers.

She pulled away again.

'Tom – this is not a good idea.'

'Why not?' he muttered into her hair. 'You want me – I know you do.'

'All I want at the moment is a shower and something to eat,' she said firmly.

He pushed his hand between her legs and found the damp patch where her juices had soaked through from her panties.

'Oh really? What's this then?'

Before she could stop him, he'd yanked down the zip of her trousers and thrust his hand inside. She gasped as his fingers made contact with her throbbing clit, then buried themselves in her hot wetness.

She moaned as he pressed her up against the side of the mini-moke in the shadows and she heard the sound of his own zip coming down. They'd undoubtedly have had it away standing up in the car park, if a car hadn't pulled up in front of them and caught them in the twin beams of its headlights.

Furious with herself, Emma jerked away and climbed into the driving seat, zipping up her trousers. 'Give me the keys!' she ordered him.

He handed them reluctantly over and they sat in silence during the short drive back to the hotel. Tom tried to follow her into her cottage but she slammed the door in his face.

He stamped back to his own cottage and found Sophia applying her make-up, seated at the dressing table in a black silk slip and a pair of high-heeled shoes.

'Just where do you think you've . . .' she began, then tailed off as she saw the expression on his face.

Without a word he dragged her to her feet and threw her on the bed. He tore off his trousers and fucked her savagely, his face contorted with frustration and rage.

Sophia was more than ready for him and responded eagerly, ripping the shirt from his back and scratching him with her long, pink-painted nails.

He grabbed her wrists and held her hands above her head, pounding into her mercilessly while she writhed and moaned beneath him. He came in a long, boiling gush, pumping it into her rhythmically while she screamed out his name.

When he'd finished, he jerked out of her and went to take a much needed shower. While he was still standing under the tingling jets of water, she opened the door of the cubicle and stepped in to join him.

The sight of her plump honey-coloured breasts stirred him again and, with his hands on her shoulders, he made her kneel on the floor and take his dick in her mouth, while the water soaked her freshly washed hair. When she'd coaxed it into an erection he pulled her to her feet and took her roughly from behind.

At least it kept her quiet. While they were dressing she didn't say a word, just slipped silently into her clothes with a dazed expression on her face.

She was just about to step into a pair of black silk camiknickers when he stopped her.

'You won't need those,' he told her.

'I can't go out without any underwear,' she protested, scandalised. 'What if I trip? Or the wind blows my skirt up?'

'You'll just have to hope that doesn't happen,' he told her determinedly, taking her arm and hurrying her towards the door.

The whole cast and production team dined at a large table set among the tropical foliage in the hotel gardens. Tom was sitting directly opposite Emma, who was looking exquisitely beautiful in a smoke-blue silk dress, which left her arms and shoulders bare.

Still in a bad mood and hoping to make his ex-wife jealous, Tom threw his arm around Sophia's shoulders and let his fingertips rest idly on the upper slopes of her breast.

Emma was chatting to Jake and didn't appear to notice. Throughout the meal, Tom became increasingly aroused again by the sight of Emma's smooth, tanned shoulders and the outline of her nipples thrusting against the fine silk of her dress. He couldn't ever remember wanting a woman so badly.

He felt incredibly horny again and was soon stroking Sophia's stocking-clad knee under the cover of the table-cloth. He could tell she was embarrassed in case anyone noticed, but excited at the same time as he trailed his fingers up over the soft skin above her stocking top.

While they were waiting for their coffee, he talked to Emma and Jake about tomorrow's shoot. When Sophia started to question the arrangements they'd made, he ran his hand up her thigh and circled his fingers over the springy hair of her bush. He wasn't looking at her, but he heard her sharp intake of breath and her voice tail off.

'Sorry, Sophia, what were you saying?' asked Emma, after waiting in vain for her to continue.

Tom chose that moment to slip his finger between Sophia's outer lips and slide it around the slick head of her clit.

Sophia blushed a deep pink and managed to say, 'I'm . . . I'm not sure.'

Puzzled, Emma shot a suspicious glance at Tom. Her suspicions were confirmed when she saw his guileless expression.

She'd have put money on it that he had silenced their difficult client by putting his hand up her skirt. She knew Tom's games of old, and had been on the receiving end of them herself many times.

Emma was torn between amusement and unbearable randiness as they continued their discussion with no further interruptions from Sophia. She saw the way the older woman clutched her glass as if it were a lifeline, her cheeks getting even pinker, and beads of sweat standing out on her forehead.

Emma was almost squirming on her seat, imagining Tom's hand up her own skirt, doing delicious things to her private parts under the cover of the tablecloth. She half envied Sophia, half felt sorry for her.

When Sophia let out a sudden gasp and tried to turn it

into a cough, Emma realised Tom was going to ruthlessly work her to orgasm in full view of everyone at the table.

He really was a bastard.

She watched covertly and at the exact moment Sophia's eyes closed and her head dropped back, Emma sent her glass of iced water flying across the table and onto Tom's lap.

Sophia's low moan went unheard as Tom let out a yell and leapt to his feet.

'Tom – I'm so sorry,' Emma apologised profusely, reaching across and handing him a napkin. While Tom mopped himself down, Sophia excused herself and went off to the ladies, reappearing five minutes later looking much more composed.

The party split up after dinner and Emma decided to get an early night – they were setting off at eight the following morning and she hadn't slept much since she'd arrived. She was desperate for sex, but told herself that a good night's sleep would do her more good than picking up some stranger and having him screw her.

Tom and Sophia went back to their cottage. Ever inventive, Tom had thought of something new he'd like to try and, as Sophia was still in a state of shock after her first public orgasm, he didn't think she'd be too difficult to coerce.

Once back there, he stripped off her dress and bent her, protesting a little, over the table in her black slip, stockings and suspender belt. He lashed her wrists to one end, then parted her legs and tied an ankle to each of the table legs.

He pulled up her slip to reveal the full globes of her pale buttocks. Her legs were so widely parted, and she was bent so far forward, that her gleaming labia was very much on display, protruding through the damp thatch of her reddish bush. Between her outer lips he could see the moist, intricate folds of her pussy and he found the sight extremely arousing.

'You look *so* sexy like that,' he told her. 'So sexy and so absolutely, completely fuckable.'

Sophia's breath was coming in little gasps.

'Tom – don't keep me waiting,' she pleaded.

'Waiting for what?' he enquired casually.

'For . . . for whatever you're going to do.'

He ran his hand over her ample backside, dipping his fingers into her wet pussy. He was half tempted to see how she'd react to a mild spanking. He could just imagine the way her plump buttocks would bounce as he slapped them sharply with the flat of his hand.

He was distracted from this titillating line of thought by Sophia wriggling around on the rough wicker surface of the table, moaning, 'Tom – make love to me. Don't keep me waiting.'

'I'm not going to make love to you, Sophia – I'm going to fuck you. If you ask me nicely.'

'Yes . . . yes. Fuck me, Tom – please fuck me!'

Tom knelt between her widely parted thighs and pushed his tongue roughly into her dripping tunnel. She thrashed her head from side to side as he alternated thrusting his large, muscular tongue inside her and sucking her clit.

She came with a cry which echoed around the room, then he stripped off his clothes and came up behind her.

He parted her buttocks like the segments of a ripe grapefruit and stood poised with the head of his cock nudging enthusiastically at the entrance to her honeypot.

'Fuck me!' she urged him again. He thrust into her and began to piston in and out at a steady pace. He found it extremely arousing to have her body spreadeagled into position beneath him, held open and ready for each strong thrust.

Tom had never really been into bondage, but he was beginning to see its appeal. He wondered if he could interest Emma in it. She had an inhibited streak and had to be coaxed into anything she considered too off the wall.

He could just imagine how delicious she'd look, her slender limbs restrained by silk scarves while he drove her into a frenzy by kissing and caressing every inch of her skin.

Sophia, meanwhile, was pushing her backside back against him and moaning loudly as he revved up for the final stretch. He gave it his all – at least for the next hour or so – before releasing a hot gush of juices high up in her pulsating pussy.

He withdrew from her and fell back into an armchair, taking pleasure from the sight of his semen dripping out of her, down her thighs and soaking her stocking tops.

'That was wonderful,' she gasped.

Just the sight of her still spreadeagled over the table, her legs running with his juices made his cock stir slightly. When her breathing had steadied, she turned her head to look at him.

'Untie me now please,' she murmured.

'I'm not sure I've finished with you yet,' he said, prompted by yet another stirring between his legs.

'I need to use the bathroom.'

Reluctantly he undid her bonds and she staggered from the room into the bathroom, rubbing her wrists.

It was a long time before she emerged, and when she did she was ashen.

'I don't feel very well – I think there was something wrong with the seafood,' she groaned, sinking weakly onto the bed.

He brought her a glass of water, but as he handed it to her she lurched to her feet again and rushed back into the bathroom. It was over an hour before she emerged and he had to help her into bed.

'Try and get some sleep. I'll bunk down with Jake for the night so I won't disturb you,' he said, thoughtfully leaving the wastepaper bin within reach.

Her only reply was another groan.

Emma was fast asleep when a sudden noise made her sit bolt upright in bed in a panic. To her horror, she saw a dark figure slipping across the room towards her. She opened her mouth to scream, just as the figure launched itself onto the bed and clapped a hand over her mouth.

She knew immediately that it was Tom; she could smell his distinctive cologne. The knowledge made her furious.

What the hell was he playing at, creeping into her bedroom in the middle of the night, nearly giving her a heart attack?

'Em – it's all right it's me,' he reassured her. She struggled with him and managed to hit him hard on the shoulder, then, as he still had his hand over her mouth, she struggled even more.

'Emma! It's me, Tom!' he exclaimed, taking his hand away.

In reply she hit him on the side of the head, then leant over and switched the lamp on.

'You hit me,' he said accusingly, rubbing his temple.

'And I'm just about to hit you again,' she blazed, her blonde hair tumbling down over her shoulders, her breasts bare. She aimed a slap at his face, but he was too quick for her and grabbed her wrist.

'What was that for?' he demanded aggrieved.

'What was that for?' she repeated furiously. 'Try frightening me half to death by creeping into my room and throwing yourself on me! I thought you were an axe murderer at the very least!'

'Sorry – I didn't mean to scare you,' he mumbled, his eyes on her breasts.

'And just what did you mean to do, dare I ask – or is that a stupid question?'

He grinned at her and released her wrist.

'What do you think?' He reached out a hand and covered one breast, his palm warm and slightly rough. He was taken aback when she slapped him again, then drew back her hand to aim another blow.

'Have you lost your mind?' he asked, grabbing both her wrists and pinning her down on the bed.

'I think I'm going to, if you don't get out of here!' she yelled, trying to knee him in the groin.

He swore and trapped her legs under one of his hard thighs.

Emma was almost speechless with fury. It was bad enough that she'd masturbated herself to sleep fantasising about him, but to have him think he could just come into her room straight from Sophia's bed, was unbelievable.

She fought him like a wild cat, adrenalin pumping through her body as she tried to free herself, but he was much stronger than she was. Unfortunately, she could tell that their struggle was turning him on.

Not that it took much.

She could feel his rock-hard erection digging into her hip as he held her down on the bed, and she realised reluctantly that she was turned on too. He raised his head and looked down at her, his eyes lingering on her heaving breasts, the nipples jutting out like small, pink thimbles.

'You're so beautiful and so sexy,' he murmured, then bent his head and took one hard nipple between his lips and drew it into his mouth.

Emma knew she was lost, but she wasn't going to make it easy for him. She lay like a statue as he held both her wrists above her head and caressed her naked body with his free hand.

When eventually his hand made its way between her legs and he felt how wet she was, he gave a sigh of satisfaction.

'You bastard,' she hissed.

'Do you want me to stop?' he muttered, nuzzling her neck.

'Would it make any difference if I said yes?'

'Do you want me to stop?' he repeated, releasing her wrists.

'Not really,' she sighed, winding her arms around his neck, 'but I'm going to hate you in the morning.'

'I can live with that,' he assured her, slipping his fingers inside her again.

Chapter Nine

No one watching Tom and Emma efficiently organising the following day's shoot, would have known that they'd managed only couple of hours' sleep the night before.

An early start meant that they'd foregone breakfast in favour of one last sweaty, breathless coupling amid the damp, crumpled sheets.

After he'd showered, Tom had gone reluctantly to check on Sophia and pick up a change of clothes. He felt guilty but relieved to find her pale and wan – and obviously still much too weak to leave her bed. He rang reception to ask if someone could check on her from time to time, then put her out of his mind.

The morning's shoot went well. With her usual efficiency Rosa rustled up coffee, banana bread and fruit, and Tom and Emma stood behind the camera enjoying a belated breakfast while the make-up girl touched up the sweat that kept breaking though on Melanie's face.

Emma had come to a decision. With only two days to go before returning to England, she thought she might as well give in to it and enjoy Tom's body and sexual expertise, whenever the opportunity arose.

Once back at home, she would make it clear that it had just been a holiday fling and that the situation between them was unchanged.

So when Tom touched her breast with the back of his hand and muttered, 'How about slipping away for half an hour at lunchtime?' she didn't take too much persuading.

She was wearing a daffodil-yellow sun-dress, which buttoned down the front, and it was all Tom could do to stop himself undoing it to release her creamy breasts. He knew that beneath the dress she was naked except for a pair of cream silk panties, and he kept getting a hard-on just thinking about it.

Rosa and Dominic were occupied making a similar arrangement. They'd spent the night together and although both of them were aching all over and had tender, swollen private parts, they just couldn't wait to fall on each other again.

'Did anyone here spend last night alone, do you think?' Emma wondered aloud, watching all the meaningful glances and furtive fondling taking place while they waited for the next shot to be set up.

'Doubt it,' said Tom laconically through a mouthful of fresh mango. 'You know what it's like on a shoot – everybody gets the hots for somebody, particularly when the temperature's in the nineties.'

When they broke for lunch, Tom and Emma took the mini-moke down the coast to a deserted cove. Tom parked the car under a palm tree, then, as Emma climbed out, he lifted her onto the bonnet and parted her legs.

The heat from the sun-warmed bonnet of the moke struck through Emma's dress and met the heat which was radiating outwards from her groin. Tom drew her panties down over her thighs, tossed them onto the passenger seat and reached for the bottle of sun oil.

'I don't want you getting burnt,' he told her, pouring some oil onto his fingers.

'I'm covered from head to foot in factor twenty-three,' she said, her bare backside squirming slightly on the dusty bonnet, partly from the heat and partly from a sense of anticipation.

'You missed a bit,' he said firmly, reaching between her thighs and applying a liberal coating of oil to her swollen clitoris.

'I'm not going to get burnt there,' she protested, squirming all the more as he intensified the pressure.

'You might with what I have in mind for the next hour,' he assured her.

In the late afternoon, Tom decided they would need several giant shells for the following day's shoot, so Rosa set off in the mini-moke in search of them.

Dominic was appearing in the scene being shot, so she left a hastily scribbled note sticking out of the pocket of his jeans which he'd left with his other clothes on a nearby rock.

It was about seven by the time she arrived back at her cottage and after a much needed shower she lay down on the bed wearing only a pair of beige silk camiknickers to await Dominic's arrival. A fine film of perspiration was already gathering between her full, bare breasts and she stroked them gently as she relaxed for the first time that day.

A fast and furious fuck in the dense undergrowth behind the beach at lunchtime had left her hot for more. Her note would have left Dominic in no doubt as to how she wanted them to spend the time before they went to join the others for dinner at around nine.

Rosa had been up early after snatching only a few hours of sleep between bouts of screwing the night before and she was tired. She drifted into a languorous doze, thinking sleepily that it would be extremely erotic to be awakened by Dominic climbing onto the bed next to her and caressing her into wakefulness.

Darkness had fallen when she awoke some time later. The flimsy curtains were billowing in at the open window as he crossed the room towards her. She yawned and stretched, her dark hair tumbling around her on the pillow, her naked breasts gleaming in the dim light.

Swiftly, he removed his clothes and knelt beside her on the bed, making an appreciative noise deep in his throat as he covered her breasts with his hands and bent to kiss her.

Rosa reached out and pulled him on top of her, rubbing her groin against his erection like a cat scratching itself against a table leg. He grabbed her backside and pulled her against him even harder. His hard-on felt like it was carved from granite as he slid a hand between her legs from behind and massaged her crotch through the thin satin of her camiknickers.

Rosa was hot and ready.

She reached for his cock and slipped it up the loose leg of her camiknickers. It felt massive, even bigger than she remembered, throbbing in her hand like a piece of high-voltage electrical equipment.

She squeezed it hard and heard him grunt in response, then she guided it between her legs and gasped in turn as he entered her.

She relaxed her internal muscles until he'd sheathed it to the hilt, then wrapped her legs scissor-like around his waist and began to move under him.

Rosa's engine always ran hot, but the sensation of his huge cock filling her completely as he plunged in and out, his broad-shouldered body covering hers, his hands on her breasts, made her climax even faster than usual.

Her back arched and her pelvis angled upwards so he could thrust even deeper into her, then she cried out as she came. She wound her hands into his hair as the shudders of sheer wanton pleasure washed over her.

In the aftermath of her climax, she became suddenly aware that something was terribly wrong. The hair she had her hands wound in was longish and tousled, but Dominic's hair was short and sleek.

And come to think of it he didn't smell like Dominic either.

Abruptly, she stopped the rhythmic circling of her pelvis and dragged his head back by the hair. Even in the dim light she realised, too late, that it was Jake.

'*Jake!*' she exclaimed in shock.

He slipped his hand between her legs and stroked her throbbing clit, without ceasing to thrust in and out of her.

Of its own volition her pelvis resumed its rhythmic circling as she ground out between clenched teeth, 'What the hell do you think you're doing?'

'To state the bleeding obvious – screwing you,' he replied amiably.

Part of her wanted to kick him out there and then, but the insidious heat of another climax was building insistently in her groin as he continued to stimulate her clit.

'You . . . you devious shit!' she gasped, dragging his head down and sinking her teeth into his lip. He let out a yell and jerked his head away, holding her down on the bed as she attempted to claw at his face.

They struggled together with Rosa twisting and turning under him like a wild cat, slamming her groin against him again and again at an increasingly fast pace. She wrenched one hand free, dug her nails into his back and tightened her legs around him like a vice.

Jake grabbed her wrists with one large hand and held them down on the bed. He continued to shaft her without a break in rhythm, worked up to boiling point by her body writhing wildly beneath his.

He came with a grunt which changed into a strangled groan, then sank on top of her, pinning her to the bed with the weight of his large body, just as she came for the second time.

After a few moments she thumped him on the shoulder and gasped, 'Get off me!'

He rolled to one side and lay there panting while she switched the lamp on and demanded furiously, 'How dare you just come wandering in here and start screwing me!'

'You invited me!' he protested, a look of outraged innocence on his face.

'I damn well didn't,' she snapped. He rolled onto one side, extracted a slip of paper from the pocket of his jeans and passed it to her.

It was the note she'd left for Dominic.

'You knew this wasn't for you!' she accused him.

'No I didn't. You left it in my pocket – I saw you do it. I thought you'd realised at last what you'd been missing,' he said triumphantly.

Rosa subsided back onto the bed as he continued, 'I didn't hear you telling me to stop. Come off it, Rosa – you enjoyed it just as much as I did – you certainly came fast enough. Man, you're one hot lady.'

Almost speechless with rage, Rosa closed her eyes. She knew she should have called a halt as soon as she realised it

142

wasn't Dominic, but the demanding heat in her groin had got the better of her and she knew it.

She sat up and reached for his limp cock, grasping it firmly in her hand as she said slowly and distinctly, 'If I *ever* hear you've told anyone about this, I'll put a Romany potion in your coffee, which will make your prick grow mould and then drop off.'

Slowly but surely his cock began to swell into another hard-on, then he sat up and covered one of her full, high breasts with his hand.

'Fancy another go while it's still in working order?' he asked winningly.

On the last evening they had a party on the beach with a calypso band and barbecue organised by the hotel.

Sophia had already flown back to England, accompanied to the airport by a reluctant Tom. Fortunately for him she was still feeling fragile, so the question of a farewell fuck didn't arise.

'What's going on between Jake and Rosa?' asked Emma curiously as she stood with Tom's arm around her watching the party hot up.

'What do you mean?' Tom downed his rum punch and looked around for another.

'I mean that Jake's been walking round for the last two days looking like he's just won the pools, and I think it's something to do with Rosa. He keeps smirking at her, but she just glares at him and snaps his head off whenever he speaks to her.'

'Those two are always arguing,' replied Tom vaguely.

'It's more than that,' insisted Emma. 'Has he said anything to you?'

'Nope.'

The party was going well and most people were pairing off, their inhibitions numbed by vast quantities of rum punch. Rosa, looking particularly dark and exotic, was dancing with Dominic and attracting a lot of attention, as her lithe body undulated to the music in a manner guaranteed to raise the blood pressure, if not the dicks, of all the men present.

Jake stood to one side watching her, with his arm slung casually over the shoulders of one of the actresses.

'He looks as if he'd like to eat her,' commented Emma.

'To fuck her would be more accurate,' remarked Tom. 'But that hardly singles him out from all the other males present. Let's face it – to see Rosa is to want to fuck her, at least as far as any man with functioning apparatus is concerned.'

'Including you?' challenged Emma.

'Not if you're around,' was his diplomatic, if not altogether truthful response.

Rosa did look stunning in a sheer, white silk camisole through which the dark circles of her nipples were clearly visible. She was also wearing a full, vividly patterned skirt which from time to time blew up in the warm breeze to reveal a glimpse of tanned bare legs and lacy white panties.

Large, gold hoop earrings flashed among her dark curls and as she danced barefoot on the sand, she looked exactly like the Romany gypsy she claimed to be.

Rosa was enjoying herself – she just wished they didn't have to leave tomorrow. She saw Jake watching her and threw him a fulminating look from beneath her long, thick lashes – she was already plotting her revenge.

Jake was going to rue the day he'd taken advantage of her.

For now, she contented herself with winding her arms around Dominic's neck and kissing him lingeringly, her curvaceous body pressed close to his.

'How about taking a walk along the beach?' muttered Dominic, stroking her bare back and shoulders.

'Okay.'

They strolled away from the party, their arms around each other, and wandered along the water's edge. Dominic slid his hand inside her camisole and stroked one full, high breast as they walked along.

They came to a deserted beach bar, the bar itself locked up for the night behind a metal grille. Rosa led the way into the shadows under the thatched roof, among the tables and chairs, and they kissed again.

She dropped to her knees and unzipped his jeans, freeing his cock from where it had been straining against the faded denim. With the tip of her tongue she circled the head, then ran down the shaft with little flicking movements which made him shiver.

She licked her way over his balls, circling and probing, then worked back up to the glans with a series of soft kisses which made his already hard member stand rigidly to attention.

When she drew it into her mouth, exerting a gentle suction with her full lips, she heard him inhale sharply. She sucked harder, tugging softly, taking him deeper and deeper until the head of his cock was lodged against the back of her throat.

When she eventually released it and stood up again, he was panting hard. He reached under her skirt and peeled her lacy panties down her shapely legs, then seized her by the waist and sat her on the bar.

She wound her legs around his waist as he took his cock

in his hand and positioned it at the entrance to her honeypot. In one smooth movement he was inside her.

He slipped her shoulder straps down her arms, baring her luscious breasts, and began to thrust in and out.

Rosa could feel the cool, smooth surface of the bar beneath her bare backside as she slid backwards and forwards in response to each of his urgent movements. She could feel moisture dripping from her well-filled pussy, making the surface even slippier, and gripped the edge of the bar with her hands.

She worked him with her internal muscles as he paused for a moment and bent his head to close his lips over an olive-hued nipple. When he resumed plunging in and out, it was fast and furious until he exploded within her, with one last dizzying thrust.

Rosa was very close to her own climax and not about to let it go. She tightened her legs around his waist and leaning back on her elbows, tilted her hips and rubbed herself against the base of his cock. Dominic pushed his fingers between them and deftly rubbed her clit for a few seconds, while her head dropped back.

'Harder ... yes, that's it ... now faster ... Aaah!'

The hot tingling emanating from her clitoris swept over her like white lightning, as her vaginal muscles went into orgasmic convulsions.

When it was over she lay weakly back on the bar with her legs still around Dominic's waist. He stroked the damp fuzz of her bush then eased out of her and fumbled in his pockets for a handful of kleenex.

'Let's get back to the party,' suggested Rosa after she'd dried herself off and rearranged her crumpled clothing.

The party was still in full swing. When Rosa and Dominic

rejoined it, Emma and Tom were sitting next to each other on a couple of canvas chairs in front of the low wall separating the beach from the hotel grounds.

'No prizes for guessing what they've just been doing,' said Emma, taking in Rosa's damp, crumpled silk camisole and dishevelled hair.

'Does it turn you on to think about it?' he teased. 'Maybe we should have followed them and watched.'

Emma was reminded of how she'd come across them in the minibus and told Tom about it. She was wearing a cornflower-blue silk top with a row of tiny buttons down the front and a tight, cream silk skirt. The next thing she knew, Tom was undoing the zip at the back of her skirt. He slipped his hand down the back of her silk camiknickers and began to stroke the upper slopes of her backside.

She interrupted her story to say, 'Tom, don't – someone will see us.'

'Everyone's too interested in getting laid themselves, to be interested in what we're doing,' he assured her, slipping a finger into the cleft between her buttocks and circling the tight bud of her anus. 'Carry on.'

Emma gulped and tried to remember what she'd just been saying. She started again, then her voice tailed off as she felt Tom's fingers pushing even further under her.

'Lift up,' he muttered.

Obediently, she raised her backside and gasped as she felt one of his long fingers slip inside her. She lowered herself onto it and couldn't stop herself wriggling slightly as he began to move it around inside her.

She took a gulp of her drink and stared at the inky blackness where the sea met the sky. She could just make out the white crests of the waves where they broke noisily against the sand. The night breeze was warm and laden with moisture – just like she was.

She knew that Tom's fingers were releasing a flood of creamy juices to join the perspiration she could feel gathering in the creases of her inner thighs as her excitement mounted. She sighed and bore down on the finger that was skewering her so pleasurably.

It was joined by another and she shifted position to accommodate them more easily. It was hard to keep her legs together, she wanted so desperately to part them and lean forward so Tom could gain greater access to her pulsating private parts.

Emma heard a faint sound behind them and glanced round in alarm, just in time to see Jake swing his long legs over the low wall to join them on the beach.

He began to ask Tom about the arrangements for tomorrow, but he was grinning so knowingly that Emma was suddenly convinced that he knew what they were doing. She wondered how long he'd been standing behind them.

Had he been there when Tom had unzipped her skirt?

No one looking at them from the front could really see what was going on, but anyone behind them would be left in no doubt.

The worst thing was that it was impossible for Tom to withdraw his hand while Jake was standing so close to them. The least Tom could have done was keep it still, thought Emma, but he redoubled his efforts, and she knew a slow flush was rising through her body as she tried not to move.

She gritted her teeth and fiddled with her hair. Damn Tom – he always found it very arousing to touch her in public, but even though she found it exciting too, the deep embarrassment she felt at the moment outweighed it.

At last, Jake moved on and Emma hissed, 'He knew what we were doing. Get your hand out of there, Tom, before someone else decides that this is the ideal moment to engage us in conversation.'

She raised her backside so he could remove his hand, but his only answer was to push it further under her until he could reach her clitoris.

'Calm down,' he said soothingly. 'What does it matter if he did know?'

He rubbed his finger up and down her clit as she said between gritted teeth, 'Tom – stop that, or I'll throw my drink into your lap.'

Tom remembered an occasion a couple of years ago when he and Emma had been hard at it on the sofa in his office. She'd been on her back with her skirt up around her waist and her eyes closed.

Tom had glanced up to see Jake standing just inside the room. Their eyes had met briefly, then Jake had left as silently as he'd come and Tom had continued to move above Emma without breaking stroke.

He hadn't thought it a good idea to mention it to Emma at the time – he didn't want her putting an embargo on sex in the office – but after that he'd always remembered to lock the door.

Now, he put his free hand behind her head and kissed her on the lips, sliding his tongue into her mouth as she opened it to protest. By the time he'd finished kissing her he'd also worked her skilfully to a climax.

Emma's eyes fluttered closed, her legs splayed apart and her back arched as she came; then Tom withdrew his hand

and zipped up her skirt again. She rose unsteadily to her feet and reached for his hand.

'Where are we going?' he asked as he followed her along the beach to the steps. He thought it was probably as well not to tell her that there was now a large damp patch on the back of her skirt.

'Back to the cottage where I'm going to make you pay for that,' she returned sweetly. 'We're going to do it my way.'

She was as good as her word.

Twice she worked him to the point of orgasm with her hands and her mouth, and both times she stopped and pinched the end of his dick hard before he could come.

Then she sat astride him and lowered herself slowly onto the massive column of his shaft, wearing only the blue silk top with all the buttons now undone.

She kept control, using him shamelessly to pleasure herself. His eyes were riveted on her naked breasts as they bobbed up and down in front of him.

When he was almost there for a third time, she raised herself so high that he slipped out of her. She took his cock in her hand, but instead of lowering herself onto it again, she began to rub it tormentingly against her clit.

He thrust hard upwards in an attempt to penetrate her, but she shook her head.

'Oh no – we've got a long way to go yet, before I let you come.'

'Like hell,' he growled, grabbing her by the waist and rolling her onto her back. He pushed her legs up over her head so that he could see the glistening folds of her vulva, then sank his face into the soft, warm flesh.

She squirmed and wriggled, but he held her in position with his hands behind her knees.

When he'd finished exploring every crevice with his

tongue, he pulled her legs over his shoulders and positioned himself above her.

'My turn,' he said, and plunged into her.

Chapter Ten

England felt cold after the humid heat of Barbados.

Despite the fact that it was mid-summer, and most of the population were walking round in light clothing, Emma wore sweaters for a couple of weeks after their return while she re-acclimatised.

They were all working overtime, shooting the rest of the chocolate commercials. They'd gone over budget in Barbados and Sophia was adamant that the overall cost remain the same – which meant less money for the last two films.

Emma urged Tom to persuade Sophia to let them have more money, but knowing the price he would probably have to pay, Tom refused. He took someone with him to every meeting with Sophia and told her, almost truthfully, that until after the final edit he would be too busy to see her socially.

Jake was happy to be working so hard – inactivity made him restless. But after a gruelling week of working long hours, he was ready for a little relaxation. On Saturday evening, having put in a straight twelve hours, he left Soho at around nine and rode out of London on his Harley.

He stopped for a drink at a pub near Henley, which was frequented by bikers, and stood with a group of his acquaintances having a pint.

His eye was caught by a petite, blonde girl standing by the jukebox with her friends. She had a face like an angel – except that, as far as Jake knew, angels didn't wear lots of black eye make-up and pale-pink lipstick.

But it wasn't her face that first attracted his attention – it was her clothing. She was wearing a tight-fitting, scruffy leather jacket, unzipped far enough to show a provocative amount of cleavage and, if she was wearing anything underneath, it wasn't visible.

Her small, shapely backside was encased in a black lycra mini-skirt, so close-fitting that he could see the outline of her mound. There was a hole in one of her black stockings and her black high-heeled shoes were scuffed.

She turned her head and caught his eye, giving him a knowing, come-hither look. That would usually have been enough for Jake to cross the room, abandoning the conversation he was having, in order to chat her up.

But not in this case.

She looked about fourteen.

And that made her jailbait.

Jake was a bit vague about the laws relating to sex with under-age girls, but he thought it was something you could do time for – or was that in certain states in America?

He wasn't sure, but he didn't want to find out the hard way. He gave her a rueful half smile, raised his glass in her direction and determinedly turned his back.

Later in the evening, he was in the tap room playing darts with a biker from Reading, known as Killer, when she came in with another girl.

Her friend approached Killer to suggest that the four of them play doubles. Killer was reluctant, but Jake wasn't averse to watching Angel-face twitch her pretty little arse around in front of him for a bit.

Looking couldn't do any harm.

Both Jake and Killer expected the game to be a walk-over, but Angel-face's friend proved to be very good, and both men started to concentrate rather than run the slightest risk of looking complete pillocks by being publicly trounced by a couple of teenage girls.

But it was difficult to concentrate when Angel-face hoiked herself up onto a table across the room from where Jake was lounging and crossed her legs. A couple of inches of snagged stocking top came into view as the movement made her tiny skirt slither upwards.

Killer was more single-minded, and pretty much kept his eyes on the board, but Jake's kept being drawn to the small blonde girl. When she reached up on tiptoe to remove her arrows from the board the first time, he nearly choked on his pint as her skirt rode up to show the bare skin above her stockings and her scarlet suspenders.

What he didn't get was a glimpse of any knickers.

Maybe she wasn't wearing any.

When she perched on the table opposite him again and took a long time crossing and uncrossing her legs, he was half convinced that he could make out the pale fuzz of her bush up her skirt.

If they'd been playing for money he would have sworn they were being hustled. As it was he completely missed the board with his next throw, provoking a stream of expletives from Killer.

The two men eventually won the game, but it was a close thing. Time was called while they were playing, and afterwards Jake decided to head for home – he was putting in another long day tomorrow. He said a mildly regretful goodbye to Angel-face and her friend and paid a last visit to the gents before leaving.

Out in the car park he was taken aback to find Angel-face leaning against his bike.

'How about a lift?' she asked him, smiling provocatively. There was nothing Jake would have liked better than to give her a lift – but not on his bike.

Unfortunately, he knew it was just asking for trouble and, anyway, under-age girls had never been his thing – not even one as luscious as this little chickie.

He should just have said no and left as soon as possible, but somehow he found himself asking, 'Where do you live?'

'About five miles away.'

'Can't one of your mates take you?'

She pouted at him, her pink-lipsticked mouth slick and inviting. He could just imagine it sliding wetly up and down his dick while he . . .

'They've all gone,' she told him, her lower lip now trembling. 'If you won't take me, I'll have to hitchhike.'

'Shit,' he muttered to himself. He couldn't let her hitch – not on her own, the way she looked. If she were found dead in a ditch tomorrow he'd feel like it was his fault or something.

'Hop on then,' he mumbled reluctantly, leaning across to get the spare crash helmet out. She climbed onto the bike and he tried not to look at her as he pulled on his own helmet. But even out of the corner of his eye he could see that her skirt had ridden up to show most of her thighs and scarlet suspenders.

Hoping he would have the self-control not to try to shag her in some deserted layby, he climbed on and shouted over his shoulder, 'Which way?'

She pointed left and he screeched out of the car park with her arms wound tightly around his waist and her breasts pressing into his back.

After a couple of miles he came to a crossroads and slowed to a halt. She pointed straight ahead and they roared along the deserted country lane until she indicated that he should turn left again. The lane became narrower, then deteriorated into a virtual cart track through a copse of shadowy trees.

Jake stopped the bike and turned to face her.

'Are you sure this is right? It doesn't look like it's leading anywhere.'

In reply she wound her arms around his neck and kissed him deeply. As she slid her tongue into his mouth he thought frustratedly that no male with an iota of testosterone in his body should be subjected to this sort of temptation.

Another few seconds and he'd have her on her back with her skirt up around her waist – fourteen years old or not.

He could feel his dick sending him an urgent message along those lines, and his hands tightened on her small waist, but one last remnant of self-preservation made him say, 'Look – there's nothing I'd like better than to screw your little fanny off, but no shag's worth doing time for. So just tell me where you live and I'll take you home, okay?'

He was taken aback when she laughed out loud.

'How old do you think I am?'

'I dread to bleeding well think,' he growled.

'I'm eighteen. Did you think I was under-age? Well I'm not.'

He wanted to believe her.

She dug into her pocket and produced a passport. 'Go on – have a look,' she urged him. 'I always carry it, otherwise I can't get served in pubs.'

He swung his leg off the bike and held the passport in the beam of the headlight, squinting at the date of birth then at the photo to make sure it was really her.

It was.

She was eighteen.

And that made it a whole different ball game.

He handed it back and grabbed her, fastening his mouth on hers and groping for her breasts through the thick leather of her jacket. She responded eagerly, pulling his head down and wriggling excitedly on the seat of the Harley.

He tugged down the zip of her jacket to discover that she was naked beneath it. He fondled her small, round breasts, his palm grazing her hard little nipples, then bent his head to take one in his mouth.

She smelt of sex and cheap perfume.

Jake slid his hand up her thigh and found that, as he'd suspected, she wasn't wearing any panties.

It was a mild night, with a slight wind rustling the leaves on the dark trees around them and owls hooting mournfully somewhere in the distance. But the wonders of nature were lost on Jake as he pushed his hand between her legs and felt the hot moisture soaking into her bush.

He started to lift her off the bike but she held onto the seat saying, 'No! Let's stay here – bikes turn me on.'

Jake didn't care where they did it as long as he could get his dick sheathed in her dripping little pussy as soon as possible – he'd had a boner for her all night.

He unzipped his jeans, released his cock and sat astride the bike facing her.

'I knew you'd have a big one,' she giggled, wriggling forward. He grabbed her backside with his large hands and lifted her onto him. She lowered herself onto his rearing shaft an inch at a time.

She had the tightest, juiciest little cunt he'd ever experienced. It took a minute or two for her to get him completely inside her, even though she was dripping wet.

She wriggled pleasurably and held onto his shoulders as she bore down. She didn't have much of a sense of rhythm but her wriggling was an experience in itself, as she worked herself up and down his cock with her skirt around her waist and her breasts pale in the moonlight.

She bounced up and down faster and faster as her excitement mounted, until Jake felt himself on the verge of release. He held onto her hips and jammed her down hard as, with one last thrust, he came.

She was breathing fast as she let him slip out of her and pulled her skirt down.

'I love your bike,' she told him. 'I wish I had one.'

He stifled a snort of laughter. She was so small she didn't look like she could keep a push-bike upright, let alone a real bike.

She sat astride the leather seat and wriggled again. 'I love to feel it between my legs – sometimes I can come just by rubbing myself like this.' She wriggled again and Jake felt a renewed stirring between his thighs.

'If I see a really great bike parked somewhere and there's no one around, I climb on and bring myself off,' she continued ingenuously.

Jake gulped and tried to imagine what his reaction would be if he returned to his bike and found an unknown teenage girl frotting herself senseless in the saddle.

Pretty much like the one he was having now, he imagined.

She continued to work herself backwards and forwards until Jake yanked her off the bike and bent her over it. He dragged her skirt up and paused for a moment to admire her small, pert rump, before plunging into her from behind.

While he thrust in and out of her, she continued to rub herself against the bike, so her backside jiggled erotically against his groin. Her breasts felt like firm little apples in the palms of his hand, as he worked towards a second scalding climax.

He exploded into her for the second time that night and, as he withdrew, a trickle of hot liquid ran down her leg. Panting, Jake released her and glanced at the luminous face of his watch.

'Better get you home – I've got an early start tomorrow.'

She lived in a house on a council estate a couple of miles from where their erotic encounter had taken place.

'Will I see you again?' she asked, as she took off her helmet.

'Sure. Give me your phone number.'

'We're not on the phone – it was cut off.'

'I'll give you mine then.' He scribbled the office number onto a scrap of paper and handed it to her, then roared off into the night.

Peregrine, Rosa's merchant banker lover was gratifyingly pleased to see her again. What he was less pleased about was the long hours she was working.

'You've been back for more than a week,' he grumbled to her over the phone, 'and I've only seen you once.'

'I'll be finishing at around ten tonight – you could pick me up then,' she suggested.

'Ten? Can't you make it eight?'

'Sorry, no. But if ten's too late for you it'll have to be some other time.'

'Can't you get a job with more sociable hours?'

'Sure, if I want to have my knickers bored off on a daily basis. Look, I'm going to have to go – are you on for tonight or not?'

'I suppose so,' he ended ungraciously. 'See you later, darling.'

He was waiting when Rosa, hips swinging, came out of the building just as the mid-summer dusk was falling. She was wearing an electric-blue dress with a low scooped neck, which clung tightly to her curvaceous figure and ended just below her backside.

He gave her a look in which lust vied with disapproval.

'Don't your employers mind you dressing like that?' he asked, pulling away from the kerb.

'Nope. Why should they?'

'It's hardly suitable attire for the office.'

'Don't be such a prick, Peregrine,' she said cheerfully.

He flushed with annoyance and drove in silence for a while. Rosa knew that, much as it might turn Peregrine on to see her dressed in skimpy, figure-hugging clothes, he disliked the idea of other men looking at her lasciviously.

Suddenly she said, 'Pull into that car wash.'

Startled, Peregrine swung the wheel, then when they'd turned in said, 'I handwashed the car yesterday – it can't be dirty. And, anyway, I never use car washes – they scratch the paintwork.'

He began to reverse, but Rosa leant across and placed her hand on his groin.

'Put it through the car wash,' she ordered him, curling

her fingers around the bulge in his trousers. Peregrine's eyes flicked wildly sideways then he drove slowly towards the entrance. When the attendant came out to take the money, Rosa removed her hand from his groin and said, 'Ask for the de luxe wash.'

He drove the car onto the conveyor belt then let out a grunt of shock as she unzipped his fly. Almost before the car was surrounded by soapy rollers she deftly extracted his semi-erect dick, then undid her seat belt and turned towards him.

Peregrine watched slack-jawed as she pulled down the low, scooped neck of her dress to expose her full, high breasts with nipples like small, tawny thimbles.

'Rosa . . . not here . . .' he stammered, then let out a yelp as she bent her head and took his cock in her mouth.

The interior of the car suddenly seemed unbearably warm. His nostrils were filled with the scent of her exotic perfume and, beneath that, the smell of hot, animal sex.

Peregrine's head fell back on the headrest and his hands automatically found her breasts, then his brain couldn't take in anything other than the feel of Rosa's hot, demanding mouth around his cock and her hands cradling his balls.

She wound her tongue around the glans, licking and probing, then sucking with a strength that took his breath away. The soap-streaming rollers continued to rotate noisily over the car, and the outside world was shut out by a continuous deluge of spray.

By the time the car had reached the hot air-drier at the far end of the car wash, Peregrine's eyes were shut and he was groaning loudly. The end of his cock was deep in Rosa's throat, then she pulled her head back slowly, while continuing to suck hard. There was no strength in

Peregrine's limbs as her movements quickened and his cock slid in and out of her wet mouth between her parted cherry-red lips at an ever increasing pace.

He came with a strangled groan and opened his eyes, just as Rosa sat upright and adjusted her dress, pulling it up to cover the magnificent sight of her naked breasts.

And only just in time.

They emerged from the car wash only a few yards from where a group of youths were swearing and pushing each other around.

Dazed and bewildered Peregrine automatically put the car into gear and pulled out into the road.

'Not another one!' exclaimed Emma appalled.

'Now we really *are* in the shit,' said Tom, putting his feet up on the desk and rubbing his eyes tiredly.

Rosa had just come into Tom's office to give them the unwelcome news that one of their clients had filed for bankruptcy, owing them a substantial amount of money.

Trying to keep afloat was a nightmare with client companies going under. This was the fifth one in the last two years – the money was well overdue and had been promised again and again. They'd been counting on it to settle some of their outstanding bills and now it was lost and gone for ever.

Emma walked over to the drinks tray and poured them all a drink.

'Did the company have any assets?' she asked hopefully.

Rosa shook her head. 'I don't know for sure, but it's unlikely – and even if there were any, they would probably have been transferred to a sister company before bankruptcy was filed.'

Having been through this before, they were all well

163

aware that any assets would be grabbed by the preferential creditors – the VAT, the Inland Revenue and the bank. There wasn't a hope in hell that there would be anything left for them.

It had become a common business strategy in recent years for companies in trouble to move assets, declare bankruptcy so as not to have to pay debts, then start up a new company from the ashes of the old. It was known as phoenixing, which to Tom and Emma was just another name for legal theft.

'Could you phone the Official Receiver anyway?' asked Emma. 'See if there's any point in attending a creditors' meeting?'

'Okay.'

Rosa left the room and Emma threw herself down on the sofa in despair.

'Now what?' she lamented. 'This is it. This is the big one. We just can't cover this sort of loss. The chocolate commercials are the only work we currently have on and the money from them won't meet our current debts.'

Tom knocked back the rest of his drink and went to pour another, before sitting on the edge of his desk, long legs crossed.

'There's only one way out,' he said slowly.

'What?' asked Emma, looking up hopefully.

'Porno films.'

She collapsed back onto the sofa.

'Never,' was her flat response. Tom had suggested this before and her response had always been the same.

'Be reasonable, Em. If we don't get a big chunk of work fast, it's over. We'll have to close down. We don't have to make porno films for ever – just until the industry picks up again. And let me tell you – it's *very* lucrative.'

'It's also illegal.'

'There's no real risk if we're careful. The most we'd be likely to get would be a fine. I'm not talking about using children, animals or unnatural artefacts – just lots of healthy, attractive young people bonking each other senseless in front of the camera. Come on, Em, it would be fun.'

'For you maybe,' retorted Emma sourly. 'You'd love it wouldn't you, Tom? I can just imagine the high old time you'd have auditioning actresses – the casting couch wouldn't begin to describe it. You wouldn't be able to keep it in your jeans long enough to find out their names.'

'Jealous?' he asked optimistically.

She ignored him as she went on, 'Anyway, it's probably not that easy a market to break into. The chances are that it's already over-subscribed. And how the hell would we go about finding a distributor?'

'No problem,' announced Tom, getting to his feet and extracting a sheet of paper from his desk drawer. He passed it to her.

'What's this?'

'A breakdown of a potential distribution deal and estimated profits for a three-film contract.'

Emma read it rapidly then looked up to meet his eyes.

'And just where did you get this sort of information?'

Tom looked uncomfortable.

'I thought it would be a good idea to do some preliminary research in the event we needed to move fast. Looks like I was right doesn't it?'

'Are you telling me that you've already had a meeting with these people?'

He looked even more uncomfortable.

'Several as a matter of fact.'

'Tom, one of the clauses in our partnership agreement states that each of us will keep the other informed of all potential deals and no agreement will be reached with any outside bodies without the other's consent. You had no right to do this.'

'I would have welcomed your involvement, but you've always refused to take the idea seriously. I thought it was very possible that we would find ourselves in this situation eventually and I took what steps I thought necessary to protect our interests.'

'You mean *your* interests.'

'*Our* interests. We each own half the company – remember?'

'If you decide to go ahead with this, you do so without me,' she warned him.

Tom crossed the room to sit next to her on the sofa. He put his hand on her knee and she could feel a tingling warmth spreading up her thigh to her groin.

'Take some time to think about it seriously. Study the figures – I've got a more detailed breakdown you can look at. Be realistic, Emma – anything's better than joining the ranks of the unemployed. If the company goes under, we go under with it, and quite frankly I'm not ready for a premature and penurious retirement. Let's face it, we both love what we do and the rewards it brings. The important thing now is to make a sound business decision based on the harsh financial facts.'

His hand slid upwards and Emma jumped to her feet.

'I'm going home,' she said firmly, and left the room without a backward glance.

Chapter Eleven

Emma arrived home, poured herself a large glass of wine and ran a bath. Leaving a trail of clothing from the bedroom to the bathroom, she pinned up her hair and immersed herself in the steaming, scented water and tried to come to terms with this latest blow.

The production company had been hovering on the brink of disaster for months now, but somehow they'd managed to keep afloat. If all the money they were owed was paid on time, by carefully juggling the bills they could continue to stay in business.

To discover that a large amount of money was never going to be paid was a terrible blow.

Emma sipped her wine and thought about Tom's devious behaviour. Whenever he'd suggested porno films in the past – and he'd suggested it several times – she'd assumed he was only half serious.

She'd always rejected the idea out of hand, never dreaming that he'd take the matter further without her agreement. To find out that he'd taken it several steps further was quite a shock.

Porno films.

Emma had seen a few – in the past Tom had occasionally brought one home for them to watch together. If the production values were good enough she found them mildly arousing, but usually her professional critical faculties got the better of her and she found herself dwelling on their myriad weaknesses.

The idea that she might actually be involved in making them was unthinkable.

A sudden sound in the hallway outside the open bathroom door made Emma turn her head sharply that way. Her heart began thumping so loudly in her chest that she was surprised the vibrations weren't making waves in the bathwater.

A shadowy figure appeared in the doorway. Emma thought her heart had actually stopped she was so scared.

'Who ... who's that?' she croaked.

'Emma – it's me, Adam.'

Belatedly, Emma recognised the CID man who'd spent the night with her after her flat was burgled.

'How *dare* you break in here?' she demanded furiously. 'I thought you were supposed to catch burglars – not be one!'

'Your front door was open,' he explained. 'I was investigating another break-in on the ground floor of this block and I came up to say hello. Your door was ajar and I thought the same burglars might be doing your place again. I crept in hoping to catch them red-handed.'

Emma thought back to her return home. She'd come in, picked up her mail, kicked off her shoes and gone to pour herself a glass of wine.

She'd thought she'd pushed the door to behind her, but obviously it hadn't quite shut.

'Sorry, Adam,' she said, embarrassed. 'You frightened me, and today's already been a pretty bad day.'

'A pretty bad day huh? Shall I get you another drink?' He indicated her empty glass.

'That would be good – pour yourself one too.'

He vanished and reappeared a few moments later with two full glasses. He shrugged out of his jacket and dropped it on the floor, then sat on the side of the bath and picked up the sponge.

'Why don't you tell me what's up, while I wash your back?'

Emma leaned forward so he could reach, and her rose-tipped breasts emerged enticingly from the scented bubbles. Adam caressed one with the palm of his hand as he lazily sponged her back and she told him about their bankrupt client.

Remembering Adam's job, she omitted all mention of Tom's dubious proposal for their financial salvation.

When he'd finished her back he turned his attention to her long, golden-brown legs, sponging them thoroughly then washing carefully between her toes.

The soles of Emma's feet were ticklish and she tried to pull her foot away, but he tightened his grip on her ankle and continued to tickle her all the way up her calf and then her thigh.

When she felt his fingers dabbling in her bush, she sighed and sank back into the water, with her arms extended along the edge of the bath. He slipped one finger inside her, then another and rotated them while she pushed her pubis hard against his hand. With his thumb, he brushed over the folded bud of her clit and felt it swell and harden beneath his touch.

'Mmm,' murmured Emma, temporarily distracted from her problems.

He continued to stroke her slippery breasts as, reaching out a languid hand, she undid his zip.

'Why don't you take your jeans off?' she suggested.

He obeyed with alacrity, tossing his jeans and briefs onto the floor, then sat on the side of the bath again.

His cock was at exactly the right height for her to take it in her mouth, the end was engorged and the skin was stretched tightly like a very ripe plum. She guided it between her lips with a soapy hand, then hastily removed it again as she swallowed a mouthful of soap suds. She dried the bubbles from his cock and then her hands on a towel, took a mouthful of wine to wash the taste away and tried again.

Her mouth was cool from the wine as she wound her chilly tongue around his strong, thick shaft and licked her way down to his throbbing balls. By the time she reached them, the heat from his cock had warmed her mouth so much that it felt like she'd been drinking coffee rather than wine.

Her tongue licked, flickered and probed until his cock felt like it was going to explode, then she got down to some serious sucking.

Adam wouldn't have believed that such a delicate-looking woman could have exerted such pressure with her pouting mouth. He felt as if she was going to suck him dry, then turn him inside out and suck some more.

He was half in the bath with her by now, his tee-shirt soaking and his hair damp from the clouds of steam swirling around them.

He kept his hand busy between her legs until she was as wet inside as she was outside. Eventually, she let his cock slip out of her mouth with one last heart-stopping, tugging motion from her shiny lips.

Emma stood up, her nude body gleaming with soap suds, damp tendrils of hair falling down around her shoulders. Her firm, high breasts were paler than the rest of her body, the rosy nipples jutting out like small raspberries glistening with evening dew.

She stepped out of the bath, lay down on the bathmat and reached out for him.

'Screw me,' she invited him simply.

Adam stripped off his damp tee-shirt and straddled her, he paused for a moment to position himself, then plunged smoothly in. In a moment they were a tangle of slippery, moving limbs as they humped their way across the bathroom floor.

It was difficult to retain any sort of hold on each other in the steamy warmth, and Emma kept trying in vain to wind her legs around his thighs, only to have them slip apart again.

It didn't matter.

In the heat of the moment, Emma managed to forget her problems and concentrate on the here and now as they both worked to a hot, urgent climax.

Tom had all the facts and figures waiting for her when she arrived at work the following day.

'I don't even want to look at them,' she told him crossly as he put them down on her desk.

'You're being unrealistic,' he replied, unperturbed.

'*You're* the one being unrealistic, if you think for a single moment that this is a good idea.'

Tom sat on the chair facing her desk and said, 'Em, darling, please look at the figures. There's nothing else we can do which is as lucrative as this. We'd be fools to turn our backs on it.'

'How about dealing drugs? I understand the profit margins in that area are sky high,' she suggested sweetly. 'You're just wasting our time, Tom – if you want to do something productive, why don't you chase up some of our other bad debts? Or even better, phone Sophia and see how soon you can talk her into paying us for the chocolate commercials.'

They'd both been so busy in the week following their return to England, that Emma hadn't found it too difficult to avoid having sex with him again. She wasn't looking forward to the inevitable confrontation when she told him that the great sex in Barbados hadn't changed anything and that she was putting herself off limits again.

When Tom had gone, Emma was sitting gloomily checking the budget for the last chocolate commercial when her phone rang. It was Lucy, an actress friend of hers, phoning to see if they could meet for lunch. Emma knew she should be phoning round looking for more work, but the idea of a pleasant, boozy lunch was too tempting.

Three hours later, she slid into the chair a waiter held out for her and immediately ordered a Martini. The Soho restaurant was bustling, with most tables already taken and Emma waved to several people she knew.

'It's not like you to drink anything stronger than wine at lunchtime,' commented Lucy, reaching for her own vodka on the rocks.

'I'm not usually staring ruin in the face,' said Emma, picking up her chilled glass as soon as the waiter set it down in front of her.

'Sounds bad – why don't you tell me about it.'

Lucy was an old school friend who made a reasonable living from minor roles on both TV and the stage. As she had a private income, the money wasn't particularly important to her, what she craved was the attention.

A beautiful, aristocratic-looking redhead, she rarely played roles that were out of character. She was always the well-bred betrayed wife, the classy girlfriend, or the up-market hero's sister.

When Emma had poured out her tale of woe, Lucy ordered another couple of drinks and said, 'Porno films – that could be a lot of fun.'

'It's easy to say that if you aren't the one who's going to be personally involved. How would you feel if it were a choice between appearing in one or starving?'

'That's a dilemma many an aspiring actress has had to face. Actually I went for an audition for something similar only last week.'

'What!' exclaimed Emma.

'Mmm, it was for a starring role in a video guide to more fulfilling love-making – there seems to be quite a market for that sort of thing at the moment. They're supposed to help couples make their sex lives more exciting by giving them ideas for new things to try. And of course they get off on watching them together.'

'That doesn't sound like your sort of thing at all,' said Emma surprised.

'It isn't. But the director is doing a TV drama in a couple of months, which has a role that would be perfect for me.'

Emma laughed out loud at this example of her friend's resourcefulness.

'Did it work?'

'He's taken me out twice since then, so it's looking hopeful.'

Over lunch, Lucy admired Emma's Barbados tan and asked how the shoot had gone. Emma's description of Sophia's unexpected arrival and subsequent behaviour, had them both laughing uproariously over forkfuls of pasta salad. Emma also brought her friend up to date on the current status of her relationship with Tom.

'You mean he spent his entire time chasing you, while Sophia was chasing him? When did he find time to direct?'

'I don't think he slept much.'

At about three o'clock they parted, both of them somewhat the worse for drink, then Emma went back to work and called Rosa into her office.

'What do you know about those video guides to making love?' she asked her.

'Not a lot – I've only seen one,' said Rosa, sinking into a chair and crossing her legs with the seductiveness that was second nature to her.

'What was it like?'

'An instructive and educational guide to sex designed to help couples who've hit a rocky patch sexually – or soft porn, depending on your point of view. There's one up for grabs at the moment as a matter of fact.'

'*What*?'

'There's one up for grabs at the moment,' repeated Rosa. 'Several production companies have put in bids.'

'Why didn't you tell me? You know we're desperate for work.'

Rosa looked puzzled. 'But we don't operate in that area – we only make corporate films and commercials.'

Emma thought rapidly. 'As from today we're widening the net. Would you get me copies of videos already on the market, together with all the information we need for putting in a bid please? Oh, and can you find out who's currently in the running?'

Rosa scribbled rapidly in her notebook then glanced up.

'Anything else?'

'Yes – don't let Tom know what you're doing.'

* * *

Rosa spent the rest of the day following Emma's instructions and eventually, at around nine, put her head round the door to say goodnight. Emma was intently watching one of the videos Rosa had been out and rented for her earlier.

'What do you think?' asked Rosa.

'Um? Interesting. Night, Rosa – see you tomorrow.'

Over the next few days, Emma worked long hours collating the information she needed and putting together a budget and a production schedule. She left the office only to attend a series of meetings connected with her new project. She also spent long hours in the editing room compiling a promotional tape to submit with their bid.

Luckily, Tom was directing a shoot in a studio on the other side of London and was rarely in the office, so Emma was able to work uninterrupted.

On the last day for submitting the bids she checked everything for the last time, then dispatched it by courier and went home early.

On Friday afternoon, Rosa undulated into the room and perched on the edge of the editing desk where Jake was busy making a rough-cut of some recent footage.

Her skirt rode up, giving Jake a close-up view of her tanned, bare thighs. She was so close he could see the sprinkling of fine golden hairs decorating her smooth skin and smell the arousing scent of her body.

He stopped what he was doing and leant back in his chair to get a better view of her luscious body.

'Hi, sweetheart – what's up?'

'Tom wants to know when that rough-cut will be ready.'

'In about an hour.'

Rosa smiled at him provocatively and ran the toe of her high-heeled shoe slowly up his shin. Jake felt goose bumps forming on the back of his neck and his cock stirred beneath his tight-fitting jeans.

'I was thinking about you in bed last night,' she murmured.

'Yeah?'

'Mmm. I was thinking about the time we were together in Barbados. In fact, I find myself thinking about it quite a lot.'

Jake looked surprised.

'I thought you hated my guts.'

'I admit I was furious at the time, but I can't get it out of my mind. It was very . . . exciting.'

Jake looked at her speculatively, then warily put his hand on her knee, half expecting the pointed toe of her shoe to make swift and vicious contact with his thigh. Instead, she smiled at him again then lowered her eyes.

'How do you fancy a repeat performance?' he asked hopefully. Beneath his hand he could feel the heat of her satiny skin and he began to massage her knee cautiously. She placed her own hand over his, then moved it slowly upwards.

He gulped as she purred, 'I was hoping you'd say that.' She was still moving his hand towards her crotch, and he jumped when his fingers made contact with her silky knickers. There was a tangible heat emanating from between her legs and he felt sweat gather on his brow.

With an unexpected twist of her hips she swung her legs off the desk and stood up.

'How about Saturday night?' she asked huskily.

Jake had arranged to go drinking with a group of friends

in Sidcup, but mentally wiped the event from his social calendar without the slightest hesitation or compunction.

'What time?' he croaked.

'Nine o'clock at my flat?'

'Great.'

'See you then.'

Rosa left the room, her hips swaying erotically, leaving him to wipe the sweat from his brow and wonder if the whole thing was just a figment of his fevered imagination.

Chapter Twelve

Jake arrived just before nine, carrying a bottle of Bulgarian wine and a six-pack of his favourite beer.

He half expected Rosa to have changed her mind, or to be pulling some sort of stunt on him, but he figured that the worst she could do was refuse to let him shag her – so it was worth turning up and risking another rejection.

He had, however, made a mental proviso that he'd resist any suggestion that she tie him up as part of some sexy game.

He wouldn't put it past her to take photos of him naked and with a dahlia stuffed up his arse – or something similar – and decorate the office walls with them.

Jake's jaw dropped when he saw what Rosa was wearing.

She opened the door clad in a scarlet basque trimmed with black lace and ribbons. The top of the basque barely covered her nipples and her full, high breasts were pushed upwards to give her a cleavage of stunning proportions.

The tight lacing emphasised both her small waist and the curvaceous thrust of her backside beneath it. The basque was cut high on the hip so her legs looked endless and her sheer, black stockings were held in place by tiny scarlet suspenders.

She took the drink he was holding out of his suddenly sweating hands and closed the door behind him.

'Take your jacket off,' she invited him casually and vanished into the kitchen.

Jake shrugged it off and wandered into the sitting room to find the curtains closed against the evening sunshine and at least a dozen candles burning around the room. The flickering light they threw was supplemented by a couple of lamps, both half hidden by gauzy scarlet scarves.

The overall effect was exotic in the extreme and Jake sank onto a large, squashy sofa draped with embroidered shawls, thinking it looked like he was going to strike lucky after all.

Rosa returned with a small tray holding a silver cocktail shaker and a couple of Martini glasses. She placed it on the coffee table and sat down next to him.

He was immediately enveloped in a warm wave of her seductive perfume and, although they weren't touching, he could feel the heat radiating from her body in a way that made his head spin.

She began to shake the cocktail and he was mesmerised by the rhythmic bobbing of her traffic-stopping breasts beneath the tight-fitting basque. He had some difficulty in stopping himself from jumping on her and grabbing her right away, but he didn't want to seem too eager.

She poured them both a glass of crimson liquid and Jake would have sworn he could see tiny curls of vapour rising from it.

'What's that?' he asked dubiously.

There was a hot, carnal glitter in Rosa's eyes as she gave him a cat-like smile, her cherry-red lips curving upwards, then the tip of her tongue darted out to lick her full lower lip.

'It's a special cocktail my Romany grandmother taught me to make.'

'I've never heard of gypsies drinking cocktails,' he said. 'I thought it was all baked hedgehogs and that sort of stuff.'

'My grandmother was a very sophisticated Romany,' she assured him.

'So what's in it then?' he wanted to know. Whatever it was, he'd prefer a beer.

'Hungarian vodka mixed with cherry liqueur and various other things. Be careful – it's very strong,' she warned him, taking a sip herself. 'In fact, drink it very slowly or you may find it overpowering.'

Jake could drink ten pints of bitter and still find his way home, so he doubted it. He took a gulp, then gasped and coughed as it seared its way down his throat, then his gullet, leaving a fiery trail in its wake.

Rosa watched him, a seductive smile playing around her lips. She dipped the tip of a scarlet-nailed finger in her glass and circled it around the rim, then slid it between her lips and sucked it provocatively.

There was a pulse throbbing through Jake's burly body, a hot, urgent pulse originating from his dick. He tried to think of something to say, but his throat seemed to have seized up. He took another gulp of his drink and immediately regretted it.

He was just about to ask Rosa if she'd mind if he got himself a beer – this stuff was foul – when, without hesitation, she tossed the remaining contents of her glass straight down her throat.

Male pride made him follow suit, then he tried not to let it show that both his head and his dick felt like they were going to explode.

She immediately poured them both another glass, and

when he tried to say that he didn't want any more, it came out as a strangled croak followed by a coughing fit.

Suddenly – and he wasn't sure how it happened – he threw himself on top of Rosa and wrenched her tiny scarlet panties off, tearing them in half in the process.

He was shocked to find himself grinding his groin against her like a madman, while simultaneously trying to yank his own zip down. His dick felt as if it were twice its usual size and red hot. The second he'd freed it, he shoved it clumsily inside her.

Within moments of gaining his desperate entry, he came in a white-hot explosion of shuddering intensity.

He collapsed on top of her, absolutely mortified, wondering what the hell had come over him – he'd *always* been able to keep it up long enough to give any woman a reasonably good time.

He managed to roll off her mumbling, 'I'm sorry. I'm really sorry – I don't know what came over me.'

Rosa picked up the scrap of torn silk, which had been her panties, and looked at him reproachfully. Feeling like a complete brute, Jake jabbered, 'I'll buy you some more – really, Rosa – I'm sorry.'

He could see the closely clipped dark fuzz of her bush erotically framed by her scarlet suspenders and, before he knew what was happening, he was on top of her again.

It was like a nightmare.

Or a bizarre erotic dream.

It was as if it were someone else frantically plunging inside her and scrabbling at her breasts, which were tightly contained by her sexy basque. He didn't know how he'd become hard again so quickly, or why he didn't appear to be able to exercise the slightest amount of self-control.

He only knew that he was thrusting frenziedly away without a hope of stopping, or even slowing down.

At least he lasted longer this time – it must have been all of ten seconds before he ejaculated again.

He sprawled on top of her, trying to catch his breath, while the same hot pulse throbbed incessantly through his large frame.

He became aware that Rosa was squirming beneath him, trying to free herself from the weight of his body, one of her breasts exposed in all its firm, luscious beauty. He tried to push himself upright, but then somehow he was inside her again, his dick forging into her like a heat-seeking missile drawn unwaveringly to its target.

He couldn't stop himself behaving like the lowest form of rutting animal, but by making a superhuman effort he managed to roll to one side, so at least he wasn't squashing her. As he came again he moaned out loud and wondered if he was hallucinating.

He'd never come three times in such swift succession.

Not even when he was a teenager.

What the fuck was going on?

This time, when he rolled off, Jake crawled weakly across the room on his hands and knees and dragged himself up to slump dazedly in an armchair. He held onto the arms as he tried to calm down and clear his head.

'I'm not sure whether I should be flattered or offended,' said Rosa, trying to tuck her naked breast back into her basque. 'Slow down, Jake – we've got all night.'

'This has never happened before,' he croaked desperately. 'Honest, Rosa – I don't know what's going on. Tell me I haven't hurt you.'

'Not if you don't count crushing me half to death.'

183

'I'd better leave.' Jake's voice was miserable in the extreme.

Rosa looked pointedly at the clock.

Nine-fifteen.

'The night is yet young,' she told him sweetly.

Jake just couldn't believe it when his dick suddenly reared into renewed and vigorous life.

He held onto the arms of the chair, but it was like being in an airborne plane with a gaping hole in the side. The suction was too strong to resist and, before he could shout a warning, he was halfway across the room towards her, his dick leading the way.

Rosa cried out and jumped over the back of the sofa. He collided with it and found himself grinding his pelvis feverishly into the cushions.

To his amazement he felt her touch his hair, 'Turn over,' she urged him. He rolled onto his back and she lowered herself swiftly onto his massive, throbbing column.

He tried to hold back, but it was no use. The feeling of her hot, juicy cunt squeezing him as she moved up and down, was just too bleeding exciting.

He came again.

She stayed astride him, and when he opened his eyes she murmured, 'Just stay where you are – we can take up where we left off in a few minutes.'

Gasping for breath and already uncomfortably aware that another hard-on was inevitable, if not imminent, Jake looked around and, suddenly, his eyes were caught by the cocktail shaker.

It hit him with the force of a ton of bricks.

'You put something in my drink!' he accused her.

'Something in *our* drinks,' she corrected him.

'What was it?' he demanded.

'A mild stimulant.'

'A mild stimulant!' he roared. 'I've just been behaving like a sex-crazed beast!'

'You always behave like a sex-crazed beast,' she pointed out.

'Not like that I don't. What's the antidote?'

His hands tightened on her waist and he shook her, then wished he hadn't as he felt his dick grow swiftly to another massive erection in response to the movement.

'Oh no – not again!' he groaned, then lost the power of rational thought as she began to move above him.

This time, she climaxed too.

When he was able to speak again, he gasped, 'Rosa! Is there an antidote?'

She shook her head, smiling down at him, then slowly tightened her internal muscles around his cock.

'Don't do that,' he begged her. 'I'm going to have a heart attack if I do it again so soon – it's not natural.'

'Everything's going to be fine,' she soothed him. 'There's nothing harmful in it – it's just an old Romany cure for impotence.'

'But I'm not impotent!' he protested furiously.

'I know that – in your case it's just increased your potency. Don't worry, Jake. You'll find you can last longer each time we do it. By midnight you'll be able to sustain an erection for hours.'

'If I'm not dead,' he said bitterly.

'It'll be the best night of your life, if you just go with it and enjoy yourself.'

Jake wanted to leave there and then, but he had a horrible suspicion that he'd be arrested for trying to impregnate a lamppost or, even worse, a passer-by, long before he arrived home.

He wanted to strangle Rosa.

No, he wanted to fuck her again.

Beneath his hot, animal desire, Jake felt an overwhelming sense of relief that he hadn't actually turned into some lust-crazed creature who only had to see a woman to jump on her – it would have made life a bit difficult to say the least.

Rosa had done this to him and Rosa could now pay the price.

He'd do everything he'd ever wanted to do with her – and more.

In a swift movement he rolled her off the sofa and onto the rug and straddled her.

As he thrust deeply into her he muttered, 'Coming – ready or not.'

After the first hour or so Jake really began to enjoy himself.

He'd never known anything like it.

'What effect does that stuff have on women?' he asked Rosa, as they lay in a heap of tangled limbs on the bed, his cock buried deep in her honeypot.

'It makes them randy as hell,' she said. 'Randy as hell, and permanently dripping wet. If I hadn't drunk some too, I wouldn't have been ready for you the first two or three times and it could have been uncomfortable – if not outright painful. As it is, I'm hot and horny.'

So was Jake.

'I need a beer,' he said, slipping reluctantly out of her – his throat was as dry as a camel's scrotum. 'Do you want one?'

'No, but I'll have a glass of white wine and soda please. There's a bottle of each in the fridge.'

When he returned, having drunk most of a can in three

swallows, he found Rosa standing in front of the dressing table trying to draw a brush through her wildly tangled dark hair.

He paused in the doorway to admire the length of her legs and the pale orbs of her buttocks, each bisected by a scarlet suspender. By now, the stockings had several runs in them, which only added to her wanton appeal.

In the dressing-table mirror he could see the reflection of her gorgeous breasts, half escaping from the partially unlaced bodice.

In the past he'd had many fantasies about Rosa, and tonight he intended to realise as many as he had the physical stamina for.

Starting with this one.

He handed her the spritzer and waited until she'd drunk it, then pulled her along behind him to the sitting room.

He helped her up onto the dining table, then arranged her on her hands and knees – a position he'd often imagined fucking her in.

He stood behind her and unlaced her basque so that her magnificent breasts tumbled free. His cock was already lodged in the cleft of her buttocks as he fondled them with one hand and pushed his other hand into the syrupy stickiness between her thighs.

She wriggled her curvaceous rump back against his groin and gasped as he found her clit. There was a mirror on the opposite wall and he could see their reflection in it, hazy and muted in the dim light from the guttering candles.

Rosa looked like sex incarnate, her hair tumbling down around her face, her magnificent breasts with their jutting nipples just begging to be handled.

He pushed into her, his cock as hard and ready as if it were the first time that evening. She edged back towards him on the polished table top and made a low purring noise deep in her throat as he commenced a series of long, smooth strokes. At each withdrawal her internal muscles tightened on his cock, then relaxed as he thrust into her again.

Her back was dipped and her well-rounded bottom was up in the air so he could achieve a deep penetration. His balls smacked against her buttocks with each movement and, leaning over her, he kneaded her breasts, teasing the distended nipples into even harder points.

Rosa began to gasp, then moan, as Jake released one breast and reached between her legs to squeeze and rub the throbbing bud of her clit.

This time it lasted much longer than their previous frenzied couplings, and Rosa sustained two prolonged climaxes before Jake let out an inarticulate cry and ejaculated forcefully, high up into her honeypot, his juices mingling with hers.

He withdrew, then bent down and fastened his lips on one satin-skinned buttock and bit and nibbled at it, sucking hard until the smooth surface was branded by a deep rose-pink mark.

It was quite a night.

He felt like he was packing a lifetime's shagging into a few short hours. They screwed in every possible position, exploring each other's bodies, probing, licking and sucking in a world where only sexual sensation existed, until in the early hours they fell asleep, exhaustedly entwined on the bed.

Jake awoke to see dawn breaking through the half-open

curtains and was immediately aware of the demanding throbbing of his cock.

He eased himself closer to Rosa, who was lying on her back with one leg drawn up, and reached between her thighs. She felt warm and moist and her clit was still swollen to the size of a large broad bean after the night's exertions.

He separated her labia, running his fingers lingeringly over their fleshy folds, then slid two fingers inside her and explored her honeypot.

Stealthily, so as not to wake her too soon, he held her open and edged his cock into her an inch at a time. He wanted to fuck her awake, from the deepest slumber to the deepest arousal.

She stirred and shifted slightly, drawing up her leg even further and giving him greater access. Once fully sheathed in her silk-lined pussy, he began to move, almost imperceptibly at first, stroking her clit at the same time.

She moaned and her head dropped back as he upped the tempo. She began to move against him, then suddenly let out an exclamation and went tense in his arms, her eyes fluttering open.

Jake carried on moving, his dick slipping easily in and out of her well-lubricated interior. She struggled against him but he held her tightly without breaking rhythm.

She struggled harder, trying to pull free, but the erotic tempo he was setting was too much for her and her hips began to move in response.

Their love-making lost its early morning languor and became hot and urgent with a fierce, undulating rhythm. Rosa reached behind him to grasp his buttocks and dig her long nails into them as she dragged him closer.

She let out a long drawn-out, choking moan as she came,

her body jerking as a series of spasmodic shudders ran through it.

Her release destroyed the last of Jake's tenuous self-control and he came too, pumping into her strongly, clutching her breasts as he did so.

He rolled onto his back and Rosa turned towards him.

'You might have woken me up first,' she protested. 'I didn't have a clue who it was for a few moments – you could have been an intruder for all I knew.'

The first ray of the day's sunshine fell across the bed and Jake looked with some alarm at his semi-erect, but massively swollen cock. The end looked like a huge, ripe plum, oozing and glistening with juice. The shaft was an ominous mottled puce and magenta, the veins standing out and throbbing strongly.

'Here, Rosa,' he asked anxiously, 'when will that stuff you gave me wear off? I'm not saying I haven't enjoyed it, but I don't think my dick can take much more of this – it's not usually that colour.'

'It should have worn off by now,' she told him. 'I made the potion too strong I'm afraid, but don't worry – it will soon. Anyway – what about me?'

She sat up and opened her legs, then held the outer folds of her pussy apart for his inspection. Her inner folds, which he remembered as being a deep rose-pink, were a luscious, dark, rich crimson, and so swollen that the entrance to her honeypot was almost hidden.

'I wasn't the one who put something in your drink,' he protested. 'What are you complaining to me for?'

But he couldn't take his eyes off the stirring sight. His semi-erect cock grew into ramrod hardness, and, of its own volition, his hand reached out to touch the jutting protuberance that was her clitoris.

'How about one more go before my dick shrivels up and drops off for good?' he suggested.

Emma was being elusive and mysterious and Tom didn't like it.

He'd been extremely busy since they'd returned from Barbados – too busy to worry about it at first. But when she'd turned down his third suggestion that they get together, he felt distinctly uneasy. Surely, after the great sex they'd enjoyed in the Caribbean, she wasn't about to back off from him again?

Because that was what it looked like.

He'd been out a lot of the time, directing a shoot in a studio on the other side of London, but Emma never seemed to be in the office on the few occasions he came back.

Now that he was in the middle of editing, she always seemed to be out at a meeting, but was evasive when he asked her who she was seeing.

Was it another man?

He tried asking Rosa, but she was similarly elusive. He tried asking Jake, but the cameraman seemed to be on another planet this week. He also looked so haggard that even Tom, not the most perceptive of individuals, noticed.

Tom eventually confronted his ex-wife in her office and suggested a drink after work. She stared at him blankly, tossing back a lock of long blonde hair then said, 'I don't think I can.'

'Why not?' he persisted.

'Because I'm busy.'

'But we need to talk.'

'What about?'

'Us for one thing. The company for another. I've nearly

finished the final edit on the chocolate commercials and then we're looking at a great big chunk of nothing. No work, no money – and no company if we don't do something about it soon.'

Emma started to search through the pile of papers on her desk and said, 'Some other time.'

Tom stared at her, taken aback.

'Is that all you've got to say when ruin and penury are just around the corner?'

'Not now, Tom, I've got a meeting.'

With that, Emma picked up her briefcase and left the room.

She didn't return to the office again that day and when Tom phoned her at the flat in the evening, all he got was the answering machine.

He spent half the night imagining her with another man and went into work the following day determined to have it out with her.

Unfortunately she didn't come in. Rosa denied all knowledge of her whereabouts and when he phoned her flat he still got the answering machine.

Eventually, at around seven, when Tom was hunched bad-temperedly over the editing desk, he heard the distinctive tapping of Emma's heels in the corridor outside.

He caught up with her in her office and noticed at once that she looked flushed and happy. In a black rage he grasped her by the upper arms and said through clenched teeth, 'Where the hell have you been until this time?'

Startled, Emma tried to pull away, but his grip on her tightened.

'For goodness' sake – what on earth's the matter with you?' she asked. 'Let go of me!'

'Who is he?' he demanded.

'What are you talking about?'

'I know you've been with another man – who is he?'

Emma looked bewildered, then laughed out loud.

Unable to control his jealous rage, Tom dragged her against him and kissed her hard on the mouth, his hand roughly covering her breast. His kiss didn't give or take any pleasure, it was one of sexual domination, re-establishing territory he felt belonged to him.

Taken aback, but nevertheless furious, Emma kicked out at his shin and heard him wince when the pointed toe of her shoe made glancing contact.

She wrenched her mouth away from his and blazed, 'How *dare* you behave like this – I'm not your possession!'

Tom had temporarily lost his grip on reality. He'd spent most of the day imagining Emma being screwed by someone else and was now convinced of it.

Lifting her bodily, he hauled her across the room to the sofa and pinned her down on it. Furious, Emma lashed out at him, only to have her wrists grasped and held above her head.

'What has he got that I haven't?' hissed Tom. 'Does he fuck you better than I do? Do you come more?'

He wrenched open the front of her dress to reveal her bare breasts and fastened his mouth over one taut nipple, while he fumbled between her legs with his free hand.

'Tom! For goodness' sake!' she cried as he managed to get his probing fingers under the elastic of her panties. As he made contact with her clit, a tremor of sensation like a jolt of electricity buzzed through her body.

She kicked out at him and knocked a metal box full of video tapes off the end of the sofa and onto the floor. The noise it made was deafening and a few seconds later the door was flung open and Rosa stood there.

'Emma – are you okay?' she asked, taking in the scene. Jake appeared just behind her and stared at Emma's bare breasts like a rabbit dazzled by headlights.

Brought back to reality, Tom sat up and clumsily pulled Emma's dress together to hide her breasts from Jake's fascinated gaze.

'Everything's fine,' he assured their two employees. 'We just knocked that box over by accident. You can get back to work now.'

Emma struggled into a sitting position and pulled her skirt down, then began to fasten up her dress.

'Would you like me to stay?' offered Rosa, familiar with Tom's jealousy and his volatile relationship with his ex-wife.

'It's okay thanks, Rosa,' Emma managed to say.

Rosa nodded and stepped back, closing the door behind her.

'If you attempt to manhandle me again, I swear I'll lay you out with that marble ashtray.'

Tom looked sheepish. 'I wasn't manhandling you,' he muttered.

'No? That's certainly what it felt like.'

'I just can't stand the thought of you with another man.'

'I haven't been with another man,' said Emma patiently. 'But if I had, it would be none of your business.'

'Where have you been then?'

'I've been at a meeting. There's a strong possibility there may be work on the horizon.'

Tom brightened up perceptibly.

'Why didn't you tell me? I thought we always pitched for work together.'

'Really? I don't recollect that being the case when you were planning to have us make porno films.'

'That was different. Tell me about this work.'

Emma rose to her feet and surveyed the front of her dress. 'I don't have time – you've ripped three buttons off and I'm meeting someone for a meal. I'll have to go home and change now.'

'When then?'

'Tomorrow.'

Tomorrow was another busy day and it was early evening before they had a chance to get together. Emma invited Tom into her office and poured them both a drink, then slotted a video into her VCR.

'What's this?' he asked with interest.

'You'll see.'

The video was one of the guides to love-making and came in at a point where different techniques were being demonstrated. Glancing at Tom, who was lounging on the sofa sipping his drink, Emma saw he was looking pleased.

After a few minutes he turned to her and said, 'I've got something much hotter than this in my office if you feel like watching blue movies together. This is okay, but it's a bit tame.'

'Let's just watch it for a while, please.'

Tom settled back on the sofa and they sat in silence until he was suddenly struck by a thought.

'If there's something new you want to try, you only have to say – you know I'm always open to suggestions. What is it? You can tell me.'

Emma was lost for words and when she didn't reply he went on, 'Is it that?' and indicated the screen. 'We've done that and I got the impression at the time that you didn't particularly like it, but if I'm wrong you only have to tell me.'

Emma smoothed her tight, scarlet skirt over her thighs and sighed – she might have guessed that Tom would take it personally.

'Just watch the video, please.'

After about fifteen minutes she stopped it and said, 'How would you feel about making something like that?'

He looked baffled.

'That isn't porn,' he pointed out. 'It's some sort of lovers' guide.'

Emma sighed. 'I know that. How would you feel about making one?'

He looked at her blankly. 'Fine, I suppose, but we can't sell that as porn – it's too tame.'

'Forget porn!' snapped Emma, thoroughly exasperated. 'Honestly, Tom, you're like a dog with a bone sometimes. Let me simplify matters for you. We're in the running to make one of these guides and now the executive producer – the money man in other words – wants to meet us both.'

Tom looked completely taken aback.

'How did you get onto this?'

'Rosa told me about it.'

'Who *is* the executive producer?'

'He's called Paul Rivers and I don't know anything about him – I haven't met him myself yet.'

Rising to her feet, Emma took a file from her desk and passed it to him.

'Here's all the information on it, together with a copy of the promotional video I put together. Paul Rivers wants us to fly over to Paris, where he's currently based, for a meeting early next week. Is that a problem?'

Tom looked delighted. 'Just the two of us?'

'Yes, but don't get any ideas – this is strictly a business trip.'

'Things are looking up – first Barbados and now Paris.'
'Have a look through the file and let me know what you think. I'll see you tomorrow.'

Chapter Thirteen

When Paul Rivers' limousine picked them up from Charles de Gaulle airport in the late afternoon, Tom commented, 'It looks like our potential executive producer is seriously rich.'

As she slid into the luxurious interior, with its cream leather upholstery, Emma was inclined to agree.

It was high summer and the bright, green leaves of the chestnut trees which spread their dappled shade along the boulevards, were coated with powdery dust.

Paris was thronging with elegantly dressed locals and somewhat less elegantly attired tourists, and all the pavement cafés were packed. Everywhere, gaily striped canopies and umbrellas proclaimed the Parisians' habit of living their social lives on the streets.

Looking out through the car windows, Emma hoped there would be time for at least a brief stroll along the teeming thoroughfares. Time to sit at one of the round, zinc-edged tables and sip a *café au lait* or a glass of wine.

When the sleek, maroon car turned in between the electronically operated, wrought-iron gates of a house off the *Boulevard de la Madeleine*, Tom whistled silently and said, 'Seriously, seriously rich.'

The house was seventeenth century, massive and set within its own well-tended grounds. A uniformed flunkey ran out to carry their bags inside then, after ascending a shallow flight of steps, they were greeted by a pale young man in an impeccably cut dark suit.

'Good afternoon. I'm Henri, secretary to Monsieur Rivers. Would you care for some tea?'

Tom would have preferred something stronger, but he smiled automatically as Emma said, 'Tea would be very welcome.'

They were led up to the first floor and ushered into a salon of overpowering and rather gloomy grandeur, furnished with a stunning array of antiques and paintings. Henri dispensed tea and made polite conversation in perfect, only faintly accented English.

They'd been invited to stay the night and the secretary told them they would meet his employer at dinner. Eventually, after they'd finished their tea, he rose and touched a bell by the fireplace.

'The maid will show you to your room. You may like to take a rest before dinner.'

Emma's face reflected her consternation.

'Room?' she echoed. 'I think there must be some mistake – my partner and I will require a room each.'

Henri looked puzzled. 'But I understood you to be husband and wife.'

'We're separated,' Emma told him firmly.

Tom had obviously expected them to be sharing a room too. He stepped forward and said, 'One room will be fine.'

'No it won't,' Emma contradicted him.

'Nothing can be done until Monsieur Rivers arrives,' said Henri smoothly. 'Perhaps you would care to discuss it with him.'

He handed them over to a maid who led them up another

flight of stairs to an opulent room twice the size of most modern houses.

She left them without a word, leaving Emma to look around, her slanting, blue eyes wide, her full lips slightly apart.

If Louis XIV had risen from the enormous, brocade-hung bed and greeted them, she wouldn't have been too surprised.

It was what she imagined a bedroom at Versailles would have looked like. The furniture all appeared to be at least 300 years old, even if the carpets and soft furnishings must have been renewed at some stage.

Three huge windows overlooked the gardens at the rear of the house, but despite the fact that plenty of light came in through them and was reflected by several large, baroque mirrors, the room seemed dark and shadowy.

It was a few moments before Emma noticed that instead of there being an adjoining bathroom, at the far end of the room there was a massive cast-iron bath on a platform reached by three shallow steps. A few yards away from the bath there was a wash basin, itself almost large enough to bathe in.

Slowly, she crossed the room and stared silently around the bathing area.

'Not exactly private is it?' she murmured. 'I wonder where the toilet is?'

Tom followed her and began opening the doors of the many cupboards at that end of the room. As he suspected, the toilet was down a short corridor behind one of the doors.

'I suppose I should be thankful for small mercies,' she commented. 'This is so annoying. It never occurred to me we'd be expected to share a room.'

201

Tom looked hurt. 'Just what's going on, Emma? I thought that after Barbados we were at least lovers again.'

'We were – now we're not. Nothing's changed, Tom. I just let my libido get the better of me while we were away – that's all.'

He started to say something, then stopped as there was a tap at the door.

'*Entrez*!' called Emma after a pause, and a maid carried in a tray holding a bottle of champagne, an ice bucket and two glasses. She deposited it silently on a table, nodded when Emma said '*Merci*', and left without speaking.

Instead of continuing with what he'd been about to say, Tom evidently thought better of it. Instead, he went over to the table and deftly opened the bottle. The cork flew out with an unobtrusive pop and he poured them both a glass of the sparkling wine.

He wandered around the room looking speculatively at the different pieces of furniture. Emma, who could read him like a book, knew quite well that he was assessing their potential for screwing on.

She sipped her champagne feeling cross. She wanted a bath before changing for dinner, but she didn't want to take one under Tom's lustful gaze.

And what was even worse, she could feel unwelcome coils of desire uncurling in her groin at the thought of them fucking their way around the room.

Some of the furniture did look as if it would lend itself to various erotic and interesting positions.

Damn. She hadn't bargained for this.

'Would you like first bath?' asked Tom amiably, throwing his lean frame down onto a strange, carved chaise-longue.

'Would it be any use asking you to read, or something, with your back turned?'

'None whatsoever,' he returned cheerfully.

Sighing, Emma decided to ignore him and began unpacking her bag. She laid out her toilet kit in the bathing area, then slipped out of her clothes with her back to him. She could feel his eyes burning holes in her as she turned on both the taps and waited for the huge tub to fill.

There was a selection of creams, lotions and bath essences around the edge, and she threw in a generous amount of rose-scented powder, which turned the water into a fragrant, milky pool.

She could see Tom's reflection in the mirror as she pinned up her hair. He was watching her with a possessive and lascivious gaze, which simultaneously annoyed and aroused her.

She sank into the steaming water and sipped her champagne.

Tom picked up the bottle and ambled up onto the platform to refill her glass, then sat on a small, gilt chair a couple of yards away.

'Can't you find something else to occupy you?' she groaned.

'Nothing half as interesting.'

Emma soaped herself thoroughly, then closed her eyes and sank further into the bath. She was seized by an overpowering desire to touch herself, and opened her eyes to glance down at the cloudy surface of the water.

She couldn't see her own body – which meant that neither could Tom.

She let her hand drift between her legs and felt her clit give a little anticipatory throb as she touched it.

If she brought herself to an unobtrusive climax, perhaps she could get through the rest of the evening without being eaten up by a hot, urgent desire to have Tom screw her.

She couldn't bear to think of the frustration it would cause if they had to spend the night in the same bed. The odds were that even if she fended off his amorous advances during the evening, as soon as she felt his hard body next to hers in the bed, she would be a pushover.

Just thinking about the possibilities made Emma feel the slow burn of sexual excitement spread over her body. Her fingers caressed her clit and explored her own smooth contours, giving herself a seductive, secret pleasure.

'Why don't you let me do that for you?' asked Tom persuasively.

Emma's eyes flew open and she saw immediately that Tom had sensed, or guessed, what she was doing.

'I don't know what you mean,' she said sulkily, feeling her climax recede as she reluctantly removed her hand. Tom came to sit on the edge of the bath.

'You were masturbating – no, don't bother to deny it, Em. The expression on your face was a dead giveaway. Not to mention this.'

The tips of his fingers traced the pink flush of arousal on her cheeks, neck and chest. He dipped into the scented milky water and touched one of her lush breasts, making her nipple harden instantly.

'Do you know what time of day this is?' he continued softly. 'It's *l'heure bleue*, when all over Paris lovers are meeting to make long, slow, sensual love. Blinds are being lowered, curtains closed and clothing removed a garment at a time . . .'

'Or more likely, all the married men are taking their mistresses to the Bois de Boulogne, parking and screwing them in the back of the car, before going home to their wives and families. Very romantic, I'm sure,' said Emma tartly, wishing she had the strength of will to remove Tom's hand from her breast. She could smell the clean scent of shampoo on his crisp, dark hair and had to resist an impulse to run her fingers through it.

'Maybe not romantic – but very, very sexy,' he persisted. 'Doesn't the idea excite you? Imagine being parked in a deserted spot of the woods and having your lover undress you until you're lying back naked on the seat – or perhaps just in stockings and a suspender belt. Imagine him kissing every inch of your skin, touching you, arousing you until you can't wait to have him inside you. Imagine him doing this . . .'

Tom's hand slid further into the water and smoothed over Emma's hip. '. . . and this . . .' His fingers brushed over her silken bush; '. . . and this . . .' He slid a finger between her outer lips until unable to stand it a moment longer, Emma stood up, with water streaming from her slender body and looked around for a towel.

Before she could stop him, Tom bent his head and kissed her dripping, fluff-covered mound, then flicked his tongue between the soft folds of her labia.

Emma was instantly paralysed by molten, squirming lust, so strong that she was unable to speak or move. Tom took full advantage of the situation by sliding his hands down over her wet buttocks and easing her legs apart.

His tongue flickered, probed and lapped at her private parts, nibbling and tasting; while Emma buried her hands in his dark hair to press him closer and stop herself from falling. His tongue finished what she'd started with her own fingers and, within a couple of minutes, she jerked into a long drawn-out orgasm.

While she was still moaning, he lifted her out of the bath, wrapped her in a towel and sat her to one side of the enormous wash basin. The towel rode up so that her bare bottom was on the cold porcelain and she gasped with shock, then gasped again as he swiftly unzipped his trousers and thrust his iron-hard cock inside her.

The force of his thrust sent her sliding back on the slippery surface and, when he pulled her back, she wound her damp legs around his waist, muttering, 'You really are a bastard.'

'But a sexy one,' he replied, then fastened his mouth over hers and kissed her deeply while they moved against each other in a fast increasing rhythm.

Emma had brought a slinky black dress to wear for dinner. It came up to her collarbones at the front, but the back was cut in a deep vee, which fell to her waist. It stopped a few discreet inches above her knee, but the overall effect was very, very sexy.

'Is that new?' asked Tom, pausing in the act of fastening his shirt. 'I don't think I've seen it before.'

'Newish,' said Emma clipping her pearl earrings in place. 'Could you fasten these for me please?' She handed him a single strand of pearls and turned her back, lifting her hair out of the way as she did so.

Tom obediently fastened the clasp, then slipped a hand down the back of her dress and fondled her bottom over her black silk camiknickers.

When he slid it even further down and touched her delicately between the legs, Emma pulled away.

'No you don't – we're due downstairs in five minutes.'

Paul Rivers was waiting for them in the main salon. A tall,

greying man in his fifties; he kissed Emma's hand, shook Tom's, then asked them what they'd like to drink.

He was courteous and charming, if somewhat enigmatic. He made it plain he didn't want to discuss business during dinner, so the three of them chatted lightly over a superbly cooked meal.

Over coffee and cognac Emma wandered around the room with unconsciously feline grace, admiring some of the finer pieces and asking him about them. Her attention was caught by a painting over the fireplace. It was of a beautiful, fair-haired woman, almost ethereally slender in a gauzy evening gown.

She stood and considered it, then turned to their host, 'This is recent isn't it?' Everything else in the room was at least 100 years old.

'You're quite correct – that's a painting of my wife.'

'Does she live in Paris too?' asked Emma innocently, then could have kicked herself when he replied, 'She died over seventeen years ago.'

'She was very beautiful,' was all she could think of to say.

'She was indeed. Not a day goes by when I don't think of her – in fact, you remind me of her just a little, my dear. Anyway – to business. I have decided that your company shall be the one to make this film. I liked your showreel, I liked your approach and I like you. It seems fitting to me that a company run by a happily married couple should get this project.'

Tom and Emma exchanged exultant but puzzled glances. Until this moment they'd been in some doubt as to whether they were the chosen company, or still competing.

But what did being a happily married couple have to do with it?

Emma was particularly baffled. She'd made a point of telling Henri that they were separated, but the message must not have been passed on, which was probably as well if their relationship had any bearing on Paul's decision to commission the film from their company.

'My wife was very active in the field of marital relations,' he explained. 'She believed fervently that couples needed to work at their relationships and sex lives to build a strong, committed life together. My primary aim in backing this film is to help as many couples as possible to enjoy their sex lives to the hilt – but I won't be displeased if it makes me a healthy profit too.'

He poured them all another glass of cognac before continuing, 'I own a house in Cheshire where I'd like you to make the film. It's very large – there'll be plenty of room for the whole production team and cast, and it will help to keep costs down. My staff there have been told to assist you in any way they can. Now, shall we go through the budget together?'

They discussed the budget and production schedule at some length. When everything had been agreed, he turned to them and said, 'There is one last thing . . .'

'Yes?' prompted Emma.

'I have a daughter. She starts university in September, but she's very interested in making films. I wonder if it would be possible for you to use her as some sort of production assistant – unpaid of course – while you're making the film, so she can gain some experience in the field.'

'We'd be delighted to,' said Emma, thinking it was a small price to pay.

'Perhaps I'd better add that Bella has led a very sheltered life. She's only just left boarding school and hasn't been about in the world much. I'd be grateful if you'd keep an eye on her and make sure she comes to no harm.'

Tom and Emma exchanged glances. If, by harm, he meant he didn't want his daughter forming any undesirable relationships, that could be a bit awkward. The film crew were a libidinous lot and if Bella was even halfway attractive, one of them was sure to have a crack at her sooner or later.

'We'll do our best,' Tom assured him, thinking they'd cross that bridge when they came to it.

'I find it reassuring that you're a happily married couple – I feel sure I can trust you to take care of my little girl – and to make a film which emphasises the importance of committed, stable relationships,' was Paul Rivers' final word on the subject.

At the end of the evening he walked upstairs with them to their room.

'I've been rather remiss,' he said, as Tom pushed open the door. 'Do you have everything you need? I should have asked earlier.'

Emma smiled and murmured, 'Thank you, we're very comfortable.'

'Love the bath,' added Tom.

'Then I'll say goodnight and goodbye – I'm leaving for Berne first thing tomorrow. The car will be ready to take you to the airport at two – please spend the morning doing as you please.' He kissed Emma's hand again, shook Tom's and left them.

As soon as he'd gone they hugged each other triumphantly.

'This should keep us in the black for a while,' said Tom. 'If we're doing the shoot at his house, with no living or studio costs, the profit we'll make will be *very* healthy.'

Weird how he kept going on about us being a happily married couple, wasn't it? Let's hope Henri forgets you told him we were separated.'

'You're right – it was weird,' agreed Emma. 'It's obviously something to do with his wife. He must place such an unusual emphasis on it because she died – isn't that sad?'

'I'm sure he hasn't lacked for female company,' commented Tom. 'He's rich and charming. I just hope Bella isn't any trouble. Would it be unkind to hope that she's a real dog? I don't relish the prospect of guarding her virtue on a location shoot – not with everyone in a permanently horny state from watching the cast demonstrating the finer points of screwing all day. Talking of which, how do you fancy fucking on that carved love-seat thing?'

In an adjoining room, a shadowy figure sat in a chair and prepared for a long night.

Chapter Fourteen

Bella Rivers started work with them the week before they went up to Cheshire. Emma and most of the team were already well into pre-production, while Tom did the final edit on the chocolate commercials.

Sophia Brentwood was very pleased with the results. She had recently become involved with a wine importer and, much to Tom's relief, had told him it was over between the two of them. With his customary charm Tom went through the motions of expressing regret, said he hoped they'd stay friends and breathed a heartfelt sigh of relief.

Bella was a slight, delicately featured girl with fine, light-brown hair held back by a black velvet band. Her pale face was devoid of make-up, and her clothes were conservative in the extreme – a navy-blue shirtwaister dress and flat navy shoes.

Rosa took the girl off to show her around and Tom asked Emma, 'What do you think, will she be any trouble?'

'Difficult to tell – she looks quiet enough. It would be better if she were ugly or overweight – she's really quite pretty, but she comes across as almost plain in those clothes and with no make-up. We'll just have to hope the crew are too busy ogling Rosa and the actresses to notice her. Have you had a word with Jake yet by the way?'

Of all the production team, it was usually Jake who presented the strongest threat to female virtue – except for Tom himself. But Emma was confident that with so much money at stake, Tom would keep his distance.

Jake was another matter.

'Do you think it's necessary?' asked Tom. 'She's hardly his type.'

'She may be mousey but she's got class, and I've known him go for that. Better to be safe than sorry. Speak to him will you?'

It was true that Jake had a weakness for humping classy, up-market women and watching their poise disintegrate when they were on the receiving end of his crude, but effective technique.

But they were usually in their thirties or forties and more often than not, married.

In his jeans and leather jacket, Jake came across as yobbier than he actually was and he liked to play it up – he was aware that to a lot of women he represented a bit of rough. In fact, he came from a comfortable, suburban semi in Sidcup – his father was a tax inspector and his mother a teacher.

Tom found Jake checking film stock and took him on one side.

'We've got to be careful how we handle Bella, since her father's putting up the money for the film. She's just out of boarding school, and he's worried she's going to be easy meat for one of the crew. Put the word around will you, that anyone caught putting the make on her will be out of a job faster than he can say, "Wham, bam, thank you ma'am" – and that includes you.'

Jake looked injured in the extreme. 'She's not my type. I like them to have been around a bit.'

212

'Well, whatever you do, don't upset her – she's led a sheltered life.'

Rosa brought Bella into the editing room late that afternoon. She wanted to phone Peregrine and make a couple of salacious suggestions, and she could hardly do that with Bella sitting primly beside her, her hands neatly folded in her lap.

'Can I leave Bella with you for a while, Jake? I have some phone calls to make.'

'I'm just in the middle of something,' said Jake hastily, remembering Tom's warning.

'Then Bella can help you with it,' returned Rosa smiling sweetly. She left the room, high heels clicking, while Jake looked for somewhere to put the pile of videos he was holding.

'Let me help you,' offered Bella, holding out her arms.

Jake took a step back, stumbled over a box, cracked his shin on the edge of a cabinet and dropped the lot.

'Fucking hell fire!' he exclaimed.

Bella shot him a glacial look. 'Would you mind awfully not using language like that?' she said coldly.

Emma opened the door. 'What's going on?' she asked.

'Nothing serious. I just barked my bleed ... I mean, I just barked my shin.'

'Perhaps you'd like to come and give me a hand, Bella,' suggested Emma, wondering who'd been foolish enough to leave the girl alone with Jake.

That evening, Tom was wandering through reception when a small, very young blonde girl came in through the door. She was wearing a scruffy leather jacket, jeans so tight that they looked like they'd been sprayed on and a pair of shabby, spike-heeled, black boots.

'Can I help you?' he enquired pleasantly. It was raining outside and her hair and clothes were wet. She reminded Tom of a bedraggled kitten.

She was also sexy as hell.

'I'm looking for someone,' she said, dabbing ineffectually at her dripping hair with a grubby handkerchief.

'Who?'

'I don't know his name,' she admitted. 'A big bloke with a Harley.'

That figured.

'Why don't you come and wait in my office while I see if he's still here?' suggested Tom, wondering whether Jake would be pleased to see her or not. He was sailing close to the wind with this luscious little Lolita – she didn't look any older than fifteen.

Still, it was none of his business.

He showed her into his office and left her huddling up to the radiator while he went in search of Jake. Maybe if the cameraman had already left he should take her for something to eat – she looked like she hadn't had a square meal in weeks.

Then he could take her home and . . .

Fortunately or unfortunately, depending on how you looked at it, Jake was still there, though just about to leave. He knew immediately who she was when Tom described her.

Angel-face.

He felt his dick stirring at the memory of their hot coupling on his bike.

'Hello, sweetheart,' he greeted her. 'What are you doing here?'

'I came to see you.'

Tom grinned as he shrugged on his jacket. 'Night,' he said casually, thinking he'd leave them to it. Everyone else had already gone. He vanished and Jake led the way back to reception.

'I was just off,' he told her. 'Fancy a drink?'

She wound her arms around his neck, pulled his head down and kissed him. She slid her pointed little tongue between his lips and wriggled her body against his chest so he could feel the taut peaks of her apple-like breasts.

He clasped her tightly to him, grasping her taut buttocks in his large hands.

'Is your bike outside?' she whispered.

'Yeah, why?'

'Let's go and sit on it.'

'It's bleeding pissing it down,' he pointed out.

She looked disappointed.

'Another time,' he promised, unzipping her leather jacket to reveal a tight, low-cut pink tee-shirt. She wasn't wearing a bra and her pointed nipples thrust alluringly against the thin material.

Jake dragged the front of the tee-shirt out of her jeans and up to her collarbones so he could fasten his mouth over one pebble-hard nipple and tease it between his lips.

He sat on the edge of the reception desk and stroked her belly and thighs through the damp, skin-tight denim. He tried to undo her zip but it got stuck halfway down and she had to help him. He peeled the jeans down over her thighs, taking the tiny pair of pink cotton panties she was wearing, with them.

He undid his own jeans then lifted her so she was straddling him. She grasped his cock eagerly and guided it into the moist, floss-covered entrance to her pussy.

She gasped as he slid into her tight little cavern and wriggled downwards until his full length was completely encased.

'Talk to me about it,' she whispered, renewing her wriggling – this time in an upward direction.

'You've got the sweetest little fanny I've ever shagged,' he said after a brief pause in which he searched his mind for something suitably complimentary.

'No, I mean about your bike.'

'Eh?'

'Tell me about your bike,' she insisted. 'Tell me how you're going to screw me on it later.'

Jake did his best to oblige as he shafted her vigorously; her wriggling was driving him wild.

There was practically steam coming off them, their fucking was so hot and raunchy.

Jake kept up a description of some future fuck on his bike, interspersing obscenities with biking terminology and grunts of pleasure.

'Then, with you kneeling on the seat, bent over the handlebars ... uuh ... I'll slip it into you ... aah ... all the way in ...'

A sudden movement glimpsed out of the corner of his eye made him turn his head.

Bella was standing in the doorway, her mouth a round 'Ooh' of surprise.

She was behind Angel-face and the luscious blonde was obviously unaware of the other girl's presence because she kept up her arousing wriggling up and down his cock at an ever-increasing pace, making little mewing noises of pleasure.

Jake was only too aware of what sort of a sight they must present to the shocked Bella. He was half reclining on the reception desk with Angel-face, her jeans and panties around her thighs, straddling him and her little rump moving up and down. Her tee-shirt was pushed up exposing her gorgeous tits and her arms were wound tightly around his neck.

He didn't know how long Bella had been standing there but she seemed frozen with shock. He just hoped she hadn't caught any of the dirty talk.

At that moment, Angel-face gave a strangled little scream of ecstasy and came, bearing down hard with her juicy little cunt so that Jake climaxed a few seconds later.

When he looked up again, Bella had vanished.

All the following day Bella avoided his eyes. Jake felt sort of uncomfortable about it – the odds were that she'd never had a boyfriend and he could see that coming across a couple humping on a desk might be a bit of a shock.

He kept out of her way, but in the afternoon Rosa sent her to ask him if he needed any more film stock ordering.

'Er, yes – tell her to just hang on a sec, I'll be out in a minute.'

Bella blushed, but instead of beating a hasty retreat she closed the door behind her and came into the room.

'I'm sorry about last night,' she murmured, 'I forgot my scarf and it was raining.'

'That's okay,' he mumbled sheepishly, edging towards the door.

'I couldn't sleep for thinking about it,' she told him.

'Er, sorry about that,' he stammered.

'The thing is ...' she stared down at the ground and clasped her hands behind her back. Today she was wearing a shapeless pale-blue dress with a white collar and her light-brown hair was held back from her face by two slides.

Jake waited uneasily. 'Yeah?' he prompted her.

'The thing is ... I'd like you to do that with me.'

217

'Eh?' he ejaculated.

'I'd like you to do that with me,' she repeated. 'Have sex, I mean.' Her voice with its cut-glass accent was so low he could barely hear her.

Jake was completely taken aback.

He was even more taken aback when she advanced towards him and unbuttoned her dress to reveal a pristine, plain white cotton bra.

He shook his head as if to clear it, then looked round with a hunted expression, wondering what the fuck was going on.

Despite her slenderness she had full, round breasts and he couldn't take his eyes from her deep, alabaster cleavage.

She kept on undoing buttons until her dress slipped to the floor, revealing a pair of equally pristine white cotton knickers, which went up all the way to her narrow waist. Jake wondered if her underwear was regulation school issue because it had no lace, frills or other adornment.

At that moment he heard the sound of Emma's voice in the corridor outside.

Within seconds, Bella had scrambled back into her dress and done up the buttons. She then glided silently to the door and slipped into the corridor, leaving Jake mopping his sweating brow and wondering what the hell he was going to do.

The following day was the final casting session.

Emma had handled the preliminary sessions. Much as Tom would have liked to have been present, he just couldn't find the time, but he'd moved heaven and earth to clear his decks for today.

Emma knew that her ex-husband would have been more than happy to audition the female actresses alone, but she didn't want the company getting a reputation for using the time-dishonoured method of the casting couch.

They'd hired a freelance casting director and the choice had already been narrowed down to a dozen men and a dozen women. The actors and actresses had to be attractive and subtly sexy. They also had to look like real people – pleasant and healthy, if not actually wholesome.

It was a difficult brief. If the cast's bodies were too good, viewers with less perfect physiques might feel inferior. But, on the other hand, no one wanted to sit and watch a sex guide featuring unattractive people with lumpy figures.

There was also a fine line between using a cast who looked like they shed their clothes so regularly that they were practising exhibitionists, and people who were obviously uncomfortable naked or partially dressed.

The guide was to feature masturbation and various simulated sex acts, so anyone with too many inhibitions would be of no use – the production schedule didn't allow time for Tom to have to coax a reluctant actress out of her clothing.

Besides Tom, Emma, Rosa and Samuel, the casting director, the audition was also attended by a sex therapist, Dr Jackson, who was acting as consultant to the film.

He was a suave and courteous man in his late forties, with a slim, well-exercised body, set off to advantage by an impeccably cut dark suit.

Bella had been asked to keep the waiting actors and actresses supplied with coffee and the rest of the production team to keep out of the way.

'Shall we begin with the men?' suggested Emma.

The first actor, Ben London, was brought in and, after another interview, stripped off for them. A painted wooden screen had been placed in a corner of the room for those who preferred to undress in privacy, but he seemed quite happy to shrug out of his clothing in front of them.

He was a good-looking actor in his early twenties who'd already appeared in the nude in two stage productions. He'd been one of Emma's choices but, when she saw him naked for the first time, she realised she might have to revise her opinion.

His detumescent cock was quite simply enormous – much larger than average. If it was proportionately huge when he had a hard-on they couldn't use him, or all the male viewers would feel inadequate.

'Would you mind masturbating for us?' asked Tom. 'We need to see you erect.'

Ben obligingly began to stimulate his cock. Casting a sideways glance at Rosa, Emma was amused to see her colleague licking her full lower lip in anticipation.

Everyone in the room was transfixed as Ben's cock rose to tower up massively between his thighs. Emma could only assume he was known to his intimates as Big Ben London – she couldn't actually imagine any woman being able to accommodate all that – however aroused.

Rosa's face was flushed and Emma distinctly heard her gulp.

'Thank you, Ben,' said Emma faintly. 'We'll be in touch with your agent in due course.'

By lunchtime they'd narrowed it down to six actors who would all take screen tests before the final four were chosen.

In the afternoon it was time for the actresses.

Jake, who hadn't come to the morning's auditions, predictably elected to attend the afternoon session. Emma felt sorry for the girls who were going to have to strip under the lustful gaze of the director, the cameraman and the casting director. She didn't know whether Dr Jackson felt lustful or not – if he did, he hid it better than the others.

But everyone present knew what was involved and if they did get a part it would be even worse when they were actually filming in front of a full crew.

For a feature-length film like this they needed a larger crew than usual and the company had been inundated with applications – several people had even offered to work for less than their usual freelance rates, presumably reckoning that the fringe benefits would make up for the reduced remuneration.

Three of the actresses were swiftly rejected. One because she had a small tattoo on her breast, which had been concealed on her publicity photos; another because she was too painfully thin; and a third because she had large, ugly hands with bitten nails.

It was a long afternoon.

Tom and Jake seemed to have permanent hard-ons, which left them pretty much unable to make any rational decisions. Tom's contribution was confined to comments like, 'Great bum', or 'Fantastic legs', and Jake appeared to have been completely bereft of the power of speech.

Samuel had his hand in his pocket, and Emma was convinced he was touching himself as the girls paraded before them.

Eventually, at around seven-thirty, they'd whittled the number down to six and were at last able to knock off for the day. Jake immediately vanished and was seen a few minutes later chatting up one of the successful actresses, Clarissa, a statuesque beauty with auburn hair,

Tom followed Emma into her office but she pre-empted the pass, which she knew was coming by saying brightly, 'I'm going to the Portofino with Samuel – he wants to discuss his fee. He says if we agree to use him on the next three films that require a cast, he'll charge less. See you tomorrow.'

Samuel appeared in the doorway at that moment, and Tom was just about to say he'd join them when Rosa called, 'Tom – there's a call for you on line two – your solicitor.'

Reluctantly, Tom went to take the call, which lasted almost an hour. When he'd finished, he thought about Emma and Samuel having dinner together and decided he wasn't happy about it. He'd always disliked the man – he was good at his job but there was something unpleasant about him. He was also bound to be horny after an afternoon of watching beautiful women strip – Emma probably wasn't safe with him.

Tom went outside to flag down a taxi, having decided to join them at the restaurant.

He was just waving at one when a voice behind him said, 'Tom! You old bastard! Long time no see.' It was one of his old college friends who'd been working in Australia for the last few years.

'Martin! When did you get back?'

'A few weeks ago. How are you?'

After a few minutes chatting on the pavement, Tom allowed himself to be persuaded into a nearby bar for a quick drink.

It was almost an hour later when he arrived at the restaurant. He was just rummaging in his pockets for some cash to pay the taxi driver, when he saw Emma emerge from the doorway a few yards away.

What was the matter with her?

Instead of her usual hip-swinging walk she was virtually staggering.

There was something wrong.

'Hey! Emma!' he called. 'Wait for me!'

His attempt to attract her attention only resulted in her quickening her pace, then she got hurriedly into her car, which was parked nearby.

Tom broke into a run, but she drove off with a crashing of gears that was very unlike her usual competent driving style. A few seconds later, just after she'd turned the corner, he heard the sickening and unmistakable sound of tearing metal and knew she'd been involved in an accident.

His heart pounding, Tom hurtled around the corner after her to find the front of her BMW embedded in the side of a parked police car.

There was no one else around and Tom reached her just as she dazedly opened her door and stumbled out of the car.

'Em!' he exclaimed thankfully. 'Are you okay?'

She looked at him blankly, then muttered, 'It was a cat ... a little grey cat ... it ran in front of the car.'

As if on cue, the cat in question stalked out from beneath the police car, where it had obviously taken refuge, and leapt daintily onto the bonnet where it began to wash one white-socked paw.

Tom realised immediately that Emma was drunk.

Not just drunk, but stinking drunk.

He didn't know what the hell was going on. Emma was an enthusiastic social drinker but when she was driving she kept her intake moderate.

And of all the bad luck, to crash into a police car.

There was no sign of the boys in blue yet, but a few interested spectators had already gathered to watch the fun. Emma would undoubtedly lose her licence – she was obviously well over the limit.

In a job like theirs you needed to be mobile. Although

they both often took taxis around central London, there were innumerable times when a car was absolutely essential.

Acting fast, Tom steered her round to the passenger seat and sat her down on the edge of it, saying urgently, 'Don't say anything – pretend you're in shock and leave it to me. Do you understand?'

At that moment a couple of policemen appeared from the doorway of a club and stopped dead when they saw the wreckage of their vehicle.

'Is that your car?' asked one of them disbelievingly, nodding at the BMW.

'I'm afraid so,' said Tom, running his fingers through his hair. 'Or rather, it's my wife's, but I was driving. Sorry, officer, that damned cat ran out in front of me and I swerved and lost control.'

The cat stopped licking its paw, stood up, twitched its backside dismissively at the policemen and stalked off with its nose in the air.

'Have you been drinking sir?' asked the second man, already taking out a breathalyser kit.

'Yes, but just a couple,' returned Tom truthfully. He obediently blew into the bag when requested to do so and almost laughed aloud when he saw the man's disappointment that he was below the limit.

'Is she okay?' asked the first policeman, nodding in the direction of Emma, who was sitting ashen faced, clutching her jacket closed.

'Just shocked I think,' replied Tom, going over to her and saying, 'Are you okay, darling?'

Emma nodded and managed a faint smile.

One of the men had already been busy talking into his radio.

'As soon as the tow-truck arrives we'll go down to the station while we sort this out,' he said grumpily. 'In the meantime, I'll just take a few particulars. Name?'

Chapter Fifteen

'It won't work,' said Rosa faintly. 'You'll never get that thing inside me – it's just too big.'

'Trust me,' said Ben London. 'Believe me – you aren't the first woman to think that.'

They were in Rosa's flat after going for a drink together. She'd accepted his invitation out of curiosity. He'd phoned her in the early evening just after the auditions had ended and suggested they get together. By the time she'd had several glasses of wine, Rosa had decided that Ben's cock couldn't possibly be as large as she remembered it.

They'd gone back to her flat and ended up in the bedroom, where she'd unzipped his jeans with some trepidation. When she saw his cock rearing up like some visiting creature from another planet, she backed away and sank down on her haunches on the other side of the bed.

'It'll be painful,' she pointed out, 'and I'm not into pain – just pleasure.'

'It won't, I promise you,' he reassured her. 'If it hurts at all, you only have to say so and I'll stop. Now just relax and leave it to me. First you need to be *very* aroused.'

Rosa sank back on the bed and tried to relax. Usually she liked her sex fairly wild, but with Ben that was out of the question. It was going to have to be slow and gentle, or he'd tear her apart.

Her blouse was already open and he helped her out of it before peeling her short, tight skirt down her shapely thighs, leaving her clad in just a hot-pink suspender belt and panties, with a pair of cream stockings.

Her full, biscuit-brown breasts still retained much of her Barbados tan and her large, olive-hued nipples jutted out expectantly.

Ben reached out and picked up a jar of rich, scented face cream from her bedside table. He unscrewed the lid and scooped out a large dollop, which he began to massage into her breasts. She flinched as the cool cream made contact with her heated flesh, then relaxed as he covered both her firm orbs with it and worked it into her finely textured skin.

It made her feel relaxed and pampered as she squirmed lazily beneath his caressing hands. When she was glistening with the rich cream from her collarbones to her navel, he drew her tiny pink panties down her legs and discarded them.

He could smell the musky scent of Rosa's sex, mingling with the perfumed cream and found it a heady mixture.

He dipped his head between her thighs and breathed deeply. Her scent made him want to taste her and he probed roughly between her legs with his tongue. Rosa sighed as she felt it pushing past her outer labia, to swirl an erotic pattern over the fleshy entrance to her honeypot.

After flickering over her clit in a way that made a deep-seated heat in her groin slowly uncoil, he thrust in deeply to explore her velvet inner chamber.

When he looked up, his face was shiny with her juices.

'I love the way you taste,' he breathed, then bent his head again and began to lick her clit with an insistent, erotic rhythm.

It never took Rosa long to come, and her muscles spasmed into orgasm within a couple of minutes.

While she was still panting, he undid her suspenders and removed the flimsy, pink suspender belt from her narrow waist, leaving her wearing only her stockings.

She was lying on her back propped up on a couple of pillows, and he pushed her legs up over her head so her curvaceous bottom and the full, pink lips of her sex were fully exposed.

Holding her legs back with one hand, he scooped out another dollop of cream and began to rub it sensually into the smooth skin of her buttocks.

Rosa was already wet, but the way he massaged her well-rounded derrière made her produce even more copious female juices.

He rubbed a glob of the scented cream into the small circle of her anus and made her shudder with delight by introducing the tip of his finger and rotating it.

When her backside and the back of her thighs had all received a liberal coating of cream, he turned his attention to her pulsating pussy. After parting her legs, he held her outer lips apart, then smeared a scoop of the thick lotion over them and massaged it gently into the silken folds.

It felt wonderfully cool in contrast to the fierce heat that consumed her swollen private parts.

Another scoop followed.

This time, he pushed it further into her, gently stretching the walls of her honeypot with his fingers as he did so. Soon she was full of it, and with each renewed application he stretched her internal walls a little further.

When her pussy was overflowing with a combination of the face cream and her own lubrications, Ben left the bed for a moment.

Rosa heard a faint buzzing sound then saw him return holding a white plastic vibrator. It was about the size of an average cock and was, in fact, virtually identical to one she had in her underwear drawer.

With her legs still up above her head, she felt him playing it over her clit, stroking the shaft, then the hood, before eventually letting it make contact with the head.

She came immediately.

He slipped it inside her, and her internal muscles clutched it hard, in a series of shuddering spasms.

Her legs, which were beginning to ache, dropped down onto the bed as he moved the vibrator in and out of her. Before she had the chance to recover, he reached down, picked up another, larger vibrator, and substituted it for the first one.

As he slid it between the hotly throbbing folds of her honeypot, Rosa caught a glimpse of it. It looked big, but not as big as Ben's own member, which was still rising up massively from between his thighs.

It was a tight fit and he had to work it carefully upwards, rotating it as he eased it into position. The vibrations made waves of pleasure emanate outwards from Rosa's groin, making her feel as if her entire lower body were on fire.

When he was sure she'd stretched to accommodate it, he withdrew it and teased her clit with the tip. Within seconds Rosa exploded into another climax.

'I love a woman who comes easily,' he commented.

'You're . . . good at this,' she gasped.

'I need to be,' he said, stimulating her inner lips with the head of the vibrator. 'A big cock is as much a liability, as it is an asset.'

When he picked up the third vibrator, Rosa stared at it apprehensively.

It was enormous.

Not as enormous as Ben, but still enormous.

'It's okay,' he said soothingly, running the end gently over her clit. 'Just relax.'

Rosa let her head flop back onto the pillows and gave herself over to the voluptuous sensations the device was causing. When he slipped it in the first couple of inches, she felt rather uncomfortably full, but the insidious vibrations kept her relaxed and soon it was halfway in.

She drew her knees up and let her thighs splay abandonedly apart as he eased it a little further up.

'Okay?' he asked.

'Umm.'

With it wedged firmly inside her, Ben used the small vibrator to bring her to another climax, causing her to cry out as her muscles tried to contract and found they couldn't.

It felt strange.

But very, very pleasurable.

At last, the moment she'd half dreaded, half craved arrived. Ben swiftly rubbed a glob of cream into the head of his swollen cock and knelt between her legs.

By now, Rosa was half delirious with excitement, her breasts heaving, her darkly lashed eyes glittering feverishly. She inhaled sharply as she felt the plum-like head nudging determinedly at the slippery folds of her sex.

The first couple of inches presented no problem, but after that he had to push ahead a fraction of an inch at a time, withdraw, then try to gain a little more ground.

Rosa was glad she was overflowing with moisture or it would have been absolutely impossible.

She wondered how he kept himself under control as he edged his way into her deepest, most secret places. After the time he'd spent on her, he must be about ready to come himself

With a last sudden thrust he was completely inside her – or as much of him as was anatomically possible.

Rosa felt as if she were about to split in two.

Or as if she were choking.

But, as he began to move in a slow, steady rhythm, she couldn't help herself moving with him, gingerly at first then with more confidence, as she became accustomed to being skewered on his huge member.

Gradually, the choking sensations were replaced by wave after wave of searing pleasure, taking over her body and sending her wild.

Their careful movements became more abandoned, then frenzied, as Rosa bucked her hips under him and clawed at his back with her long nails.

He caught her wrists and held them down by her sides grunting, 'Don't mark me – I've another audition tomorrow.'

She wrapped her legs around his waist and went with him as he thrust into her with insatiable ferocity, until, at last, in a scalding eruption which flooded her like molten lava, Ben came.

His groans of release were loud and long drawn out, but not as loud and long drawn out as Rosa's cries when she came again, pushed over the edge by the erotic sensation of his hot fluid pumping endlessly into her.

The following morning, Emma sat miserably propped up against the pillows of Tom's bed and sipped the cup of coffee he'd brought her. She looked pale and wan, with dark circles under her eyes and her blonde hair limp and tousled. She had a pounding headache and, unfortunately, the painkillers he'd also handed her, hadn't yet taken effect.

After over an hour at the police station, Tom had brought her back to the house in Highgate and put her to bed. He suspected that the police had only let him go when they did because Emma looked so ill.

Any hopes he might have entertained of a gratitude fuck, had been speedily laid to rest when she'd been sick within five minutes of entering the house and continued to be so for a considerable amount of time.

After he'd eventually got her to bed, he'd spent the night in the spare room, feeling mildly regretful that he'd not got to screw her.

But there was always tomorrow.

And the day after that.

Now he asked her, 'What happened, Em? You never drink a lot and drive. And you weren't just borderline – you were absolutely arseholed.'

'That little prick Samuel must have added several shots of vodka to the wine,' she groaned. 'He insisted on buying dinner, and then ordered a carafe of house red. I thought it tasted strange, but house wine is often such piss that I wasn't suspicious. He must have doctored it when I went to the ladies – I could taste it really strongly later on when I was throwing up.'

'He was trying to facilitate his entry to your delectable knickers I assume?'

'You assume right. He was angling for an invitation back and, when it wasn't forthcoming, he turned nasty. I left while he was paying the bill, hoping to forestall an unseemly scuffle by the car. I was already feeling strange – I thought I must be ill – I was just wondering whether to take a taxi rather than try to drive, when I heard Samuel shouting behind me. I couldn't face *another* scene, so stupidly I jumped into the car and drove off.'

Emma was wearing Tom's dressing gown, which was much too big for her and gave her a waif-like air. It had fallen apart at the front, revealing part of one creamy breast and the intoxicating valley of her cleavage.

Tom wanted to slip his hand into the front of the dressing gown and rub the palm over her crinkled nipple, until the little nub of flesh hardened and jutted sharply outwards. Then he'd slide the soft towelling down over her shoulders, leaving her naked to the waist and . . .

'. . . come to be there?' asked Emma.

'What?'

Tom realised belatedly that his ex-wife had just asked him something.

'How did you come to be there?' repeated Emma.

'I didn't trust Samuel – he's always been a devious little shit where women are concerned. I thought I'd come along and keep an eye on you, but I got held up and arrived just as you were leaving. It wasn't Samuel shouting after you – it was me. The rest you know.'

Emma put her coffee cup down on the bedside table.

'Thank you, Tom. I'm so grateful to you – if they'd realised it was me driving and that I was drunk as a skunk, I'd probably still be in the cells and I would *definitely* have lost my licence – not to mention having to pay a hefty fine. I'm sure telling them that my wine had been spiked with neat vodka wouldn't have made any difference.'

'No, I don't suppose it would. It really was sod's law, and then some, to smack into a police car. Luckily it was unoccupied at the time and there weren't any witnesses.'

'I really am grateful,' she repeated.

'How grateful?' asked Tom, a lascivious gleam in his eyes.

'Grateful enough to say that I'll leave it to you to decide what tangible form you'd like my thanks to take.'

Slowly, Tom slid his hand into the front of her dressing gown and closed it over her firm, taut-nippled breast.

'I'll think of something,' he assured her.

'I'm sure you will, but not right now, if you don't mind – I feel dreadful.'

Reluctantly, he withdrew his hand and pulled the front of the dressing gown closed.

Actually, despite her churning stomach and pounding head, Emma's body was already reacting to the arousing feeling of Tom's warm hand clasping her breast, the palm grazing over her nipple in a tiny circular movement.

But she didn't want him to know that.

'I'll let you know,' he promised her.

Tom went into the office, leaving Emma fast asleep. He spent the morning on the phone, making various arrangements for the shoot in Cheshire.

When he picked up the phone again, after pouring a cup of coffee, he realised he'd got a crossed line because he heard Rosa's voice speaking to someone at the other end.

About to hang up, he heard her say, '. . . the biggest cock I'd ever seen – and I've seen a lot. It was seriously huge. I did wonder what he usually did with it, because I couldn't imagine there were any women around who could accommodate it. A cunt can only stretch so far after all.'

'Don't tell me – you just had to find out for yourself,' said a female voice with a Scottish accent.

'I didn't plan to, but we went out for a drink and then back to my place.'

Tom listened with growing excitement as Rosa described her encounter with Ben, in the most gratuitous, explicit detail.

His own dick was threatening to burst the zip on his trousers as she told her friend what it felt like to have her breasts, backside and pussy massaged with cream.

Tom had been in a state of some frustration since yesterday's audition and this was just too much. He unzipped his trousers, grasped his cock and began to masturbate.

It was a heady pleasure: tossing himself off while one of his employees shared the details of her sex life, not knowing he was listening.

As his hand moved faster and faster Tom also spared a fleeting thought for Emma.

She owed him now.

She owed him and he was going to make sure she repaid her debt in full.

She didn't know what she was letting herself in for.

'Don't you like me?'

Jake cast a wild-eyed look around the small kitchen, then continued to stir his tea without replying.

Bella stood in the doorway, her slight body shrouded in an unattractive pale-pink suit with a drooping, shapeless skirt.

'Don't you like me?' she repeated. 'You seem to keep avoiding me.'

Of course he was bleeding avoiding her – he wanted to keep his job. And anyway, he didn't really fancy her, though that wouldn't have stopped him shagging her, once she'd made him the offer he'd never been known to refuse.

'I've got a girlfriend,' he said desperately.

'What difference does that make?'

Toby came into view at that moment and Jake hailed him like a drowning man clutching at a life-jacket.

'Toby! We need to check over the shooting schedule – can we do it now?'

'I was just . . .'

Edging his way past Bella, Jake thankfully joined his assistant, thinking that if she kept this up, he was going to be a nervous wreck by the time the shoot finished.

Emma dragged herself reluctantly into work in the afternoon. She still felt terrible, but there was too much to be done to lie around in bed all day.

Whoever would have thought that mixing cheap red wine with vodka could cause such a hangover? But then, the red wine alone would probably have given her a headache – it was undoubtedly the sort that owed more to chemicals, than to grapes.

At around eight she decided it was time to go home and get an early night – hopefully she'd feel better in the morning.

Tom put his head round the door at that moment, then came ambling in with his hands in his pockets. One glance at his face told her what he'd come about.

'I've decided,' he greeted her.

'And?'

'I've decided that the enormous favour you owe me can only be repaid by letting me wreak my brutish lusts on your fair, white body.'

'You do surprise me.'

'And not only that, I expect to have my every whim humoured – however aberrant. We're going to do things *so* perverted they don't even have a name. In fact for one *very* long evening, you, Emma my darling, are going to be my very own sex-slave.'

Chapter Sixteen

Paul Rivers' house in Cheshire was virtually a stately home. It stood among several acres of well-tended gardens, surrounded by lush parklands where deer roamed freely among the trees and around a large, water lily-strewn lake.

Pulling up on the gravel driveway at the bottom of a shallow flight of steps, Tom grinned, turned to Emma and said, 'I just hate slumming it.'

They'd driven up in Tom's car since Emma's was still off the road. Other than a delay near Birmingham, they'd made good time.

'Oh to be filthy rich,' sighed Emma. 'No wonder Paul wants to make sure Bella doesn't form an undesirable relationship – anyone who marries her is going to be made for life.'

'I'm quite tempted myself,' said Tom. 'I could handle this sort of lifestyle on a permanent basis.'

He hauled the cases out of the back, while Emma went into the enormous oak-panelled hall. Just like the house in Paris, everything seemed to be in excellent repair.

Bella appeared from a door off to one side and pulled an old-fashioned bell-pull hanging by the stone fireplace.

'Someone will show you to your room,' she told them, then vanished as silently as she'd appeared.

Emma was reluctantly reconciled to sharing a room with
Tom for the duration of the shoot. If the price they had to
pay for getting to make the film, was to pretend to be
happily married, she supposed she could live with it.

But it irked her that after a year of successfully managing
to keep Tom at a distance, this summer she seemed to be
constantly spreading her legs for him.

She was half dreading the night she had to spend as his
sex-slave. Tom was extremely inventive when it came to
sex, and in the past she'd had to draw the line more than
once, when he'd wanted her to do something she didn't like
the sound of.

Now, just for one long night, she wouldn't be able to do
that.

Their room was the last word in luxury, and Emma was
extremely thankful that it had an en-suite, rather than
integral bathroom.

'He likes mirrors doesn't he?' said Tom, nodding at the
massive baroque one which covered half of one wall and
was flanked by two smaller ones. 'Not that I'm complaining,' he added. 'I love to watch myself fucking.'

He went off to find out who else had arrived, while
Emma explored the house. Bella told her that only the
central part of the building was in use, the two wings were
closed up and pretty much unfurnished.

The rest of the day passed quickly while they tried to
decide which scenes should be shot where. There was
plenty of choice – in addition to numerous bedrooms and
various reception rooms, there was an indoor pool in an
orangery attached to the back of the house, with a jacuzzi
and sauna off to one side.

The grounds featured an extensive maze, and Tom was
keen to shoot at least one scene there. In the centre was an

open area, with statues of animals arranged in a circle around a fountain.

Eventually, at around seven, they finished for the evening. Bella told them dinner would be served in the dining room at eight. Emma made a note to check to see if meals could be served individually as and when they were requested, canteen style, for greater flexibility.

It just wasn't cost efficient for the whole cast and crew to eat at the same time – at least during the day – in what she would bet would be a leisurely fashion, when they were working to a tight schedule.

She wondered whether she should consult Bella about it, but decided to ask Rosa to talk to the forbidding-looking housekeeper direct. If anyone could charm the woman, Rosa could. The house seemed to be efficiently run, and Paul Rivers had said that his staff would do their best to accommodate them.

Putting her pen and notebook away, Emma headed back for their room, trying to decide whether to take a long bath, or to have a quick swim followed by a shorter bath.

Up in his room, Jake rummaged through his untidily packed suitcase for his swimming trunks. He could just go a swim after the sticky journey up from London.

There was a tap at his door.

'Yeah? Come in.'

The door opened a few inches and Bella slipped inside.

'What's up?' he asked, eyeing her nervously.

Without replying, she unzipped her dress and stepped out of it, then turned to face him wearing what appeared to be the same white cotton bra and knickers she'd been wearing the day she'd propositioned him in the editing room.

'Here – don't do that!' he begged her.

Without replying, she removed her pristine white bra, leaving her full alabaster breasts exposed, the nipples small and a delicate shell-pink.

Jake gulped and backed away as she moved towards him, her small face set in an expression of intense determination.

'Look, sweetheart,' he began, then stopped as she fell to her knees and unzipped his jeans. She drew out his cock, which was already half erect in response to her naked breasts, and fastened her small mouth around the glans.

Jake groaned and buried his hands in her hair, wishing he had the willpower to push her away and beat a hasty retreat. It was all very well for Tom to issue ultimatums, but he'd like to see his boss say no, when a half-naked girl had his dick in her mouth.

Bella sucked away at his cock employing the sort of delicacy with which the more up-market of his girlfriends ate asparagus.

Her pointed tongue slipped up and down the full length of him, strumming away at the ridge behind the head, then flickering back to lick away the droplets of moisture oozing from the tip.

When she stopped and scrambled to her feet, he reached out and pulled her roughly to him, fondling her full breasts and then her taut backside through the all-concealing cotton knickers.

Figuring he might as well be hanged for a sheep as for a lamb, but angry with her for putting him in this position, he dragged her knickers down around her knees and pushed her back on the bed.

If she wanted it that much, she could have it.

He'd worry about the consequences later.

He thrust his knee between her thighs then jabbed his cock at her floss-covered pussy. To his surprise she was dry and tight and flinched as he took his shaft in his hand and tried to get it inside her.

He let go of his cock and fumbled between her legs with his fingers, trying to locate the exact entrance to what should have been a welcoming, moist cavern. Instead, he found her closed tightly against him like the petals of a flower that was still a long way from opening.

This wasn't a situation Jake often found himself in. Usually the women he screwed were as hot and ready for it as he was himself.

Why had she thrown herself at him if she didn't bloody well want sex? Because her body was telling him pretty definitely that she didn't.

What the fuck was going on now?

'What's up?' he asked.

She opened her eyes to say, 'What do you mean?'

'I mean, you're as dry as the Gobi desert. I thought you wanted it.'

'I do.'

'It doesn't bleeding seem that way to me.'

'I need you to talk to me.'

'Eh?'

'Like you did to her.'

Jake stared at her in bewilderment.

'You know – talk dirty to me.'

Jake's jaw dropped.

Was this the same girl who'd told him to watch his language, just because he'd sworn in front of her?

'Go on,' she urged him.

'Er . . . you've got great tits,' he said cautiously.

She gave a little wriggle and closed her eyes.

'And a fantastic little arse,' he went on, searching his mind desperately for something else to say. 'And I think you'll be a great shag once you've warmed up a bit.'

He continued in the same vein for several minutes, then tentatively probed between her thighs again. Although not actually dripping wet, there was a definite slick of moisture around the entrance to her honeypot. He spread it around with his forefinger, while continuing to talk to her, using as many obscenities from his extensive vocabulary, as he could manage.

After a few more minutes he could get one finger inside her, though she still felt tight and unyielding.

Feeling his sexual prowess was being challenged, he bent his head and used his tongue to further wet her tightly furled folds.

He explored every crevice, licking and probing until she was wet and slippery. He managed to get his tongue inside her and plunged it in and out of her pussy, gratified to feel her relax even more.

Her clit was only the size of a small pea and it took him a while to locate it, hidden as it was under its protective fold of flesh.

He teased and sucked it until it swelled perceptibly, and he felt more moisture trickling out of her.

Poised above her, he took his cock in his hand once again and positioned it carefully. As he began to slide it in, he talked to her again, describing what he was doing in crude and explicit detail.

She made a faint moaning noise and parted her legs further, enabling him to slip in a couple more inches. At long last he was tightly sheathed inside her and began to move.

It was hard work and he was already knackered from

unloading equipment, but he persevered and, eventually, she began to move with him.

He redoubled his efforts verbally, until she was writhing beneath him, her eyes tightly closed, her slim hips rotating on the bedspread, her legs splayed abandonedly out.

When Jake came, in a series of grunting thrusts that drained him completely, he felt like he'd run a marathon. He rolled off her, dashed the sweat from his forehead and closed his eyes.

A few seconds later, she slipped silently off the bed, pulled on her clothes and would have left the room if he hadn't said, 'Hang on a minute – no need to tell anyone about this, is there? It'll be our secret.'

She nodded and left, leaving Jake praying fervently that she'd keep her mouth shut.

Dinner was served in the vast dining room around a table that was so long, they didn't quite fill it. To Jake's relief, Bella ignored him and sat quietly next to Emma, speaking only when spoken to.

He'd been half afraid that she'd come and sit next to him and give the game away somehow. He was already regretting shagging her – he should have bolted out of the room the moment she'd appeared.

Maybe now she'd take a shine to someone else. She might even work her way around the cast and production team. If she came on to every man staying there, most of them would take her up on it and then Jake would be in the clear.

Tom couldn't sack everyone – could he?

The woman Jake really fancied was Clarissa, one of the actresses, and he was hoping to have a crack at her at some stage.

Just looking at her made him randy, remembering the sight of her curvaceous body when she'd stood nude in front of them all at the auditions.

She was tall and auburn-haired, and on his way down to dinner he'd been delighted to see she had the room next to his.

She was another well-bred, debby type.

There was something about her which conjured up visions of riding gear – something which Jake had always had a thing about. The thought of her in tight jodhpurs and boots, perhaps tapping a riding crop against one thigh, made him feel feverish.

Rosa was sitting next to Dr Jackson and kept glancing at him covertly. He was years older than she – he must be in his late forties – but he was an attractive man, with his silver hair and well-cut suit.

Maybe, just maybe.

Or perhaps one of the actors. She smiled to herself and licked her lips – location shoots offered *so* many possibilities.

After dinner, Rosa wandered outside onto the terrace, then down the steps onto the lawn. She kicked off her high-heeled shoes and walked barefoot towards the lake. Twilight was falling and the grass felt cool and damp beneath her. She could feel the soft cotton voile of her brightly patterned skirt swishing over her bare thighs and felt hot with anticipation for the days ahead.

Her clit started to throb, and she glanced swiftly around before reaching beneath her skirt to drag her silk panties tightly into her cleft so the material rubbed against her clit as she walked, arousing and stimulating her.

She reached the edge of the lake and strolled around it,

until, eventually, she sank onto a rough stone bench next to a stream flowing under a humpback bridge.

On an impulse, she pulled her skirt up around her waist, then stood up and discarded her panties, sitting down again and flinching as her bare bottom made contact with the cold, damp stone.

She reached between her legs, thighs wide apart and knees bent, and squeezed her clit gently. She could feel the warm evening breeze playing over her mound and exposed labia, and began to rub herself.

She thought about Dr Jackson, and imagined the two of them fucking on a bed on the set, demonstrating a particular technique for the cast, watched by the entire production team.

Every man present would have a hard-on and wish he were the one screwing her. Maybe when she and the doctor had finished she would take the other men one at a time, until she was overflowing with their juices, taking one cock after another deep inside her . . .

A sudden movement made her freeze and turn her head, then she sighed with relief when she saw a curious deer standing a few yards away.

It wandered off and she continued to fantasise and rub herself, until a white-hot climax made her whole body jerk, then she bore down hard on the rough stone seat, the cold striking upwards in exciting contrast to the heat generated by her body.

Just before she came, she heard another noise, but thought the deer had returned and accordingly ignored it.

She was just about to put her panties back on when she smelt the unmistakable scent of cigar smoke and jumped to her feet, straining her eyes in the darkness to see if anyone was standing in the shadows of the trees.

'Who's there?' she called accusingly.

'Don't be alarmed – it's me – Dr Jackson,' said a deep voice from above her head.

Gazing upwards, Rosa saw the sex therapist leaning over the parapet of the humpback bridge, a cigar in his hand.

'How long have you been there?' she demanded.

'Long enough to enjoy the sight of a beautiful young woman taking pleasure from her own body.'

'You should have said something.' Her tone was cold in the extreme.

'Perhaps I should. But the temptation to watch you was too strong – I'm only human after all.'

Her senses still stirred, Rosa joined him on the bridge, her panties dangling from one hand.

'There's something alluringly primitive about you,' he told her. 'I noticed it at once – you're a true child of nature, despite your city sophistication. I even think you might have gypsy blood from somewhere along the line. May I?'

He took her panties from her hand and buried his nose in them, inhaling deeply.

'We've moved too far away from the primitive,' he continued, when at last he handed them back. 'Everything now is hidebound by convention and social mores, until we forget how we used to be, how our bodies were in tune with the seasons and our own atavistic urges.

'I deeply regret that because I'm what's considered to be a civilised man, I can't bend you over this ancient bridge, lift your skirts up and plunge my aching cock into you – because that's what I'd like to do.'

He threw the cigar away and smiled at her.

'Forgive me. I know I shouldn't be talking to you like

this, but your wonderfully abandoned behaviour struck a deep-seated chord. I think I'd better go back to the house and leave you to yourself.'

Rosa smiled at him seductively and said, 'You're right, I do have gypsy blood – my grandmother was a Romany. I think there are times when we *should* act on impulse – and as far as I'm concerned, this is one of them.'

She ran her hands over her breasts, then slid them provocatively over the curve of her hips, before turning her back and bending over the crumbling stone parapet of the bridge.

She looked over her shoulder at him. 'Just for once, forget you're a civilised man and behave as primitively as you like.

He hesitated, his hand on his zip.

'I want you to fuck me,' she said succinctly.

He threw her skirt up over her waist and paused for a moment to admire the smooth globes of her buttocks, pale and gleaming in the moonlight.

She felt his hand between her legs, ascertaining her state of readiness, then she heard his trousers slither down around his ankles and, the next moment, he plunged inside her with a force that rammed her against the bridge.

It was a memorable fuck.

The cool, self-contained doctor threw aside any restraint and fucked her like it was his last one on earth. There was no subtlety, no finesse, just his throbbing cock ramming in and out of her, sending her wild with lust as he worked her to a heaving, choking climax.

His hands were on her breasts and he held them tightly as he pounded away in an ever-increasing rhythm, his balls slapping against her well-rounded buttocks.

He came with an anguished cry and bent her so far over

the bridge, that she thought she would topple off and then soar up into the air from the strength of her own climax.

He slumped over her, panting, then straightened up, pulling her with him, his cock still buried deep within her.

The sound of a twig cracking sharply made them look down to see Tom and Emma strolling along the bank of the stream, deep in a discussion of tomorrow's shooting schedule.

'Hi,' called Tom when he saw them, then he and Emma vanished under the bridge as they continued to follow the stream.

'Was he screwing her, do you think?' asked Tom as soon as they were out of earshot. 'They were standing very close together.'

'The suave and sophisticated Dr Jackson, screwing a woman half his age over a bridge in full view of anyone passing – hardly likely,' replied Emma. 'Don't you ever think about anything else, Tom?'

Chapter Seventeen

Tom had decided to wait until they were in Cheshire before having Emma be his sex-slave for the night – new surroundings always turned him on.

He chose the second night of their stay, and Emma spent all day in a fever of anticipation tinged with apprehension. Rehearsals had started for the first scenes of the video and she found them extremely arousing.

When she wasn't watching the actors and actresses simulating sex, she was imagining what Tom might have in store for her, with the result that she became so wet she had to change her sodden panties three times.

Whenever he caught her eye, he grinned at her so meaningfully that she flushed and felt a hot prickle of excitement spread outwards from her groin. She felt rubbed raw by the hot carnality of his gaze.

In the afternoon he came sauntering into the library to find her standing on a small stepladder selecting a few leather-bound old books to use as props.

'I can barely concentrate for thinking about tonight,' he told her, appreciatively eyeing the expanse of thigh revealed by her short skirt. 'I'll bet you're just counting the minutes, aren't you, my love?'

'Not really,' she retaliated sweetly. 'I'm much too busy.'

'You mean that the thought of being my sex-slave doesn't excite you? That the idea of having to let me use your luscious body in all kinds of depraved ways doesn't turn you on? I don't believe it.'

'Believe it,' said Emma, passing him a pile of books to place on the table. 'It's something I'm going to have to grit my teeth and get through by thinking about something else.'

He stepped closer to her, his head on a level with her waist.

'You don't really expect me to believe that do you? I'll bet you're creaming your knickers in anticipation.'

'In your dreams, Tom. Only in your dreams.'

Jake and Toby were at the other end of the large room getting the lighting set up, but they were both facing the other way and fully occupied with what they were doing.

Turning sideways so his body blocked their view of Emma's lower body, Tom pushed his hand up her skirt and under the crotch of her panties. She gasped in outrage as his fingers slipped around in the copious lubrications he found there. She gasped again when he pushed his fingers deep inside her.

He withdrew his hand and held it out for her to see, glistening wetly in the hot, afternoon sunlight, then licked his fingers appreciatively.

'Liar,' he said amiably, then strolled off.

Emma returned to their room in the early evening and ran herself a deep bath. She locked the bathroom door then settled back for a long soak.

When at last she emerged, damp and pink, Tom was lying on the bed, his hands clasped behind his head and a tumbler of whiskey by his side.

He didn't say anything, just flashed her a barracuda-like smile, then went into the bathroom himself. She heard the shower running as she sat at the dressing table applying her make-up. When she'd finished, she curled up on the bed in her cream silk robe and pretended to read a magazine.

After he'd showered, Tom pulled on some casual clothes then said, 'This is the deal. From now until we fall asleep, you're my sex-slave. You have to do absolutely *anything* I tell you to do without question. No arguments, no saying you don't feel like it – what I say goes. Okay?'

Emma nodded reluctantly.

He led her into the bathroom, tucked her robe up around her waist, then sat her on a folded towel on the side of the bath. She blanched when she saw him pick up his shaving brush and begin to work up a lather.

He was going to shave her pubic hair.

He'd often suggested doing so in the past, but she hadn't liked the idea and wouldn't agree. She was sure it would look strange and, even worse, it would itch when it was growing back.

'Tom . . .' she began, then stopped when he raised his eyebrows at her. She could only sit with her hands clasped protectively over her blonde floss and watch him work up a rich creamy lather.

'Move your hands, darling,' he ordered her.

Slowly, Emma let them slide down by her side, then flinched as he worked the foam into her silken muff. The shaving brush tickled as he spent far longer than necessary over the task. She kept her thighs tightly closed, but he parted them and drew the brush arousingly over her vulva, circling over it, then dabbling at her clit.

All too soon, he picked up the razor and, with intense concentration, began to remove her bush, an inch at a time.

Emma couldn't bear to watch. She was certain that he was going to cut her, so she kept her eyes closed throughout the entire procedure. At last, after a final rinse, Tom stepped back.

'Beautiful,' he said reverently.

He pulled her behind him into the bedroom, posing her in front of the largest baroque mirror with her robe still tucked up around her waist.

Emma gulped when she saw herself, her labia now clearly visible, her cleft smooth and hairless. He ran his fingers over it, tracing the outline of where her fine thatch had been.

'I've always wanted to do that,' he told her. 'Now you're completely exposed to me whenever I want to look at you.' He touched the pink bud of her clit, which was protruding between her outer lips and she shivered.

'Time to dress for dinner,' he said cheerfully. He delved into a drawer and brought out a small carrier bag. She took it from him and peered suspiciously inside.

It was worse than she'd imagined.

The bag contained a bra and panties made from soft black leather. The bra had two circular holes over the nipples and the panties were of the split-crotch variety.

Emma owned a wide range of sexy underwear, but it was all of satin, silk, lace or the sheerest cotton voile. Never in her entire life had she worn underwear as unashamedly *fetishistic*.

Tom slipped her robe from her shoulders and hooked the bra into place, then sat her on the edge of the bed and drew the pants up her long, slim legs, adjusting them carefully around her freshly depilated private parts. He handed her a pair of black fishnet stockings with garters at the top, then finally her highest-heeled black shoes.

'You're a wet dream,' he said at last.

Emma could barely bring herself to look in the mirror.

She almost didn't recognise herself.

She didn't want to recognise herself.

Her breasts were tightly encased in the black leather bra, which jacked them up higher than her usual bras. Her nipples protruded rudely through the circular holes, pink and very prominent.

As if that wasn't bad enough, even with her legs closed she could see the whole of her vulva, lewdly framed by a tight casing of black leather, which Tom had arranged so that it was holding her labia partially apart. The black fishnet stockings and high-heeled shoes added the final touches.

She stood facing the mirror, completely lost for words, while Tom devoured her with his eyes.

'Open your legs,' he ordered her.

Slowly and unwillingly, she did as he asked, showing him the innermost folds of her honeypot.

It was as if she was looking at a stranger. Emma's honeypot was half concealed by her blonde, silken bush, this woman's was blatantly on display.

She looked vulgar.

She looked depraved.

She looked very, very sexy.

There was a tap at the door and Emma bolted into the bathroom. There was no way *anyone* except Tom was going to see her dressed like that.

'It's okay – you can come out,' he shouted after a brief pause. Emma listened for a few moments, then peered cautiously around the door to see him opening a bottle of wine. She picked up her robe and would have slipped into it, but Tom twitched it out of her hand.

'No you don't,' he said reprovingly. 'Sit on the chaise longue and drink your wine – and keep changing position, I want to admire you from all angles.'

Emma could see herself reflected in one of the mirrors, as she drew her legs up, the knees bent. It didn't matter how she arranged herself, the tight leather kept her private parts held wide open for him to admire. He could see everything from her smooth mound, right round to the valley running up between her buttocks.

He sipped his wine reflectively, then said, 'Bring yourself to a climax.'

'I . . . I don't think I can,' she stammered.

'Never mind – we can both enjoy watching you try.'

Emma gulped down the rest of her wine, then touched one nipple tentatively with the tip of her forefinger. A little shudder of erotic anticipation ran through her body, then she circled delicately around it, smoothing her hand over the leather of the tight-fitting bra.

She teased her own nipples until they swelled and thrust even harder through the holes in her bra, before turning her attention to her private parts.

She stroked herself softly at first, watching carefully in the mirror. She saw a slow flush spreading over her body and realised, almost to her shame, that her arousal was mounting.

She pushed her fingers deep inside herself and explored the velvet walls of her tunnel, feeling it moisten and expand ready for whatever erotic adventure was on Tom's agenda.

When she turned her attention to her clit, she realised immediately that she would have no trouble climaxing. The little bud of flesh grew as she stroked it, emerging completely from its covering hood.

Her strokes became more rapid and she forgot that Tom

was watching her avidly, his long fingers curled loosely around his wine glass.

She became oblivious to everything except her own reflection in the mirror and the pleasure she was giving herself.

She was propped up against the end of the chaise longue, her knees bent and her legs wide apart, her hand moving faster and faster as she neared the release she craved.

It came in a sudden rush of heat, which made a fine dew of perspiration appear between the tight leather and her skin. She moaned and her back arched convulsively, as a long drawn-out spasm of pleasure consumed her.

Tom fell to his knees beside her and pushed his tongue into the musky haven of her pussy, tasting the surge of orgasmic moisture her climax had released.

He sat back on his haunches and licked his lips.

'See what you can do if you try,' he admonished her.

He glanced at his watch, then went to sit at the small circular table by the window. It was covered in an antique lace cloth, thrown over another in deep rose-pink brocade.

'Get under the table and go down on me,' he ordered her, unzipping his trousers.

Reluctantly, Emma dropped to her hands and knees and crawled under the table. The cloth fell to the floor behind her, leaving her crouched in a dim, circular tent. Tom drew his chair up to the table so that his knees and lap were in the tent with her, his erection massive in the shadowy darkness.

She crouched in front of him and took his cock in her mouth. She began to swirl her tongue around the glans as if it were a lollipop she was tasting.

It tasted good.

She withdrew it from her mouth and let her tongue swirl its way down the shaft to his balls, licking them lightly in the way she knew he liked best. She kissed her way back up, then let it slip into her mouth as far as it could without choking her. Sucking hard, she slowly withdrew her mouth again. The suction she was exerting made it a tantalisingly long drawn-out process.

When only the tip remained in her mouth, she began to suck it back in, her full lips opening and closing around his shaft, varying the pressure for maximum stimulation.

Almost the full length of his huge cock was crammed into her mouth, butting up against the back of her throat, when, to her horror, Emma heard a knock at the door.

'Don't stop, Em,' he said in a low voice, then he called. 'Come in.'

Emma couldn't believe it as she crouched there on all fours, almost gagging in panic as she heard Jake's voice.

Why the hell had Tom told him to come in?

Jake only had to sit at the table and he'd realise there was someone underneath. Then he'd undoubtedly raise the cloth, to be met by the startling sight of his employer, wearing a black leather peephole bra and a pair of matching split-crotch panties, performing fellatio on her ex-husband.

Emma could feel a pink flush of shame surging over her body at the thought of being discovered in such an embarrassing position.

Jake would tell everyone.

She'd never be able to look anyone in the face again.

It was all Tom's fault.

If she hadn't been afraid it would lead to her discovery, she would have given his cock a nasty nip with her teeth. As it was, when she felt him move his hips slightly as a signal to her to continue, she did so.

She sucked, licked and lapped at his dick for what seemed like an eternity, while he held a long conversation with Jake about lighting the jacuzzi for tomorrow's shoot.

It hit her suddenly like a bolt of lightning.

Tom had planned this.

The devious bastard.

She remembered the way he'd glanced at his watch before making her get under the table. He'd asked Jake to come at a prearranged time, knowing she'd be squirming with embarrassment.

She'd get him back for this, if it was the last thing she did.

Eventually, Jake left the room and Tom said, 'You can come out now.'

Simmering with rage, Emma crawled out from under the table, aware that Tom's eyes were devouring the cleft between her buttocks and the whole of her exposed labia again.

She opened her mouth to give him a piece of her mind, but he raised a warning finger.

'You're my sex-slave, remember? No complaints or protests please, or I'll make you do something you'll really hate.'

He drew her to her feet, sat her on the edge of the table, then pulled her legs up over his shoulders so she was forced to lean back, her weight on her elbows.

He used the end of his cock to stimulate her. He circled it around the entrance to her honeypot until her rage began to abate and sexual arousal blotted out all other emotions.

He pulled her closer and, without warning, plunged his cock deep inside her to the very hilt, then withdrew it with agonizing slowness, sucking one taut nipple as he did so. He repeated the procedure half a dozen times then suddenly, to Emma's surprise, groaned and came.

'Fuck it,' he muttered under his breath. He withdrew and passed her a handful of tissues. 'Sorry, Em. I intended to last much longer, but this is just so bloody exciting I couldn't help myself.'

Emma wished it had lasted long enough for her to come too, but she knew that in the course of the evening she'd undoubtedly sustain many climaxes.

Tom would be hard and ready again soon enough.

He rummaged in the wardrobe and passed her a short black dress.

'Time to eat. Much as I'd like to parade you through the house dressed like that, it's not on I suppose. Wear that.'

Thankfully, Emma pulled the dress over her head, then allowed Tom to lead her downstairs to the hall, where he picked up a wicker hamper which was waiting for them.

'We're going to have a picnic,' he announced.

They went into the grounds then entered the maze. Tom fished a map out of his pocket and studied it.

'I got this off Bella,' he told her, 'otherwise we'd be walking round for hours trying to find the centre.'

A couple of the crew had already got themselves lost and had to be rescued by the gardener.

The setting sun was too low to shine in between the tall, closely clipped yew hedges, making the narrow paths dark and claustrophobic.

Emma shivered. The maze gave her the creeps.

But she forgot about it when Tom pushed his hand up her skirt from behind and began to massage her pussy with the palm of his hand as they walked along.

'Just to keep your motor running,' he told her cheerfully.

It did more than that.

Every step she took was intensely sexually exciting, as Tom kept his fingers moving. Her outer lips were still held apart by the tight-fitting leather pants and that alone made walking an unusually arousing activity.

She came three times as they followed Bella's map.

The open space in the centre of the maze was still in sunlight, the last rays catching the spray of the fountain and turning the droplets of water into multi-coloured jewels.

While Tom laid out a rug on the grass, Emma wandered around examining the animal statues, consciously flexing her internal muscles, which were still tingling after her recent climaxes.

Carved from some sort of shiny black stone, a lion, a bull, a tiger, a bear and a wolf, crouched in a circle around the fountain.

'Come and eat,' said Tom. 'Oh, and take your dress off again – there's no one here except us.'

Emma stared at him mutinously. There might be no one here now, but someone could come along at any moment. She knew that most of the others would be sitting down to dinner in the house soon, but that was no guarantee.

While she hesitated, Tom pulled her down onto the rug and dragged her dress over her head, leaving her wearing only the demeaning underwear, her stockings and high-heeled shoes.

He sat her crosslegged, her honeypot gaping wide open in the evening sunlight, then began to unpack the food. Tom had always liked mixing food with sex, while Emma preferred to keep them separate, but tonight they were obviously going to do things his way.

It was a delicious-looking picnic, but Emma wasn't hungry. She kept glancing nervously over her shoulder towards the entrance to the maze.

'Relax,' he said, opening a bottle of wine after a slight struggle. 'Here, have a drink.'

She tossed down the first glass in a few seconds, then held it out for a refill. Maybe if she was fairly tipsy, the evening would just slide by unnoticed. The sex was great, but the constant fear of discovery was keeping her too much on edge to relax.

There was a dip to start with, to be eaten with long, thin strips of carrot and celery. 'There's nothing to hold the crudités,' complained Tom.

About to say, 'So what?' Emma gave a start of surprise as he picked up a celery stick and murmured, 'The very thing.'

He slid the first three inches of the stick into her gaping pussy while she inhaled sharply. He followed it with another, then a carrot stick, then another, until the entrance to her honeypot was crammed with them.

She would never have let him do that under normal circumstances.

But these weren't normal circumstances.

Tom placed the pot of creamy dip between them and slowly withdrew a piece of celery from its impromptu holder.

'Enterprising, aren't I?' he asked, coating the end with dip then pushing it between her lips. He fed them both a stick at a time until only one remained. Leaning forward, he pushed it all the way into her, then drew it out with his teeth, eating it slowly.

She squirmed on the rug. His lips were warm against the folds of her private parts, arousing and exciting her again. She wished he'd just screw her instead of, literally, making a meal out of it.

Throughout the picnic, he used Emma as a plate, feeding them both from whichever part of her body he thought most appropriate.

For the next course, he made her lie on her stomach, then peeled the tight-fitting leather pants down to her thighs. He spread pâté thickly over her bottom with a knife, then proceeded to mop it up with chunks of crusty white bread.

He told her to roll over, then laid out slices of quiche and chicken legs surrounded by tiny tomatoes and lettuce leaves on her stomach.

After that, he removed her bra and coated her bare breasts with ripe, runny brie and scraped it off a bit at a time with savoury biscuits.

'I can only assume you like your women covered in grease and crumbs,' she commented, as he licked the last morsel of brie off one taut, sugar-pink nipple. 'I dread to think what the last course is,' she added, as he delved into the hamper for the final time.

When she saw what he brought out, she couldn't help but laugh.

A doughnut and a chocolate eclair.

He pushed the eclair into her pussy, the cream squashing out over her shaven mound as he did so, then unzipped his trousers and dropped the doughnut onto his cock.

'You should have let me throw it on,' she gurgled.

'You'd have missed,' he said sternly. 'Okay, Em, straddle me on your hands and knees, facing my feet.'

Her leather bra and pants were back in position and she could feel crumbs chafing her where they were pressed into her skin by the tight-fitting leather.

Dusk was falling, which was some comfort. Even if anyone did come upon them unexpectedly, it would be hard to make out what they were doing in the dark.

Which was just as well.

With the chocolate eclair sticking obscenely out of her

pussy above Tom's face, Emma crouched over him on all fours and bent her head to nibble at the doughnut.

They ate the cakes, their lips and tongues all over each others private parts, until only a few greasy crumbs remained.

'Now for the after-dinner entertainment,' announced Tom. 'I think we'll start with the lion.'

He led Emma over to the statue of a lion with its head on its paws and made her climb astride it; the smooth black stone felt cool and strange against her exposed vulva.

'Rub yourself on it,' he ordered her.

With the remains of the cream from the eclair acting as a lubricant, Emma rubbed her clit backwards and forwards along the lion's back, her feet in her high-heeled shoes just making contact with the ground.

Tom moved slowly around her, watching from every angle as she pleasured herself. She was just approaching her climax when he climbed on behind her and thrust his cock deep into her cunt as she shuddered into an orgasm.

She gasped and leant forward so he could penetrate her even further, winding her arms around the lion's neck. It felt strange and very wanton to be fucked from behind while astride a statue.

She was riding the lion while Tom was riding her thrusting into her with the long, smooth strokes that always whipped her into a frenzy.

She climaxed again, then Tom withdrew and murmured, 'The bull next, I think.'

Without waiting for his instructions, Emma lay along the bull's broad back, her nipples jutting upwards towards the rapidly darkening sky, her legs wide apart, her feet searching for a resting place on the statue's legs.

'You look fantastic,' breathed Tom, caressing her heated

nipples, then burying his hand in the hot, stickiness of her honeypot. 'Like a maiden from some primitive culture waiting to be ravished.'

He leapt onto the statue and plunged into her. She wrapped her legs around his waist and they screwed feverishly until Tom suddenly withdrew and led her to the statue of the bear.

'Bend over it,' he told her shortly.

She obeyed, her legs wide apart. The inner part of the globes of her buttocks, exposed by the split-crotch panties, gleamed lewdly in the moonlight as he entered her again.

This time, he fucked her long and hard, until they both climaxed, Emma's swollen clit further stimulated by the carved fur of the bear's coat.

Just as she came, there was a dazzling burst of light outside her closed eyelids, which she put down to the strength of her orgasm, until she opened her eyes a few seconds later.

A time switch must have operated, because, suddenly, the centre of the maze was flooded with light.

A moving shadow caught her eye and, to her horror, she could have sworn she saw a dark shape vanishing back into the maze.

Chapter Eighteen

When Jake walked into his bedroom, he knew someone else was already in the room a couple of seconds before he saw Bella crouching inside the wardrobe.

'What the fuck are you doing?' he asked, taken aback.

She straightened up and stepped out before saying frostily, 'There's no need to swear.'

'That isn't what you said yesterday, when you wanted me to screw you,' he pointed out.

Bella's usually pale face was flushed and there was a strange glitter in her eyes, which made Jake uneasy.

'What were you doing in there?' he demanded. She dropped her eyes to the carpet and stubbed at it with the toe of her shoe.

'Nothing,' she mumbled

Jake wasn't in too good a mood. He'd tried to chat up Clarissa over dinner and got nowhere. Then he'd been ignominiously beaten at snooker by the female make-up artist and, having decided to drown his sorrows in the local pub, had set off on his bike and blown a tyre before he'd gone half a mile.

He really wasn't in the mood for Bella acting weirdly.

He went over to the wardrobe, which was really a walk-in closet, and peered inside. Outside, dusk was falling and it was becoming gloomy in the room, so his eyes were immediately caught by a chink of light at the back of the wardrobe.

Stepping inside, he stooped and found he could see right into the next bedroom. The same thin partition of wood obviously formed the back of both wardrobes, because his view was partially obscured by clothes hanging just beyond the crack.

'There were a set of communicating doors between this room and that one,' he heard Bella's voice behind him. 'Some previous owner of the house built closets over the opening, so if the wardrobe doors are open you can see right into the next bedroom.'

He was just about to say something, when Clarissa walked out of her bathroom wearing only a towel around her luscious body, her auburn hair pinned up. Jake was frozen to the spot as she closed the curtains, switched on another lamp and shed the towel.

She had the most fantastic body. Wonderfully high breasts, a narrow waist swelling to lushly curved hips and a pair of legs that went on forever.

He gulped audibly and felt Bella squirming in front of him to peer through the same crack.

Clarissa picked up a bottle of body lotion and began to massage it into her arms. Jake knew he was being a Peeping Tom, but he just couldn't tear himself away.

He'd spent part of the day watching her rehearse a couple of scenes with one of the actors and it had left him as horny as fuck.

That had been a big enough turn-on, but this was something else.

Clarissa had no idea she was being watched.

Which made him even hornier.

She continued to massage cream into her silken skin.

When she reached her breasts, Jake found he was holding his breath as she poured a generous amount of lotion into her hand and spread it luxuriously over her silken orbs. He could see her peach-coloured nipples hardening as she circled them with her fingertips, then massaged them with the flat of her hand.

He could feel his hard-on, hot and heavy, straining against his jeans. He groaned when she turned her attention to her gorgeous arse, covering every inch of her skin with cream.

When she sat on the edge of the bed, her legs apart, and poured some more into the palm of her hand, he could feel sweat breaking out on his forehead.

She dabbed a blob of it onto the deep-pink kernel of her clit, then proceeded to spread it around the soft folds of her private parts, carefully avoiding her russet muff.

Jake was just thinking he couldn't stand it any longer, when he heard a soft tap at her bedroom door. Clarissa pulled the towel back on and went to open it. A few seconds later Rosa strolled into the room, her hips swinging provocatively.

Jake couldn't believe his eyes when the two women immediately embraced, their mouths meeting in a long, deep kiss.

He didn't know Rosa went both ways.

In front of him, he heard Bella gasp, but she didn't move away from her vantage point.

The two women kissed for a long time, then Rosa loosened the towel around the other woman's body, so that it slid to the ground leaving her naked again.

He watched dumbfounded as Rosa stroked Clarissa's breasts, then bent her dark head to suck one distended nipple. Clarissa deftly unfastened Rosa's dress and it fell to the floor leaving her clad in only a beige lace bra, panties and suspender belt, holding up a pair of sheer stockings.

The two women sank onto the bed, kissing and caressing each other's bodies in a way that made Jake long for his camera.

They made such an erotic picture, Clarissa with her auburn hair and pale colouring, in contrast to Rosa's golden, biscuit-brown skin and dusky curls.

Jake felt like he was choking to death, the blood pounding furiously through his veins with a thunderous noise. He realised suddenly that he'd not drawn a breath for about a minute and hastily gulped down some air before he passed out.

When the women moved so that they were lying on their sides facing each other in the *soixante-neuf* position, he thought that if he didn't jack himself off, his dick would explode.

As Clarissa drew Rosa's panties down her legs then dropped a kiss on the other woman's dark bush, he couldn't stand it a moment longer and unzipped his jeans.

But he'd forgotten about Bella.

When she heard the sound of his zip going down she hitched her skirt up around her waist and pulled her knickers down.

Even better.

He'd shag Bella, while he watched Clarissa and Rosa.

Grabbing her around the waist, he thrust his throbbing dick into her with no preliminaries. Luckily she was dripping wet – a far cry from her unyielding dryness of the night before.

She was obviously as turned on as he was.

She still felt very tight and it was difficult screwing her while trying to keep his eye on what was going on in the

270

next room, but he managed it. It was even more difficult not to make a noise.

Jake didn't attempt to hold back and came in record time, his juices spurting high up inside Bella's moist little cavern.

His dick remained clutched tightly inside her and he was still clasping her around the waist as Rosa and Clarissa kissed, licked and nibbled at each other's private parts. Rosa came first – he knew from personal experience that she climaxed quickly – but Clarissa took much longer.

Rosa changed position to kneel between the other woman's legs and bury her face in her mound, giving Jake an intoxicating view of her well-rounded rump and swollen vulva, glistening with her own female lubrications and Clarissa's saliva.

Somewhat to his surprise he'd remained hot for Rosa after his night with her, but she'd turned down several suggestions that they have a repeat performance – preferably without the love-potion.

It wasn't that he hadn't enjoyed himself – he had. It'd been one of the best nights of his life, but he didn't think his dick would take the sort of ferocious activity the love-potion induced, without dropping off.

He hadn't been too worried when she'd turned him down – he was sure they'd get it together again at some point.

But it gave him a powerful charge to be secretly watching her making it with another woman he had the hots for – it was like a wet dream come true.

After a while longer of Rosa's oral attentions, Clarissa shuddered into orgasm, crying out loudly and grinding her pelvis upwards against Rosa's face.

Jake could feel his dick harden again and as it was still

inside Bella, he began to move it. She pressed back against him, and as the two women in the next room were now talking softly, he thought he could afford to give Bella his undivided attention for a few minutes.

He pulled open her dress at the front, pushed her bra up out of the way and covered her breasts with his big hands, grazing his palms over her small, hard nipples.

She jammed her bottom back against his groin and began to rotate her pelvis in a way that drove him wild. His dick was tightly sheathed in her wet little pussy, but moving it was easier now that she was full of his juices.

She really did have great tits and a nice little arse, he liked the feel of it, firm and smooth against the rough denim of his jeans. He heard her wince and realised she'd caught herself on the edge of his zip fastener.

'Just a sec,' he muttered, suspending movement for long enough to ease his jeans and briefs down around his ankles.

That was better, now he could feel the smooth flesh of her rump against his hairy balls.

He reached between her legs from the front and located her hard little clit. He stroked it and she let out a moan of pleasure. Her eye was still firmly pressed to the crack in the wood, and he gathered something new was happening in the room next door, but he couldn't sustain the long, slow strokes he was using and lean forward at the same time.

Thrusting in and out of Bella's sweet little pussy suddenly seemed more urgent, and he redoubled his attention to her clit as she began to gasp excitedly.

She let out a cry and came, her head falling back against his chest. He came himself a few seconds later, after speeding up his strokes until he was giving it to her hard and fast.

She was virtually lifted off her feet by the last, strong

thrust and he tightened his arms around her and buried his face in her hair to muffle his grunts of pleasure.

When he pressed his eye to the crack again, Rosa and Clarissa were nowhere in sight, but he could hear the sound of splashing from the bathroom and realised they'd decided to take a bath together.

His legs were killing him because he'd been semi-squatting for ages. He slipped out of Bella, then stepped backwards out of the wardrobe and tried to straighten up. He let out a yowl of pain as one of his legs spasmed into cramp and then fell back on the bed clutching it.

'What's the matter?' asked Bella anxiously, following him out, her knickers still around her ankles hobbling her movements.

'Bleeding cramp,' he groaned.

She kicked off her knickers and knelt beside him, massaging his leg with surprisingly strong fingers. Her skirt was still hitched up around her waist and he could see her bush and the tiny pink tip of her clit. There was a snail's trail of clear secretions sliding down her thigh and he felt unexpectedly turned on again.

As soon as his cramp vanished, he reached out for her, but she slipped out of his grasp and swiftly tidied her clothing in front of the mirror.

'Here – you don't have to go yet, do you?' he asked, disappointed. He wanted to see her sitting astride him, bouncing around on his cock.

Without replying, she picked up her knickers, slipped them into her pocket and silently left the room.

Further down the corridor, Emma emerged from the shower and found Tom had laid out a new outfit for her to wear. He'd told her she was imagining things when she'd claimed someone had been watching them in the centre of the maze.

She wasn't so sure.

With the grease and crumbs washed from her body, she pulled on the black basque Tom had laid out for her, then fastened a clean pair of black seamed stockings to the suspenders attached to it.

The basque was another of his purchases and, although she found it a little uncomfortable, she had to admit she preferred it to the leather bra and pants.

Tom had to lace her into it. It jacked her in tightly at the waist and pushed her boobs up so that they spilled enticingly over the black lace at the top. Her shaven mound was raunchily framed by the two front suspenders and looked very much on display.

He gave her a tight-fitting scarlet dress to pull on over it, then said, 'Lie down and open your legs.'

She did as she was told, then swiftly closed them when she saw him taking something out of a bag.

'What the hell are those?' she demanded.

He held up two small balls joined together by a piece of thin cord, with a long loop extending from the second one.

Japanese love-balls.

'You're not putting those inside me,' she said flatly.

Tom raised his eyebrows at her.

'You're my sex-slave. Remember?'

Emma looked mutinous. In the past, whenever Tom had tried to introduce sex toys into their love-making, she'd refused. The only one she'd agreed to was a vibrator, which she sometimes used herself anyway.

'Come on, Em,' he said persuasively. 'They won't hurt you, and you're not allowed to say no. Just try it.'

Reluctantly, Emma parted her legs, determined to call a

halt if they were the least bit uncomfortable. Tom knelt between her legs and inserted the tip of his forefinger into her, checking that she was still wet.

Then he slipped the first of the balls inside her. It felt cold and heavy, and she tried to tighten her internal muscles against the unwelcome invasion, but Tom tickled her clit with his finger and she unconsciously relaxed long enough for him to push it high up into her pussy. The second followed, and the loop remained hanging out, just brushing the tops of her thighs.

Next he slipped a pair of very tight pants up her long legs, pulling them up so high that they felt skin-tight over her vulva and pressed arousingly against her clit.

'Okay, stand up,' he told her.

Emma slid to her feet then gasped as she felt the balls roll around inside her. She automatically tightened her internal muscles to stop them falling out, then gasped again as their weight made her clit press against its hood, sending a tiny spasm of pleasure through her.

There was a sensation of pressure within her groin that made her feel short of breath, and she moaned as Tom put the flat of his hand against her pussy and pressed upwards, intensifying the feeling.

'Shall I make you come?' he asked. Then without waiting for a reply continued, 'Perhaps not now – later.' He took her hand and drew her towards the door.

'Where are we going?'

'To while away an hour or two until I get my second wind.'

He led the way downstairs. With every step the balls moved around inside her, stimulating her stretched love-channel and sending little shocks of nerve-jangling pleasure through her belly.

They went into the study where an impromptu bar had been set up.

'What would you like?' asked Tom.

'Dry white wine please,' responded Emma automatically. She lowered herself thankfully into a chair, then nearly cried out as the balls spread her outwards, dragging at the nerve endings running directly to her clit and making it pulse hectically with alarm and anticipation.

She inched herself back into the chair, trying to keep her breathing as shallow as possible.

This was sheer torture.

She sat and sipped her wine, while Tom chatted to Dr Jackson who was sitting in a leather armchair near to them. After a while, the erotic sensations in her groin quietened down and she was able to join in the conversation.

Toby, Jake's assistant, put his head round the door and called, 'Tom, we're on next.'

To Emma's horror Tom looked across at her and said, 'I told Toby and Ed we'd have a game of snooker with them.'

'I . . . I don't want to play snooker,' she stammered, only too horribly aware what sort of effect all the bending and stretching over the snooker table would have on the heavy metal balls nestling deep in her honeypot.

'Sure you do,' he urged her, pulling her to her feet. She could feel the flesh tugging demandingly between her thighs, and her clit throbbed urgently.

She allowed him to lead her into the deserted hallway then stopped and hissed, 'If you make me play snooker I'm going to come in front of everyone – don't do this, Tom.'

'It'll be the most exciting game of snooker you've ever played,' he grinned. 'You've always had a lot of self control, Em – use it.'

Seething with rage and renewed excitement as the balls continued their lethally arousing movements within her, particularly when she had to pick her way over the banks of cables snaking along the hallway, Emma followed him into the billiard room. She could cheerfully have hit him with her cue as he leant over to start the game.

She was only an indifferent player at the best of times – and this certainly wasn't one of them.

She nearly leapt out of her skin when she bent over to take her first shot. The sudden pressure on her clitoris was unbearable, stretching it to its fullest extent and holding it there while her nerve endings shrieked in protest.

Even worse, she could feel Toby and Ed's eyes burning into her as she bent forward and was embarrassingly aware that her stocking tops were probably showing.

She stepped backwards away from the brightly lit table and into the shadows, and tried furtively to adjust the tight fitting pants so they didn't press so hard against her pussy.

Tom slipped his arm around her and murmured, 'Enjoying yourself?'

'You bastard,' she muttered.

As the game progressed, Emma's pants were soon sticking to her with moisture as the balls kept up a relentlessly arousing pressure inside her. Her clit was so swollen and throbbed so hard that it felt about the size of a snooker ball itself.

There was a deliciously painful, heavy weight filling her belly and she knew several times that she was hovering·on the brink of a climax but, by exerting super-human self-control, she managed not to come.

There was a fine beading of sweat on her upper lip and she felt red-hot inside the restricting basque. She tried to distract herself by plotting a terrible revenge on Tom, but the insistent throbbing of her clit kept bringing her back to reality.

It would have been so easy to relax and let herself enjoy the ecstatic release of an orgasm – she would only have to squeeze the balls with her internal muscles – but not in front of Toby and Ed.

At long last the game was over, won not surprisingly by the other two, and Emma hoped her torture was now over and they could return to their room.

Tom had other ideas.

He led the way into the drawing room and said to Emma, 'Sit there.'

She sank thankfully into the seat, then let out a barely suppressed shriek as she realised she was sitting in a rocking chair. The room was empty, but there were other people in the library, visible through a pair of open double doors.

'You really do have remarkable self-control,' he remarked admiringly. 'I was certain you'd come at some stage during the game. Now let's see how you manage in the rocking chair.'

Speaking through gritted teeth, Emma said, 'I'm going to get you back for this, if it's the last thing I do.'

'I'll look forward to it.'

As he spoke, Tom began rocking the chair backwards and forwards, gently at first, then more forcefully.

Her clit was pulled against its hood, then pushed back beneath it, chafing against her tight, sticky pants, making the whole of her pelvic regions unbearably hot and heavy.

She felt the intense build up of prickling heat and held her breath, but it was no good – as the chair rocked forward she was unable to hold back a second longer and with a low, strangled cry she came.

And came again.

And again.

Tom stopped the chair and moved between her and a couple of people gazing curiously through the open doors.

The strength of the climaxes, after hovering on the brink of them for so long, was too much for Emma and she blacked out for a few seconds.

Tom knelt beside her.

'As soon as you can walk we'll go back upstairs and I'll fuck your brains out,' he promised her.

Chapter Nineteen

Jake woke up early, missing the sounds of heavy traffic he could usually hear outside his flat. He felt restless, and decided to go and assess the damage to his bike. After the tyre had blown he'd been thrown off – luckily he'd only been going slowly and had landed unhurt in the long grass by the side of the road.

He'd pushed the bike back, but it had been too dark to see if there was any other real damage, so he'd left it in the cobbled courtyard by the old stables block.

Before leaving his room, he peeked through the crack in the back of the wardrobe, but Clarissa had closed her door at some stage and his view was blocked.

The early morning air was cool and fresh; the sun was just putting in an appearance over some distant hills, colouring the sky on the horizon a pale, clear primrose.

The bike didn't appear to have sustained any serious injury and Jake was just about to go back inside, when he heard the sound of horse's hooves on the cobbles behind him.

Turning round, he saw Bella trotting into the yard astride a chestnut mare. She didn't see him and rode over to the stables before slipping from the horse's back.

Jake was transfixed.

The ride had given her usually pale cheeks a pink glow

and her hair was windblown and fell becomingly around her face. Best of all, she was wearing a crisp white shirt with nothing beneath it, tight-fitting jodhpurs and a pair of gleaming black boots.

Jake had always had a thing about women in riding gear and he felt a strong kick of lust deep in his loins. He'd never felt that way about Bella in her shapeless dresses, but now the blood pounded through his body as she dismounted, her shapely rear enhanced by the skin-tight breeches.

She led the horse into the stables and, like a man in a trance, he followed.

She hitched the horse to a hook in the wall, her small hands encased in soft leather gloves, her riding crop under her arm.

She jumped when she turned and saw him.

'It's all right – it's only me,' he reassured her. 'You look absolutely great in that get-up – it really turns me on.'

Without a word she undid her shirt to reveal the naked perfection of her full breasts, the small nipples pink and swollen.

'What happened to the passion-killer bra?' he asked, drinking in the sight.

'I never wear underwear when I'm riding,' she told him matter of factly. 'I like my nipples to rub against my shirt.'

'What – no knickers either?' he asked.

In reply, she slowly unzipped the jodhpurs until the dark fuzz of her bush came into view.

'No knickers,' she said. 'It's more exciting that way.'

'I'll just bet it is.' Jake had heard about girls and how they got off on horseback.

'Er, how do you fancy riding me?'

He covered one breast with his hand as he spoke, grazing the pebble-hard nipple while his other hand cupped her mound. Even through the riding breeches he could feel how wet she was. The material was soaked through.

'Does riding make you . . . you know . . . come?' he asked with interest.

'Oh yes, many more times than any man.'

Jake dragged his jeans down and glanced around him, then pulled her down on top of him on a bale of hay that lay at the bottom of a pile which went halfway up to the ceiling.

His dick reared up, hard and ready, as she swiftly peeled her breeches down and climbed astride him, still holding her riding crop.

She knelt, poised just above him, then used her hand to rub his straining dick over her swollen vulva. She felt wet and slippery and Jake thrust his hips upwards, impatient to sheath himself in her hot, aroused flesh.

He let out a yelp as she flicked his hip with the tip of her crop.

'Don't be so impatient,' she said reprovingly.

She grabbed the ends of his leather belt and gripped them as if they were reins. 'Let's see if I enjoy riding you as much as Dancer.'

Jake had never experienced anything like it – she rode him as if he were a difficult horse. She squeezed him with her thigh muscles, first at a trot, then a canter, then finally at full gallop, flicking him with the whip if he wasn't responding the way she wanted him to.

After the third flick he snatched it off her. He was half tempted to smack her across the backside with it, but settled for throwing it into a corner.

He grabbed her hips and jammed her down hard each

time she bounced on his ramrod-hard shaft, making her cry out with pleasure as she rose and fell above him. Her breasts bobbed and jiggled, partially hidden by her open white shirt, her nipples popping in and out of view with each movement.

She came twice before Jake finally erupted in a spectacular climax, which felt like it was pumping the life force from his body.

He lay back on the bale of hay with his eyes closed, while Bella climbed off, pulled up her breeches and sat down beside him.

He felt a tickling sensation at the end of his dick and, opening one eye, saw that Bella was drawing a piece of straw across his limp member.

'I think, on balance, Dancer makes for a better ride,' she said softly. 'I only came twice with you. Maybe I should have used the whip more.'

'Only if you wanted your backside tanning with it,' he growled, annoyed at being compared unfavourably to a bleeding horse. 'Anyway, I haven't finished yet.'

She prodded at his slumbering cock with the piece of straw. 'That isn't what it looks like to me.'

He grabbed her and turned her over onto her stomach, so she was bending over another bale of hay higher than the one they were lying on. She looked at him over her shoulder.

'Do you want to spank me with my riding crop? You can if you want to.'

Jake paused in the act of peeling her breeches down over her pert backside.

'You're a weird one,' he said, taken aback by the suggestion.

She shrugged and opened her legs, so he pushed his hand

between them, feeling for her clit with his fingers. He massaged it until her breath began to come in little gasps and she moved her rump in circles.

His dick hardened rapidly. He waited until she was on the brink of coming before thrusting it into her forcefully. Her muscles clenched tightly around it as she climaxed.

He shafted her from behind, bringing her to another climax, then withdrew and turned her onto her back.

'My turn for a ride,' he told her, covering her breasts with his hands and spreading her legs as wide as he could with the restricting breeches still hobbling her. 'Let's see if you can stand the pace.'

Emma stretched and then winced as she felt her muscles twinging in protest. She ached all over, her pussy felt sore and her swollen clit was still throbbing after all the attention it had been paid the night before.

When they'd got back up to their room, Tom had removed her dress to reveal the tightly laced basque and then brought her to two more climaxes with the heavy Japanese love-balls still inside her. The first, by sitting her on his knee and rocking her backwards and forwards; and the second, by massaging her pussy with the flat of his hand over her sopping panties.

The sensation when he'd at last removed the balls by pulling gently on the loop attached had been exquisite. He'd taken a long time over it, slowly drawing them down through her dripping love-channel, until at last they'd popped out, each making an obscene plopping sound.

Then, with silk scarves, he'd tied her wrists and ankles to the posts at each corner of the bed, so she had been helplessly spreadeagled.

After that, her memory was a bit blurred. Tom had used

a vibrator on her until she'd been unable to take any more pleasure and had screamed at him to stop. He'd put his hand over her mouth and carried on while she'd strained futilely at the scarves and writhed around on the bed, her body shaken by climax after climax.

Emma also knew she'd spent a long time with Tom's cock in her mouth after he'd finally released her. She could still taste him, and ran her tongue languorously around the inside of her mouth at the memory.

The evening had eventually culminated in a marathon screwing session, incorporating practically every position known to man and involving uses for the bedroom furniture Emma wouldn't have thought of in her wildest imaginings.

She swung her legs silently out of bed and pulled on her jeans and a sweater, wincing anew at the pressure of the harsh denim against her tender vulva.

She left the sleeping house through a side door and strolled across the lawns at the front of the house, breathing the cool, fresh air of the early morning deep into her lungs.

She stopped and looked up to their bedroom window. Had Tom woken up and missed her yet? A movement at the window of the room next door caught her eye and she wondered who it was.

She could have sworn that the shadowy figure saw her at the same moment, because whoever it was stood stock still for a few seconds, then vanished.

Emma frowned as she realised that the room next door to theirs was in the west wing, which Bella had told her wasn't used.

So who was that?

Emma wasn't of a particularly nervous disposition, but several times during their stay she'd had a creepy feeling she was being watched. A couple of times in their bedroom, she'd felt the hairs on the back of her neck stand on end and spun round, half expecting to see someone.

And last night, despite Tom's scepticism, she was certain that someone had been spying on them in the centre of the maze.

She continued to walk slowly around the house, glancing up at the windows from time to time, but didn't see anyone else.

When she turned a corner into the stable yard she thought she'd go and look at the horses. She stepped into the stables, then stopped dead when she saw Jake straddling a woman on a bale of hay, screwing her energetically a few yards from a pretty chestnut mare.

Jake's broad-shouldered body blocked Emma's view of the woman. All she could see was that she was wearing riding boots and jodhpurs. Emma wondered if it was Clarissa – she hadn't missed the lustful way the cameraman had been looking at her the night before.

She slipped silently away.

By lunchtime, everyone was in a state of intense sexual arousal after spending the morning watching Clarissa and one of the actors demonstrating various erotic techniques and positions in front of the camera.

It was a warm day and most people took their lunch outside to eat on the lawns in front of the house. Emma kept glancing up at the window where she'd seen the shadowy figure early that morning, but didn't spot anyone.

When Bella came to sit with her she asked, 'Are the empty wings used for anything at all?'

Bella lifted her gaze from Rosa and Clarissa, who were laughing together in the shade of a tree, and said, 'Only for storage.'

'How do you get into the west wing from the main block?'

'There are doors on every floor round the corner at the end of the main corridors, but they're kept locked.'

'Would it be possible for me to go for a wander round? I'm interested in old houses.'

Bella took a dainty bite from her sandwich before replying. 'My father and mother lived in the west wing – the rest of the house was only used for entertaining when she was alive. When she died he had it shut up and moved into the main block. He wouldn't like anyone to go in there, I don't think.'

Emma lay back on the grass and closed her eyes. There must be some way to get in without anyone knowing.

A morning spent watching simulated sex acts had its inevitable effect and after lunch people began to disappear back to their rooms or into the woods.

Jake looked around for Bella but she was nowhere in sight. He went up to his room in the hope of finding Clarissa doing something interesting he could watch. If she wasn't there, he could do with a rest anyway – he was shagged out after getting up so early then screwing Bella in the stables.

Still waters definitely ran deep in her case. For a girl who'd supposedly led a sheltered life, she was full of surprises.

Unfortunately, Clarissa's room was empty, so he stretched out on the bed and hoped Bella would put in an appearance. He got hot just thinking about her in her riding gear – he'd ask her to wear it again next time he saw her. He was relieved she was being so discreet – when there was anyone else around she ignored him, but they'd have to be careful not to be seen together.

He'd found his eyes straying to her more than once during breaks between filming. That morning she'd been dressed like bleeding Alice in Wonderland in a pale-blue dress with a matching blue velvet band holding back her hair.

And no doubt underneath she'd been wearing the passion-killing bra and pants again. He wondered why she dressed like that when she had such a great figure; she should be showing it off.

Maybe he should take her in hand.

Emma waited until everyone was busy shooting another scene, then slipped into Paul Rivers' study and closed the door.

The keys to the doors between the main block and the west wing must be kept somewhere. But his desk was locked, as were the various cupboards in the room. She searched the library and the drawing room to no avail, then the small sitting room. After that, she went outside and walked around the west wing looking for any sign of an unlocked window or door.

But she drew a blank.

When they'd finished for the day, Jake searched for Bella but couldn't find her anywhere. He decided to take a swim and, after picking up his trunks and a towel, went down to the pool.

He dived in and swam several lengths, then floated on his back, wondering where Bella had vanished to. He didn't even know where her room was.

Despite the cold water, he could feel his dick getting hard as he remembered Bella sitting astride him that morning and riding him wildly.

A muffled sound from the sauna made him raise his head.

Maybe she was in there.

The door was a couple of inches ajar and he began to push it open, then stopped dead at the sight that met his eyes.

Rosa, Clarissa and Dr Jackson were in there together, and what they were doing made his mouth go dry and his dick rear up out of the front of his trunks like a periscope breaking water.

Rosa, her body bent in the shape of a bow, was in the crab position, her head thrown back and her breasts thrusting outwards.

The heat in the room made her lithe, tanned body glisten with perspiration as if she'd been oiled, and her nakedness was adorned by fine gold chains around her neck and ankle. Her thighs were wide apart, exposing the deep, coral folds of her honeypot.

Clarissa was kneeling beside her, wielding a bundle of birch twigs, with which she was systematically striking Rosa's mound and exposed vulva with gentle strokes.

Dr Jackson had his cock in Rosa's mouth and was working his way over Clarissa's naked thighs and backside with another bundle of birch twigs. He wasn't putting any force behind the blows but, even so, her buttocks and thighs looked slightly pink.

Jake wondered what Tom would say if they got carried away and the birch twigs left marks. It wouldn't look good on a sex guide to have the leading lady's nether regions bearing the signs of a recent thrashing.

He felt like he'd been turned to stone – particularly his dick – as he watched the trio's abandoned enjoyment of the proceedings. When all three were moaning and breathing heavily, Rosa let Dr Jackson's cock slip from her mouth and eased herself down onto her back.

'Can't hold that position a second longer,' she gasped. 'My pussy feels like it's on fire.'

They rearranged themselves.

This time Dr Jackson knelt between Rosa's thighs and, after filling the ladle used to throw more water on the coals, he let it trickle slowly through the dark tendrils of her bush and over the over-stimulated folds of her honeypot, while stroking her clit with his forefinger.

While he did that, Clarissa lowered herself so she was squatting over Rosa's face. Rosa began to lick and nibble Clarissa's private parts in a way that made Jake feel like he was about to shoot his load.

Clarissa meanwhile was gently beating Dr Jackson with the birch twigs, starting at his shoulders and working her way slowly downwards.

A noise behind him made Jake start and step back from the door. A couple of the film crew came in and after shrugging out of their robes, dived into the water.

Feeling as if he were on the point of erupting like a volcano, Jake charged out of the pool room and back into the house. He caught a glimpse of a blue dress vanishing into the library and followed it.

Bella was reaching for a book from one of the shelves when he grabbed her and threw her onto a high-backed leather sofa in front of the stone fireplace.

Within five seconds, her skirt was up halfway over her face, her knickers were around her thighs and his cock was desperately trying to gain entry.

She felt dry and tight.

Not as dry and tight as the first time he'd fucked her, but enough to make entry difficult.

In an urgent undertone, he told her what he'd just witnessed, and felt her tight little tunnel moisten and expand until he was able to thrust deep inside her.

Within a couple of minutes, she was as turned on as he was and wrapped her legs around his waist while they screwed wildly on the cool, cracked surface of the old leather sofa.

Jake's surge of boiling release was accompanied by a strangled, tonsil-wrenching groan, which echoed around the library.

His breathing was just returning, if not to normal, at least to that of someone who had just done the hundred-yard dash in record time; when to his horror the library door opened and he heard the unmistakable voices of Tom and Emma.

He was still sprawled on top of Bella with his swimming trunks around his thighs and his limp cock deep inside her after discharging its load.

They were hidden from his employers by the high back of the sofa – but only if they stayed on the other side of the room.

He didn't dare move a muscle.

Bella stared up at him wide-eyed and they lay there in an agony of suspense while Tom and Emma discussed some changes to tomorrow's script.

Suddenly the conversation stopped, then there was the rustle of clothing and Tom said, 'How about a quickie on the sofa?'

Emma laughed softly. 'I'll never understand your penchant for screwing in public place. But not here – how about the woods?'

To the relief of both Jake and Bella the other couple left the room.

'Shall we follow them and watch?' suggested Bella, adjusting her clothing.

'I'd rather we went upstairs and shagged each other senseless,' replied Jake, whose dick was stirring again. 'And Bella . . .'

'Yes?'

'Will you wear your riding gear?'

Chapter Twenty

The filming went well.

England was in the grip of a late-summer heatwave and although the mornings dawned cool and crisp, the days and evenings were warm and humid.

Everyone seemed to be permanently horny and, as the heat intensified, it was not uncommon to stumble across copulating couples in the grounds and in shadowy corners of the house. Even the household staff were affected by the pervading air of carnality, as they too were sucked into the libidinous world the cast and crew had brought with them.

Emma was still unable to shake off the feeling that she was being watched.

She was pinning her hair up one evening in front of the large baroque mirror that dominated the room, when the fine hairs on the back of her neck stood on end.

She was wearing only a pair of satin camiknickers and automatically crossed her arms across her chest to cover her bare breasts. She looked nervously around the room, but she was completely alone.

It was very unnerving to keep feeling like that.

She took to trying the door between the two wings every evening before returning to their room, but it was always locked.

The final week of production was particularly hot. Tom

and Emma had arranged for a wrap party to be held on the last evening and in the afternoon, while the final scene was being shot, Emma went upstairs to their room to lay out the clothes she was planning to wear.

She turned into the corridor, just in time to see a dark figure vanish round the corner which led only to the locked door between the wings.

She followed swiftly.

There was no one there.

Cautiously, she tried the door.

It creaked slowly open and she stepped into the dusty corridor on the other side. She stood immobile for a few seconds while her eyes adjusted to the dimness, then she moved silently to the first door on the right – the one that led to the room where she'd seen someone standing at the window.

In contrast to the dim, dusty corridor, the afternoon sunlight poured through the window into a large, sumptuous bedroom decorated in shades of pale-blue, green and ivory.

The room was immaculately clean and obviously in use, because there were fresh flowers in a vase on the windowsill, and several items of women's clothing thrown over a chair in the corner.

Emma went over to the dressing table and studied the scent bottles and make-up laid out there.

Was this Bella's room?

If so, why hadn't she said so when Emma was asking her about the west wing?

But Bella didn't wear make-up and Emma had certainly never seen her in any of the elegant, diaphanous clothes lying on the chair.

She walked thoughtfully over to the window, passing a

large mirror on the wall between this room and the one she was sharing with Tom.

She stopped dead.

Something was wrong.

She hadn't seen her reflection as she walked by.

She pivoted slowly around and realised to her heart-stopping horror, that she was looking directly through the glass into their own bedroom.

It was a two-way mirror.

Emma's legs wouldn't support her and she sank into an armchair. Her head was spinning and her heart was thudding noisily, as she realised that someone had obviously been spying on them since the day they'd arrived.

Her face flooded with hot colour as she mentally reviewed some of the things that she and Tom had done in there.

Particularly the night she'd been his sex-slave.

She let out a low moan and closed her eyes. She'd never felt as embarrassed about anything in her life – and that was saying something, considering that Tom seemed to revel in living a semi-public sex life.

A sound at the door made her open her eyes.

'You,' she said slowly, as Paul Rivers stepped into the room.

'I'm sorry, my dear – you were never meant to find out,' he told her, as she sipped from the glass of water he'd brought her from the bathroom. She'd almost fainted when she'd seen him, and he was alarmed by her pallor.

Emma was trembling in every limb, wondering if anyone would hear her if she screamed. Did he intend to harm her?

He seemed to read her mind, because he went over to the window and opened it a couple of inches.

'There are people on the grass just outside,' he said, moving away and sitting on a chair by the bed. 'You only have to call out and they'll hear you. Please believe me when I say I mean you no harm – quite the contrary. Will you allow me to explain?'

She nodded, trying to will herself to stop trembling.

'This was the bedroom I shared with my wife,' he began. 'After she died I moved into another room but I've kept this one just the way it was when she was alive, so that I can come in here and pretend she's still with me.

'I loved my wife deeply and I truly believe that we had the most fulfilling sex life any couple ever had. There was nothing we didn't do, nothing we wouldn't try, to give each other pleasure.

'After she died, I decided no one could ever replace her, and I have been faithful to her memory ever since – there has been no one else.

'As I think I told you, my wife was active in the field of marital relations and believed firmly that a good sex life was essential for a lasting relationship. I had no interest in sex for many years after she died, and in fact became impotent, until one day, by chance, I witnessed a married couple of my acquaintance making love, and realised that for the first time since her death I had an erection.

'Since then my only pleasure in life is to watch happily married couples having sex. I've tried pornography, but that doesn't work – it has to be a married couple. So I had the two-way mirrors put in here and in my house in Paris.'

'You mean . . . you watched us in Paris too?' stammered Emma, blushing as she remembered the bath on the dais at one end of the room.

'Yes. I think I mentioned that you look a lot like my wife. The sight of you stepping into the bath stirred me to tears. I know I've shocked you deeply, my dear – but please will you at least try to understand?'

He looked so upset that, despite her horror at her unwelcome discovery, Emma was moved.

'Doesn't it bother you that you've invaded our privacy in the most unforgivable way?' she asked.

'You were never meant to know,' he said simply. 'It seemed a harmless enough thing to do, but I can see how appalling it must appear to you. I'm afraid you've become somewhat of an obsession with me because your rich and varied sex life reminds me so much of our own. Once I'd watched you in Paris, I had to watch you again and again.'

He picked up a photo from the bedside table and passed it to her. 'You made me feel as if I were still as alive as when this photo was taken and I owe you a great debt of gratitude.'

The photo showed a younger Paul Rivers and the woman Emma had seen in the painting in Paris, laughing and gazing into each other's eyes.

She felt his sorrow almost as if it were her own.

'And now I expect you're going to tell your husband, then the police.' He replaced the photo on the table.

'No. No I'm not.' The words were out of her mouth before she realised that she was going to say them. She glanced at her watch. 'I must go – I'll be needed downstairs. I'd like to talk to you again – will you meet me here later?'

'I'll do anything you wish – I owe you that much.'

Emma spent the rest of the afternoon in a daze, trying to behave normally. In the early evening she went into the impromptu bar to check on the supplies of booze and found Rosa emptying a clear liquid from a small glass bottle into the punch.

'What on earth's that?' she asked curiously, staring down to where a thin vapour was forming above the punch bowl.

Rosa started guiltily.

'Oh – nothing really. Just a special ingredient to help the party go with a bang.'

'What sort of special ingredient?'

Rosa smiled conspiratorially. 'It's an old gypsy love-potion.'

Jake came into the room at that moment. 'Here, Rosa – you haven't really put that stuff in the punch have you?' he asked in alarm. 'It'll be like the fall of the Roman Empire tonight.'

Emma was intrigued. 'Have you had some?' she asked.

'Yeah. She spiked my drink with it once. I tell you, Emma, that stuff is lethal. I'd have screwed a giant turtle if one'd showed up. You're asking for trouble putting it in the punch – they'll all be like rabid dogs.'

'I've only put a small amount in. I admit I did overdo it when I gave it to you – my hand slipped when I was mixing the drinks, but I wouldn't usually make it so strong.'

Jake went on to describe its effect on his libido in graphic detail until Emma was struck by an idea.

'I don't see that it'll do any harm – if you're sure it's much weaker than the dose you gave Jake. It might even be interesting. But let's keep it our secret shall we?'

She went upstairs humming to herself.

Now she'd have her revenge on Tom for the things he'd made her do as his sex-slave.

Emma dressed in the bathroom that evening. She didn't

know whether Paul Rivers was in the next room or not, but she wasn't taking any chances.

Tom arrived just as she was spraying herself with scent. He paused in the doorway and whistled silently.

'You look fantastic,' he complimented her. She was wearing a short emerald-green dress with a plunging neckline, and her blonde hair hung down around her shoulders like a golden cloud. 'The question is,' he said, advancing on her, 'what underwear are you wearing?'

Emma backed hastily into the bathroom and only when they were out of sight of the mirror, did she allow him to pull up her skirt to reveal her oyster silk camiknickers and matching suspender belt, holding up her sheer, seamed stockings.

When he slipped his hand between her legs she wriggled away.

'Later,' she breathed. 'I have to go downstairs to check on the food.'

Tom turned on the shower and began to shed his clothes. 'Okay,' he said reluctantly. 'But not *too* much later.'

When Jake saw Bella gulping down a glass of punch, he felt a twinge of apprehension – if she threw herself on him in front of everybody, it would give the game away. On the other hand, if she threw herself on someone else, he wouldn't feel too happy about it.

'I'm not sure this was such a good idea,' he muttered to Rosa, taking a swig from his can of beer.

He wasn't about to touch the stuff himself. The evening with Rosa had been unbelievable once he'd got into it, but the memory of falling on her like a crazed beast and shooting his load almost immediately, still made him break out in a sweat.

'Party pooper,' she teased him.

Rosa was wearing one of her gypsy outfits: a long, brightly patterned skirt with a white, low-cut bodice, which showed off a lot of tanned cleavage. Her gold hoop earrings glittered in the candlelight, and a similar glitter in her dark eyes made Jake suspect that she'd been at the punch herself.

He looked at her speculatively – he was very keen to fuck her again, particularly after secretly watching her, but he'd leave it a while – the more punch she consumed, the better.

Clarissa came sashaying into the room at that moment, causing quite a stir in a shimmering, gold-coloured dress, which left a lot of her marvellous body on display. Every man in the room had spent a good part of the day salivating over her nubile nakedness, and more than one of them hoped to get into her knickers later.

Jake realised that he had an advantage over the other men – he knew what sort of effect the punch had on the female libido. If he played his cards right, he might even strike lucky with Clarissa.

The fact that she went both ways only added spice to the idea as far as he was concerned.

When she approached the bar, he poured her a large glass of punch and passed it to her, smiling blandly.

The party had only just started, but Rosa's love-potion was already working and several couples were groping each other unashamedly.

Jake saw Bella accept an invitation to dance from Toby and was annoyed to see his assistant, eyes glazed with lust, immediately start fondling her bottom.

He made his way over to them and pulled Toby to one side, not noticing that Rosa took the opportunity to slip a few drops of the potion into his can of beer.

'Worth losing your job for, is it? Find someone else to grope before Tom or Emma sees you.'

Toby turned away and grabbed the next woman who came his way, who happened to be the stern-faced, middle-aged housekeeper carrying a plate of canapés.

When Tom came down, Emma was waiting for him and gave him a large glass of punch, which he drained in a couple of gulps. She sipped a glass cautiously herself – one couldn't hurt surely.

After fifteen minutes and two more glasses, Tom, always sexually voracious, had Emma backed up against the wall in a dark corner and was showing every inclination to screw her on the spot.

'Tom – not here!' she chided him as he attempted to ease her camiknickers down under her dress. 'Come upstairs.'

The third glass of punch must have hit him as they turned the corner at the top of the stairs because, without any warning, he dragged her skirt up, her camiknickers down and was inside her before she could coax him the few further yards to their room.

After three strong thrusts he came, looking completely bewildered as he did so.

'Sorry, Em,' he gasped, pulling out of her. 'I don't know what came over me.'

Emma did.

But she wasn't telling.

Not yet anyway.

'Come to our room,' she urged him, as he pushed his cock back inside his trousers. His bewildered expression became even more bewildered when his dick grew swiftly into another erection and resisted his attempts to tuck it away.

Taking his hand, Emma led him along the corridor and into their bedroom. She was just bending over to reach for one of the stockings she'd left on the bedside table, intending to tie him up, when he grabbed her by the waist.

He fell on top of her and she tried to squirm out of his grasp – she'd no intention of letting Paul Rivers see them screwing again.

But she hadn't bargained for the potency of the punch.

Without even taking the time to drag her pants down, he plunged his straining erection up the loose-fitting leg of her camiknickers and deep into her honeypot.

After a few rapid thrusts, he came again and collapsed onto her, breathing hard.

'What the fuck's going on?' His voice was that of a baffled man. 'I haven't come twice in such quick succession since I was fourteen. I couldn't have stopped just then to save my life.'

Emma wriggled away and grabbed a stocking.

'You obviously need restraining,' she admonished him.

'I think I do,' he agreed, and didn't object when she swiftly lashed his wrists to the bedposts. She dragged his trousers and briefs off and secured his ankles, then covered up the mirror with a towel.

'Why have you done that?' he asked puzzled, then let out an incredulous groan as his cock reared skywards. He began to yank at his bonds. 'I don't believe this,' he croaked. 'There must be something wrong with me. It's my dick's final fling before dropping off. Untie me, Em, I need a doctor.'

Then as his cock throbbed urgently he added, 'No – I've got a better idea. Sit on it quickly – I'm going to come again.'

To Tom's frustration, instead of kneeling astride him and

engulfing his furiously pulsating member in the soft folds of her pussy, she slipped out of her dress and stood bare-breasted in front of him.

The sight of her naked orbs, with the candy-pink nipples jutting towards him, was too much.

'Touch me! Just touch me!' he begged. In reply, she stroked one firm, full breast with her hand, lingering on the nipple. Tom thrashed about on the bed like a madman, but the stockings held him firmly spreadeagled.

'How does it feel, Tom?' she asked softly. 'How does it feel to want to come and not be able to?'

'Bloody torture,' he ground out through gritted teeth.

She knelt beside him on the bed, close enough for him to smell her perfume and the heady reek of sex, which lingered on her from their previous swift couplings. He could see that the crotch of her camiknickers was sodden, as the fluid he'd pumped into her trickled slowly out.

She slipped her hand between her legs and began to rub herself, slowly at first, then more urgently as the one glass of punch she'd drunk sent her spinning towards her own climax far faster than usual.

It was explosive and left her weak, trembling and wanting more.

Ignoring Tom's anguished pleadings, she removed her oyster satin camiknickers and knelt over his face.

'Maybe if you give me enough pleasure, I'll take pity on you,' she said, lowering herself.

He lapped desperately at her labia, using all his considerable expertise to work her to another earth-shattering orgasm.

She could see the veins throbbing wildly on his engorged member and, as her back arched and the first shudders of pleasure rippled through her body, her hand closed on his cock and he came instantly, covering her naked breasts with his hot juices.

Emma lay next to him and massaged the liquid into her breasts, taking a long time about it. Long before she'd finished, Tom was hard again and begging her to climb onto him.

This time she took pity on him and lowered herself lithely onto his granite-hard cock. It took him a little longer this time, and Emma managed to come herself just before he did.

By now, the punch had taken full effect on her and she felt a molten itch, which needed permanent scratching, deep inside her honeypot.

She felt that he'd been punished enough, so she gave in to his pleadings that she release him, and cut him free with a pair of scissors. Anyway, she wanted his hands and mouth on her, as well as his cock deep inside her.

For what seemed like an eternity they fucked each other to climax after climax. Eventually, when they were both covered in sweat and each other's juices, they lay exhausted on the bed, Tom's shaft still buried up to the hilt in her swollen pussy.

'My cock's been taken over by an alien life force,' he muttered. 'Either that or it *is* just about to drop off.'

'It was the punch,' returned Emma weakly. 'There's nothing wrong with your cock – quite the reverse actually.'

'What?'

'There was something in the punch – some Romany aphrodisiac of Rosa's.'

Tom sat bolt upright, his member slipping out of her, though she automatically tightened her internal muscles in an attempt to keep him inside her.

'Why the fuck didn't you tell me before?'

'Because it was much more fun this way.'

'What does this aphrodisiac do?'

'What it just did – increases potency on a temporary basis.'

'Did you have some?'

'One glass.'

'And how has it affected you?'

'It's made me want to fuck like a rabbit.'

Tom lay back on the bed and considered the situation.

'Has everyone had some?'

'Most people, I think.'

'Hmm. Why don't we go downstairs for a while and watch the fun while we get our second wind? This should be interesting. But first . . .'

'What?'

Tom flipped her over onto her stomach and slid inside her again. He began to hump her vigorously, his fingers on her clit, squeezing and stroking.

When another hot, ecstatic climax broke over her, Emma threw back her head and cried out.

It was at that moment she noticed the towel had slipped from the mirror.

While Tom was in the shower, Emma dried herself off and pulled her dress on over her naked body, standing out of sight of the mirror.

She didn't know when the towel had slipped off, but if Paul Rivers was watching, he'd just had quite a show.

She slipped silently out of the room and through the door leading into the west wing.

He was waiting for her in the next room.

'Thank you,' he said simply.

She sank onto the bed.

Maybe it was the punch, but she suddenly felt enormously turned-on that he'd been watching them.

'May I ask you something?' she enquired.

'Anything.'

'Did you follow us into the maze that evening?'

'Yes. I couldn't resist it.'

'And was it you who turned the floodlights on?'

'Yes. It was almost dark, and I wanted to see you properly. You were both absolutely magnificent.'

They sat in silence for a few moments, then Paul Rivers said, 'Would your company be interested in making feature films?'

Feature films.

The ultimate goal of any production company.

'Yes,' she said without prevarication.

'Splendid. I've just bought a studio in Buckinghamshire and I want to use it. As soon as you've finished the sex guide, perhaps you'd like to start pulling together a few treatments. Incidentally . . .'

Emma looked at him expectantly.

'We'll need to meet occasionally to discuss our joint projects . . . would that embarrass you at all?'

Emma would have suffered any amount of embarrassment to produce feature films. She shook her head slowly.

'It may mean your staying here, or at my house in Paris from time to time.'

Their eyes met.

Emma understood the bargain being struck.

Paul Rivers wanted to watch them again.

'That won't be a problem,' she murmured.

When Emma went downstairs, Tom was searching for her.

'Where have you been?' he asked, putting his arm around her amorously and closing his hand over one breast. 'You're missing all the fun.'

Emma was too dumbstruck to reply.

Everywhere she looked, half-naked people were openly copulating in twos, threes and larger groups. Her mouth fell open and she hastily closed it again. The film crew were generally a randy lot – particularly on location – but this was something else.

'And come and look at this,' Tom urged her, dragging her away from her fascinated contemplation of Toby, who was feverishly screwing the forbidding, middle-aged house-keeper.

The woman's dark-coloured dress was undone, revealing that her thick stockings were held up by a flesh-coloured suspender belt and if she had been wearing briefs of any kind, they were no longer in evidence.

Her hair had come free from its bun and she was clinging onto Toby crying, 'Yes! Yes!' as he thrust vigorously into her and clutched at her surprisingly ample bosom.

Tom pulled Emma into the library where, in a tangle of slender female limbs, a burly, naked Jake looked as if he'd finally found heaven on earth.

He had his cock inside Clarissa, who was riding him ecstatically, and his tongue inside Bella, who was sitting astride his face.

Rosa was half lying across him with her head angled towards his feet and he had a hand buried inside her crotch, while she, in turn, stroked Clarissa's breasts.

Bella and Clarissa, who were facing each other over Jake's prone body, were kissing, their arms wound around each others's necks, moving above him with erotic grace.

'Shall I film it?' asked Tom, unable to take his eyes from

the scene. Then, when he realised that Bella was one of the participants, he let out a strangled cry.

'Quick, Em – help me drag her off. Paul Rivers will have my goolies for gobstoppers if he finds out about this.'

'He won't find out,' she assured him. 'Who's going to tell him? We're not. Anyway, I've got a better idea . . .'

The punch had made Emma temporarily lose her inhibitions.

'What's that?'

'Let's join them.'

More Thrilling Fiction from Headline:

Scandal In Paradise

A chronicle of outrageous lechery

A N O N Y M O U S

Playtime in Paradise

Amanda Redfern may be blonde and
busty but when it comes to finance she's
no booby. This former escort-girl and
owner of the Paradise Country Club is not
usually taken in by men. Flattered and
fondled, stroked and willingly seduced,
yes. But diddled – in the business sense – definitely no.

Then comes demon debaucher Roger Vennings, a man
who can roger like a stallion and sweet-talk the knickers off
a nun. In his hands Amanda is putty, so how can she resist
his latest scheme? Which is to use the Country Club as a
base for his sex rejuvenation clinic. Unfortunately for
Amanda, Roger's business plans all have their shady side.
And this one has a shady lady to boot – a redheaded
dominatrix with a cupboard full of sex toys...

PASSION IN PARADISE is also available in Headline Delta.

FICTION/EROTICA   0 7472 4358 0

Headline Delta Erotic Survey

In order to provide the kind of books you like to read - and to qualify for a free erotic novel of the Editor's choice - we would appreciate it if you would complete the following survey and send your answers, together with any further comments, to:

> Headline Book Publishing
> FREEPOST (WD 4984)
> London
> NW1 0YR

1. Are you male or female?
2. Age? Under 20 / 20 to 30 / 30 to 40 / 40 to 50 / 50 to 60 / 60 to 70 / over
3. At what age did you leave full-time education?
4. Where do you live? (Main geographical area)
5. Are you a regular erotic book buyer / a regular book buyer in general / both?
6. How much approximately do you spend a year on erotic books / on books in general?
7. How did you come by this book?
7a. If you bought it, did you purchase from: a national bookchain / a high street store / a newsagent / a motorway station / an airport / a railway station / other........
8. Do you find erotic books easy / hard to come by?
8a. Do you find Headline Delta erotic books easy / hard to come by?
9. Which are the best / worst erotic books you have ever read?
9a. Which are the best / worst Headline Delta erotic books you have ever read?
10. Within the erotic genre there are many periods, subjects and literary styles. Which of the following do you prefer:
10a. (period) historical / Victorian / C20th / contemporary / future?
10b. (subject) nuns / whores & whorehouses / Continental frolics / s&m / vampires / modern realism / escapist fantasy / science fiction?

10c. (styles) hardboiled / humorous / hardcore / ironic / romantic / realistic?

10d. Are there any other ingredients that particularly appeal to you?

11. We try to create a cover appearance that is suitable for each title. Do you consider them to be successful?

12. Would you prefer them to be less explicit / more explicit?

13. We would be interested to hear of your other reading habits. What other types of books do you read?

14. Who are your favourite authors?

15. Which newspapers do you read?

16. Which magazines?

17. Do you have any other comments or suggestions to make?

If you would like to receive a free erotic novel of the Editor's choice (available only to UK residents), together with an up-to-date listing of Headline Delta titles, please supply your name and address. Please allow 28 days for delivery.

Name..

Address...

....

....

A selection of Erotica
from Headline

SCANDAL IN PARADISE	Anonymous	£4.99 ☐
UNDER ORDERS	Nick Aymes	£4.99 ☐
RECKLESS LIAISONS	Anonymous	£4.99 ☐
GROUPIES II	Johnny Angelo	£4.99 ☐
TOTAL ABANDON	Anonymous	£4.99 ☐
AMOUR ENCORE	Marie-Claire Villefranche	£4.99 ☐
COMPULSION	Maria Caprio	£4.99 ☐
INDECENT	Felice Ash	£4.99 ☐
AMATEUR DAYS	Becky Bell	£4.99 ☐
EROS IN SPRINGTIME	Anonymous	£4.99 ☐
GOOD VIBRATIONS	Jeff Charles	£4.99 ☐
CITIZEN JULIETTE	Louise Aragon	£4.99 ☐

All Headline books are available at your local bookshop or newsagent, or can be ordered direct from the publisher. Just tick the titles you want and fill in the form below. Prices and availability subject to change without notice.

Headline Book Publishing, Cash Sales Department, Bookpoint, 39 Milton Park, Abingdon, OXON, OX14 4TD, UK. If you have a credit card you may order by telephone – 0235 400400.

Please enclose a cheque or postal order made payable to Bookpoint Ltd to the value of the cover price and allow the following for postage and packing:
UK & BFPO: £1.00 for the first book, 50p for the second book and 30p for each additional book ordered up to a maximum charge of £3.00.
OVERSEAS & EIRE: £2.00 for the first book, £1.00 for the second book and 50p for each additional book.

Name ....

Address ....

....

....

If you would prefer to pay by credit card, please complete:
Please debit my Visa/Access/Diner's Card/American Express (delete as applicable) card no:

Signature .... Expiry Date ....